Three Days by the Sea

Three Days by the Sea

Helen E. Mundler

www.hhousebooks.com

Hardback ISBN: 978-1-910688-69-4

Cover design by Ken Dawson Creative Covers
Typeset by Polgarus Studio

Published in the UK

Holland House Books
Holland House
47 Greenham Road
Newbury, Berkshire RG14 7HY
United Kingdom

www.hhousebooks.com

For Urias, now and always

Michigan seems like a dream to me now.
Simon and Garfunkel, "America"

Prologue

It was three days, Gina said when she got the invitation, because Janet wouldn't be able to stand any more. Not for Janet the week-long family gathering or the open-ended invitation. Three days meant she could psyche herself up to it, pace herself and start on a huge sigh of relief as they all packed their bags. There wasn't actually a check-out time on the card, but there might as well have been: after breakfast, once the third full day was over, it would be time to leave.

The card read, *"Dear _____. "You are invited to a,"* followed by a blank line on which Janet had inscribed neatly, "Three days by the sea". The grammar glitch, "a" and "three", made it rather touching. There were two other lines, beginning *"On"* and *"At"*, which were also filled in: an address in Falmouth, dates to arrive and leave. At the bottom was printed RSVP.

It was rather an attractive pre-printed card, although probably intended for children's parties rather than the summoning of adults from their various, far-flung busynesses. It was in the retro style which was the new language of desirability: sailing boats were superimposed palely on the print, an indigo haze crept up to the top where it solidified, a yellow sun shone from the west.

Janet had sent one each to Gina, Robert – and Nadège. It had occurred to Gina to wonder how many had been in the pack; perhaps five or six? Had she tried to send one to Susie? She could have scanned it and sent it by email. (This was, in fact, how Gina's own invitation had arrived, since she was no longer reachable at any address known to her mother, although Janet was not to know that. The Susie situation was complicated enough. Two lost daughters might be too much to bear.)

As for Robert, there were different ways, Gina sometimes thought, of being lost. St Agnes Mount, where Robert lived now, if it could be called living, was apparently some sort of monastery, or perhaps that wasn't the right word, since there were women there as well. Some were *Sisters*, according to Robert's latterly more frequent emails, and these were more or less nuns, while others were *Ladies*. The Ladies were recently-released prisoners serving out probation, from what Gina gathered. The place was run as a charity, Robert had told Gina, and, when pushed, he had agreed that yes, in a way, it was a *sort* of prison, but only in that the Ladies had to stay for whatever term was decided. It was like Robert to say "in that", in a sentence: this was one of the many things about Robert which could tip Gina over into raging impatience, given the right, or perhaps wrong, circumstances.

"So how long do they stay?" Gina had asked during a fairly recent conversation on Skype.

"Usually six months or a year," Robert had said. "It's for women who have... you know, helped kill their mothers. That sort of thing."

"Their mothers?" Gina had echoed.

"You know," Robert had bumbled. "Helped them on their way."

2

"Polite murder," Gina had said. "The pillow over the face, the—" but she couldn't think how to go on. Her friend Karin was expert on these matters, but it wasn't something Gina had thought about much on her own account. But the Ladies, Robert said, had, specifically, committed family crimes.

"Attenuating circumstances, then," Gina said to that, but Robert didn't get it.

In spite of herself, Gina was fascinated by St Agnes Mount, with what she hoped was not a prurient interest. Besides imagining the Sisters and the Ladies, which she could not help, she was also interested in imagining Robert, how he managed, how he fitted in – bumbling, ineffectual Robert, who had never greatly interested her before. Did he get ragged by the Sisters? Did the monk-in-chief despise him? Or was he flourishing into some sort of superior spiritual being of an order she could ill imagine?

More oddly, she had begun to dream of Susie somehow arriving at St Agnes Mount: one sibling for another, a sort of unconscious displacement, the mind playing tricks, or so she supposed. This was a new version of an older recurrent dream, in which Susie was in prison. The prison was always very clean and well-ordered, and Susie would be sitting alone in her cell with that haze of hair framing her face and shoulders, cloaked in unspoken questions, unguessable answers. Sometimes Gina wondered if Robert wasn't in some way looking for Susie, at St Agnes Mount, or perhaps looking in some more indirect way to solve the Susie problem and unlock the mystery.

How hard to imagine Susie's hair paler now, beginning to be silvered. But, more than that, how hard to imagine Susie, sweet, clever, pretty Susie, Susie of the thousand silly habits and sayings, in prison. What could have gone so wrong? At one very basic level, the dream seemed to be about Susie being locked away, inaccessible, but it was also a dream which turned things around: in making herself inaccessible, in removing herself from them, it was her family Susie had put in prison. They were the ones serving out a sentence of indefinite duration.

And so in dreaming of her sister in prison Gina was, she concluded, dreaming also of herself, of the impotent frustration which was her own, and yet which, she suspected, the other members of her family shared, to one extent or another.

Ashwick

I

Georgina, Robert and Suzanne. They had never been the sort of people you might expect to allow one of their number to get lost, to slip off the edge of the world. The Ellises at first glance seemed too stolid, too rooted, too *English* for nonsense of that kind. They stood in plain sight, they were pillars of the community, a tiny nerve in the backbone of England. Gordon and Janet, parents to these three, were a part of things; they were, in their small way, public figures. You would not have expected what happened, as family life unfolded, to happen to them.

In later years, during a bad time about a year prior to Janet's invitation, Gina saw herself as very slightly cracked, like a Chinese porcelain vase with a hairline fissure from top to bottom which had been turned to face the wall. Probably family life had been like that too: it had looked, not perfect, but completely and utterly respectable, and it had not been that, not quite. A very public family in a small and local way, very much on display, but what they had seemed and what they were had never quite coincided.

Still, when Gina found out about Robert and St Agnes Mount, it seemed to her a continuation of the family story, an unsurprising episode, a coda. Robert, as Gina saw it, was continuing Gordon's path, in his own way. They had always been part of something bigger, Gordon had wanted that, had needed it, but the contexts he had chosen, the institutions into which he wove his family, were to have unexpected consequences in later years. The places Gordon chose made them what they were. They never really left: Coombe's and Crick House, Gordon's chosen fiefdoms, formed the bedrock of their lives, whether they liked it or not.

It was better to think of it as bedrock than prison. The Ellis children were not brought up in a prison or a monastery, it was just that prisons and monasteries always lurked, somehow, in the background. Even Coombe's had had its prison aspect. This had been Gordon's first post, after he and Janet were married; he was a master, except that Coombe's was just grand enough to say *beak*. It was a rather minor public school in Warwickshire, and there the boys were more or less interned, "called over" morning, noon and night, and subjected to a regime of terrible food, physical discomfort and small, pointless tyrannies which was in some ways not so different from prison. There was at that time still something brutal about both public schools and many of the masters they attracted. It wasn't until new legislation on child welfare went through in the late eighties and early nineties that the caning stopped, the chilly dormitories with their bare boards, uncurtained windows and thin blankets were grudgingly transformed into carpeted nooks of private space, and masters were "vetted" before appointment ("dreadful expression, like farm animals", said Janet, but by this time Gordon and Janet were long gone).

At Coombe's, the boys were not simply boys, they were Boys, with the capital somehow clearly enunciated. The boys seemed, to Janet always and to Gordon occasionally, under their sports coats and their neat haircuts and their "Sirs" and "*Mrs* Ellis" (always that emphasis on the Mrs, as if there was something inherently odd about speaking to a woman), to be only just under control, seething with some threatened violence, some insurrection, some overthrow of authority, although Gordon was good at diffusing any trouble that arose. While his teaching was reputed to be only "solid", and never attained the flights of brilliance for which some of the masters were reputed, he was considered "good with the Boys", and was envied for it, although not all his colleagues appreciated that this was achieved by Gordon's refusal to enforce petty rules for their own sake. He ignored small latenesses and lapses in dress and pretended not to hear cheek, qualities which would stand him in good stead later on.

As was the way of it then, a job had been found at Coombe's for Janet in one of the boarding houses, where she was under-matron. This meant "ironing and mending", as she complained bitterly, so bitterly that it was decided after the second year that she would go to college in Birmingham, and train to be a psychotherapist: "The worst psychotherapist in the world," her disloyal children would later giggle, but at least it got her out of being, to all intents and purposes, a maid.

Gordon had loved the teaching: history and English literature, and a little history of art as an elective. The problem was not, in a sense, the school: impossible not to love the Victorian buildings, the close and its chapel, a clear imitation of their more august neighbour across the county, although on a much smaller scale; impossible not to rejoice in leading the boys through the O and A-level syllabuses, a year early, two years early, the iron discipline of no talking in class and no getting out of prep, of "optional" reading lists and extended essays making it easy to pull the final rabbit out of the hat. As Gordon saw it, that rabbit was not so much the exam A grade, but knowing the boy capable of sustaining a proper conversation about literature, or politics, or art, while at the same time something of himself was transmitted, went on and out into the world.

Gordon was torn about Coombe's. On the one hand, the place exuded a certain provincial ease and comfort: sherry in the common room, staff dinner parties, gardens to sit and drink Pimms in in summer, the beautiful outdoor arcaded swimming pool, known as the Tosh. Once in his first year there, walking through the close and hearing Elgar's cello concerto drifting languorously from a window, Gordon had thought, yes, this is it, *this* is England, this *is* England as it should be. Overall, perhaps, there was – notwithstanding the actual work, which was intensive – a sort of relief, a restfulness, in the perpetuation of the myth that in the 1970s and on into the 80s sports coats were still the default clothing for young men, and chapel on Sunday morning still the norm. There was a period during which Gordon, who had grown up if not in poverty at least in occasional hardship, gave in gratefully to these consolations, and enjoyed the pretence that this was, if not what he was born to, what he now, with his education, had a right to expect.

But what began to bother Gordon increasingly, through the seventies, could be called, in short, class. The scholarship interviews with the local boys each May were a case in point. In they would come, the expectant twelve-year-olds, the self-conscious fifteen-year-olds, scrubbed and in new suits, cowed by this one chance to shine, to, in effect, win the lottery, to climb a straightened and foreshortened ladder up to the Establishment. Not that Ashwick Boys' Grammar was in any way inadequate; the boys might even have been better off staying there. Entry to Coombe's guaranteed them, as well as five or two years of free private education, an equivalent period of ceaseless bullying on the subject of their inferior accents or parents or whatever it was the boys who were there as of right chose to pick on, a spectacle which did little to edify Gordon's own grammar-school-boy soul. The final straw came when one of Gordon's best A-level English students, a fairly certain Oxford admission – he would be coming back for seventh-term, which was the way of it at the time – allowed himself to be dragged into an illicit outing to a nightclub in a nearby town. This boy, Stopford, was a local boy, one of the pupils known as "town", although in fact Coombe's had, at that time, a boarding-only policy, and so those who would have been day-boys elsewhere lived among the paying pupils. This meant that instead of looking down on the day-boys, the school looked down on the local boarders.

Since the adventure involved breaking a number of fundamental school rules on the driving of cars, the smoking of cigarettes and the consumption of alcohol to name but a few, there was no choice but to expel three of the four boys concerned, and off they went to face various degrees of parental displeasure. The fourth boy, however, was not expelled, because it happened that he was the son of a prominent politician who had risen to be a cabinet member (his rise had taken place since the enrolment of his son at the relatively minor Coombe's). And because of this, that boy would somehow stay on, take his A-levels, and depart to take up his place at Bristol as if nothing had happened.

Gordon called Stopford into his study on private side and told him he was a fool. "Six weeks," he told him, "And you could do what you like, drink where you like, for the rest of your life Five years of damn hard work"—here Gordon brought his hand down on the table to stop the tears pricking behind his eyes, because Stopford was of course, in this instant, himself —"And you throw it all away for the sake of trying to keep up with a couple of minor Hooray Henries? Those boys," Gordon continued, waving them away with the other hand, "they're not here because they've got brains. They're here because their parents have got money. And you had the chance —"

And there was Stopford, blond and lanky, letting the storm rage on, saying nothing. "Oh, get out," said Gordon in his own voice, suddenly devoid of the omnipotence of beak or housemaster. He allowed his shoulders to slump. For a brief moment something flickered over Stopford's face as he registered this change, and then he left, closing the door very quietly behind him. There was nothing more to be said.

Of course Gordon went to see the headmaster; of course he pleaded for Stopford, elevating him to dead cert for Oxford, praising his intellect, his determination, his talent for art. The headmaster – known as the Bodger, since the masters were beaks – looked at Gordon from out of his fat and his complacency and said, "Those boys need to be set an example. We can't have behaviour like that here." Gordon had been too furious to ask what he meant by "those boys", and why they, in particular, needed to be taught how to behave, and why the fourth boy was exempt. There was no point, because he knew the answers. Hearing them rehearsed, in that context, would simply undermine his own position, which began, suddenly, to look less tenable. Smoking his pipe in the common room on a May evening, Gordon started to think seriously about other lives.

While for Gordon the Stopford affair was a turning point, Janet had different reasons for disliking Coombe's, chief among which were the family's living arrangements (the children at this time were ten, eight and three). Gordon "had a house", and so they, as Janet saw it, were condemned to live in it. At Shakespeare House – all the houses were named after venerable authors – the Ellis family existed in a space for which "private side" was a cruel misnomer. It was the flat above the shop, said Janet, without the saving grace of separation by stairs.

Tradition had it that visitors, unless they were hopelessly alien to the school, like Avon ladies or Jehovah's witnesses, did not ring the bell at the front door. Masters requiring Gordon's opinion or advice, boys from the house on various errands or from other houses wanting help with their prep or extensions for their essays, cleaning ladies, the chaplain, all of these moved constantly through their family living space. Janet, coming out of the bathroom, in a housecoat and with her hair done up in a turban, had once found herself confronted with a boy of about sixteen, looking vastly amused, who had informed her that so-and-so had been missing from call-over – as if, Janet had screamed at Gordon, as if she *gave a damn*.

Between what was supposed to be their home, a vertical slice cut off the end of the boarding house, and each of the three floors, was a door, a simple, wooden door with a polished brass knob. Although they were not intended to be used – the boys were supposed to go round and use the front door, which served little purpose in Janet's opinion since they didn't ring – these doors could never be locked, as a matter of safety. Moreover, on the ground floor, you could actually see how a room had been divided in half when the conversion was done: a drawing-room was split between the two sides of the house, the plaster mouldings and curlicues and picture rails beginning on Gordon and Janet's side, where the family gathered to watch television and the children practised the piano, and continuing on the other, which was used as a common room for the house tutors: "On the other side of the wall! I can't even relax in my own home!" said Janet. But of course it was not their own home.

When Janet was preparing food in the kitchen on the first floor, the boys were less than twenty feet away; when the family ate in their dining room, the distance was six inches. It wasn't like living in a flat or a semi, or simply having neighbours, in a normal way. Even on the second floor, where the family's bedrooms were, Janet could never lose her awareness of the boys effectively at the end of the corridor, probably thinking it was hilarious, in their nasty adolescent way, that Gordon had a wife, and wondering how often they had sex and how they did it. She hated the insolence of their studied politeness, their awful pack behaviour, the smell of old games shoes making its way into her side of the house.

In term-time, and term-time was thirty-six weeks of the year, the boys could not be forgotten for a moment. It was like being on stage all the time, said Janet. And it wasn't only the boys: there was also having to keep up the ridiculous pretence with the other masters and their families that they were somehow an ideal family, harmonious and completely functional. As the children got older, Janet would disappear for days out, not come home for hours after her mornings at her part-time job, make a point of not being available. She didn't want to be the kind of housemaster's wife who baked birthday cakes for however many of the boys' birthdays did not fall in the holidays, like Sarah Gill in Dickens. After all,

14

there were house tutors to see to the boys' moral welfare, and there was Marks and Spencer if they wanted cakes. (They took notes into the town and got credit. The bills were sent to their parents at the end of each term. It was, Janet said, another world.)

Psychologically, Janet said, the whole arrangement was untenable, and now that she had her psychotherapist's diploma, when Janet said "psychologically", it carried some weight. It was perfectly true that the Ellis marriage was not a peaceful one: rows, of necessity stifled, were breaking out more and more often, and once or twice, Janet had threatened to leave. But in the end, they all left: the nightclub debacle in May was the catalyst, and by the end of June Gordon had been interviewed, successfully, for a job at what was called, at the time, Crick House, and only much later became Fairfields – once, ironically, the fair fields in which it stood had been dug up and built over. And although she had at first been appalled by the idea of the move ("A reformatory!"; "Not exactly that," said Gordon), Janet at last had her house.

*

Looking back on all this, Gina sometimes wondered if the Ellis children had been irreversibly institutionalised. Could that be Robert's problem? And perhaps it was Gina's, too. Unlike Robert, she could clearly survive in the outside world, but into that world she took, like a heavy suitcase she would rather have left behind, a deep need to belong to something bigger than herself, to truly belong, without ever seeming to find what that thing was. As for Susie, who knew what she wanted, or needed, what she tapped into or didn't? Maybe she had fled from the whole idea of institutional life – after all, in many ways, she was the one who had borne the brunt of Crick House, the one who grew up with it, who lived with through its many idiosyncrasies and its rise and fall, once Gina and Robert had left to pursue their own affairs. Or in Robert's case, to be dragged along by fate, or circumstance; or something.

II

The move to Crick House, a mere four miles down the road from Coombe's, brought all sorts of changes, not only in the Ellises' living arrangements, but also in their in social circle. They were drawn into a new life with the new school – although Crick House was not exactly a school. It had in its time been an approved school, although it had started out in the late nineteenth century as a prep school, one of the feeder schools for Coombe's. But gradually the rolls had fallen, part of the land had been sold off, and what was left of the estate been taken over by the local education authority. In the early seventies it had been officially reclassified as a Community Home with Education. This was a mix of children's home and what most people would understand as a reformatory, as Janet had said. But Crick House still had endowments, both from private sources and from the Anglican church, and these had not entirely been lost when it changed use, and became what would later be known as a public-private partnership.

The place had always been run along the most philanthropic lines. There were places for only eighteen pupils, all boys aged between fourteen and seventeen. Past seventeen, in those days, they were expected to get jobs and make their own way in the world, although places were found for some at the county colleges. The stated aim of the institution was to steer boys from difficult backgrounds into useful, upright lives, and the means by which this was, at least in most cases, achieved, were both liberal and humane.

The boys who came to Crick House ranged from criminals – car thieves and burglars, but no boy with a history of violent assault – through chronic truants, to boys whose home lives had collapsed around them for one reason or another (the reasons often involved poverty and addiction, but there was also, Janet pointed out, a certain amount of simple fecklessness). Crick House was supposed to provide the nurturing environment the boys needed, to mend their ways or themselves, as necessary. Gordon saw Crick House as a mirror-image of Coombe's: you took boys who were as they were by virtue of their socio-economic background, and you tried to make them better according to the means at your disposal. As at Coombe's, schooling, in the form of lessons and work handed in, was part of it, but it wasn't all.

For two hours in the afternoons the boys were taught more or less individually by a Mrs Johnson. Most of the boys were academically indifferent, but Mrs Johnson had ideas about giving them elocution training, functional French or German and a few cultural references, even if they did read these from a series of simplified hand-outs, in order to equip them for life outside and counter their disadvantage. Gordon's role was to provide a pared-down curriculum for three hours every weekday morning in the hope of preparing them for CSEs, the simplified school-leaving exams of the time (O-levels, which were what they did at Coombe's, were not hoped for). But Gordon also had carte blanche to provide, as he saw it, the real education of the boys: working on the school smallholding, hiking and camping, and looking after the school animals, which included, to his own children's delight, a donkey named Arthur, who lived in a small paddock with a pair of goats.

In spite of the move, Coombe's was a continuing presence, since Robert was there now, plodding along, and when sixth-form scholarships for local girls were launched (sixth-form girls were all the rage at that time – many boarding schools counted on them for their continuing survival), Gina got one. Ashwick Girls' Grammar was a perfectly good school, but it was a time of strikes and spending cuts, and besides, Gina was keen to give Coombe's a go, since it was relaxing its rule about boarding only. If there must be Girls, it was felt day-girls would be a lot less trouble.

Janet was believed to leave Coombe's behind her. The new house was a constant source of pleasure: in warm Victorian brick, it was not architecturally dissimilar to the one they had had at Coombe's, except that it was a building in its own right. There was a waist-high iron gate set in a low wall, with a lichen-encrusted plaque on which was engraved the name "Oak Lodge," although such oaks as there were stood outside the perimeter of the garden. There was a gravel path leading through a small front lawn. Inside, the rooms were evenly distributed, not sliced off as before: a sitting room on one side of the flagged, square hall, a dining-room on the other, a large kitchen, and a breakfast-room, angled to get the morning sun. There were bedrooms enough for them all to spread out over two upper floors, and even a roof terrace. Crick House itself stood some thirty yards away: you went out of the front gate and turned right, crossed a lane and followed it – an effective *cordon sanitaire*, in Janet's view.

Of course, it was not theirs, which was something Janet occasionally worried about. Oak Lodge was tied to the job, or jobs, since Janet was also to be taken on by Crick House as part-time counsellor to the boys. There were to be group sessions, to help them to come to terms with their past behaviour. As at Shakespeare House, there was no rent to pay in the new job, but Gordon's salary was less generous than at Coombe's and Janet's would not entirely compensate the shortfall. They continued to save, as they always had, with vague plans for a holiday home in the future, but still, the joy of living in what at least felt like their own house at last, with other people employed to supervise the boys in the evenings and at night – and generally deal with the more unwholesome side of things – detracted from this anxiety.

The real fly in the ointment for Janet was the lack of neighbours. Although the proximity of the boys at Shakespeare House had tried her patience, with that had gone the easy availability of other School households, other kitchens to be popped in to for coffee, other gardens to be sat in for tea in the afternoon or drinks in the evenings in the summer term. There were people – wives – for conversation and complaint. Gordon and Janet had seen a lot of Stella and Peter Carr, who were in charge of Swift. He taught maths, she did some part-time English-language tutoring for foreign boys. There had also been the Thomsons, an older couple whom Janet liked because they didn't take it all too seriously, and were more interested in planning their retirement to northern Italy than the daily goings-on at Coombe's. Oliver taught geography, Felicity had been a specialist cancer nurse, but no longer worked. They had a house on the outer reaches of the grounds, which meant you had to walk past it to get into town, and Janet would often drop in.

But no ready-made social circle came with Crick House, and for all she was no more than four miles up the road, Janet sometimes felt as if she had fallen out of some vital circuit, and began to look back rather uncomfortably on the figurative doors she had slammed. The new house was much more isolated. For a time Janet's outside clients were her closest contacts, and she was rapaciously interested in them, as she would never manage to be in the Crick House boys. But this, as Gordon pointed out when she relayed details of their sessions over the dinner table (two acts of intimacy in a dozen years, a husband who liked to put on his wife's apron and stockings, a marriage ruined by the wife's excessive attachment to the dog), was not healthy. "Or ethical," he added. Janet looked up and saw censorious looks on the face of both her husband and eldest daughter and disliked them intensely, for more than a moment.

Mrs Johnson dropped in on Janet once or twice and sat at the kitchen table with a cigarette between her index and middle fingers and one foot up on the opposite chair, under her long gathered skirt. She was a classics scholar who had abandoned a part-time post at Oxford – not so many miles distant – to look after her husband, who had a degenerative illness. While the classes she taught had been described as "challenging" in the job description, the hours were short and there was little marking. She liked to talk, and had been interested to find out that Janet was a psychotherapist, but her idea of conversation was to launch some theoretical question: could one still be a Freudian, had Melanie Klein been right about Little Dick, what was Janet's relationship with the Tavistock Institute? Janet ignored these lines of enquiry and answered with anecdotes about the state of her clients' marriages too seamy for the family dinner table, or their asinine mistakes in bringing up their children, and Mrs Johnson first looked quizzical, then did not come again.

The only other nearby house, a three-minute walk down the lane, belonged to the Allinghams, mother and son, whom, although they did not know it at that time, the Ellises were never to shake off. The mother was a Dr Allingham, recently retired from a famous London girls' school. She had taught English, and written a thesis on the metaphysical poets. She had also published a number of articles on minor French poets of the same period, and was intensely francophile.

She lived in a world of great formality, and had called and left her card the day after Gordon and his family had moved in. The children had been entranced by this; Janet had said what patronage, and how *grande dame*. She had nonetheless phoned and invited her to tea, but Dr Allingham had said she wouldn't hear of it with the Ellises still at sixes and sevens, and had invited them instead. They had sat around a wrought-iron table in the garden and been served home-made lemonade from a glass jug, Janet frowning at the children to keep them quiet and sitting up straight. Dr Allingham took a great fancy to Gina, and asked her about the books she was reading.

The strain of the occasion had been broken by the arrival of Dr Allingham's son, introduced as Gerry. Tall, spare and auburn, wearing a striped shirt with sleeves rolled up to the elbows and a hand-knitted sleeveless jumper, he looked like Bertie Wooster dressed for the country, but this sat ill with his face which was sallow and raddled. He sat and made gentle, courteous, and wholly ironic conversation.

"You notice," said Janet afterwards, "that she didn't say what he does."

"Perhaps he doesn't do much," said Gordon, lightly. "Strange set-up." And so it proved. Janet came home a week or two later with the news that Gerry had been in prison in the Far East, "for something unspeakable", and that his health had never quite recovered.

Gina, who got into the habit of going over to see Dr Allingham to have books lent and then explained to her and to be conversed with in French, had once found her unexpectedly out. As she hesitated on the doorstep, Gerry had leaned from his upstairs window and called down to her to have tea with him instead. "No, not in his bedroom", she had said afterwards, to allay Janet's fears: "He has a flat."

In fact there was a large central room, containing a baby grand piano and a great many piles of sketches and books on art, open and turned face down, and round the walls stood various canvases, waiting to be hung. Clearly visible through double doors was Gerry's wide bed, with bedposts and a maroon silk eiderdown; but Gerry had no interest in getting young girls into it. He sat at the piano and played abstractedly – bits of Scott Joplin, bits of Bach, in a desultory way – and said things designed to make her talk: what did her parents make of Crick House? Gina would tell him, and he would laugh and encourage her when she imitated Janet being furious or Gordon do-gooding. But he wanted to know about her life, too. It did not take Gina long, as the visits went on (always when Dr Allingham was expected to be out) to understand that what Gerry liked was to hear about girl-things. He liked to hear details of bra-shopping, eyebrow-plucking, the application of make-up, and also more intimate things. He liked Gina to sit on the immense, faded navy-blue velvet sofa behind the piano, legs tucked under her, or later legs spread out with her skirt up, and tell him about these things, or simply to say nothing and do things he liked to hear. He never turned round, he never looked, never acknowledged that it was going on.

It took Gina a much longer time to understand what it was all about. What was in it for him, this strangely cloistered life in his mother's home? He had qualified as a solicitor, it turned out, but barely left the house, only walked around the lanes and to a couple of local pubs, sometimes took the train to London, sometimes stayed away for a few days. There had apparently been a bad marriage, a child he no longer saw. It was rumoured – by Janet, who heard things, "through her consultations" (she never said during, since it would have been unprofessional), that he had women friends, liked to take them out for dinner, take them to bed. But what was the deal, with the young girls? There must have been others, it was all so easily slipped into, so well-rehearsed ("No, you just sit there. Lie down if you like. What you were saying about … in the bath… if perhaps you—?") He was the master of the unfinished sentence, the incomplete suggestion. He was, Gina saw later, an arch-manipulator, but he also seemed to her intensely sad. He could have been a war veteran in another age, a shell-shocked shell of a man, but what had happened to him to make him like this? Was it simply public school – he had been at Harrow – and Oxford? She had no idea. He did not like to talk about himself. He would say, with a self-mocking smile, but one which also deflected criticism, "I'm a bad lot, Gina. Through negligence, through weakness, through my own deliberate fault." And sip more whisky, still doodling on the piano with the other hand.

*

Gordon, meanwhile, was eternally busy with what Janet called, "his utopia", Crick House. He would sit in his study, drawing up programmes for the betterment of the boys, and, he said once, to Janet's annoyance, his own family. Mixing the two was part of Gordon's philosophy. As Gordon saw it, it was vital to expose his children, who, if not "privileged" themselves, had always bordered privilege, to the other side of life, to boys who had been driven to delinquency by neglect and abuse, to boys who had nothing but their wits to fall back on. Conversely, Gordon wanted his own family to serve as some sort of background – not exactly an example, he explained to Janet, not as a pageant of traditional family life, but as a glimpse of "what was normal". It became usual for Gina and Robert, and on occasion Susie, to frequent the film evenings and talks Gordon laid on. What he wanted, he went on, was to set up something real and shared, for all of them to give their best and get the best from each other. To this end, he also invited the domestic staff. Janet, with her diploma in psychotherapy, snorted at all this.

"I don't know why you bother," she said once. "These boys have no understanding of that sort of thing. They're not capable of it." This was after an attempt at Ken Loach's *Family Life*, to be shown over two evenings, with discussion led by Janet. The Ellis children had not been present on this occasion, as Gordon had not deemed the theme suitable. The boys had looked bored and had had nothing to say about the impact of family background on children.

"Oh for God's sake," Janet had snapped finally, looking round at the dozen blank faces, the fingers drumming on her "Larkin/R.D. Laing" handouts. "'They fuck you up, your mum and dad': if you've got nothing to say about that, who has?" But she had already tried them with "Not waving but drowning," with the different parts read out by different boys in a stumbling monotone, and the friends by several boys at once, and that hadn't gone down too well either ("What is this crap? Sounds like a five-year-old." But Mary, who did

25

the cooking and cleaning at Crick House, had asked Gordon for a copy some days later, and he had lent her one of the school anthologies).

"I don't think you should swear, Miss," said one of the boys laconically after Janet's outburst, and Janet had snapped "You can call me Mrs Ellis! I'm not the housemaid."

"Housemaid called by first name," said Mary, arms folded, legs planted squarely and a little apart, and Janet humphed in her direction, because what did Mary know about housemaids or about anything at all, with that unwholesome, unwashed look about her. But on the other hand Mary must not be offended, because she kept things ticking over on the domestic front without reference to Janet, who had made it abundantly clear that it was not her job to deal with missing invoices for dry goods, silverfish in the school kitchen, or anything else of that nature. Gordon said Mary had had a hard life: he took an interest in her nonsense about orphanages and being so terrorised with Bible verses that she had become unhinged. Janet pretended no interest in her whatsoever. So she said nothing more, gathered up her papers and her RD Laing, and swept out.

There were other, more innocuous, film evenings – hard chairs and never quite dark enough for the old-fashioned projector, spatters of light over the screen. Sometimes there were comedies, "good, clean fun" as Gordon put it, with the Ellis children, he felt, on an equal footing with the boys. He always encouraged the staff to come too. The house supervisors tended not to – to be fair, they probably had enough of the boys in the hours in which they could not avoid dealing with them – but Mary would usually come. Most of the boys pretty much ignored her, but they didn't look down on her, or refer to her as a wench, which was how the boys at

Coombe's had spoken of the domestic staff in spite of Gordon's best efforts. There were a few boys she got on with, and one or two she was quite thick with.

Broad-faced and with cinnamon skin which people wrongly supposed to be Indian, her hair cut straight and high across her forehead, Mary had been placed at Crick House by some sort of scheme which found jobs for women in difficult circumstances. Circumstances probably didn't come much more difficult than Mary's: Gordon had seen her file (a failed adoption, incomplete education, a long spell in a psychiatric hospital). The jobs were predictably domestic, the great advantage being, of course, that many of them came with accommodation. Mary moved around with an air of resentment and said little, but the film evenings seemed to cheer her up. And the boys seemed happy enough with them too: or at least they were quiet, their restlessness contained.

*

Much later, Gina said to Robert, on hearing about the making of mead and the cultivation of seedlings, the evening talks and indeed the criminals at St Agnes Mount, "Don't you feel as if you're back at Crick House?"

"What do you mean?" Robert had said in astonishment, which just confirmed Gina's view that it was impossible ever to get away, however hard you tried: it was just a question of which form this impossibility took.

From what Robert had said, St Agnes Mount seemed to be a hotchpotch of a community, not really a convent at all, not in the sense of being the end-point of centuries of unchanging tradition. Even the name was a mere two decades old. Anthony, the self-elected Father Anthony, came from Saginaw in the late nineties, with a passion for the north-east of England and a huge inheritance, settling around him a small group of men devoted to God and to Anthony himself. Robert's devotion to God was new, or else Gina had been unaware of it, but she could quite see that he had needed a passport out, the way things were.

The Brothers were Daniel, Matthew, Michael and now Robert, and they formed Anthony's inner circle. There were also the lay Brothers, Nathan, Charlie, Gareth, Tim and Paul. They did not live in all the time – Nathan and Charlie were still students, the others had part-time jobs outside – but rules had been worked out about how much time they must spend in the community, and at least two of them were present every day.

Two of the five Sisters came when one of the few remaining houses in the Scottish borders finally expired (neither was Scottish: Sister Agnes was from Yorkshire and Sister Philomène originally from Madagascar). The other three, Sister Angélique, Sister Bénédicte and Sister Maria, were respectively from Belgium, France, and Solihull. The first batch of Ladies arrived two years after the Brothers and Sisters, when even Anthony's money began to run out. The charitable foundation that supplied the Ladies also helped with other things, like tax relief and upkeep, but according to Robert it also seemed to help everyone to know what they were for. According to Anthony, their purpose had latterly been revealed.

"So can a Lady ever become a Sister?" Gina had asked, with light malice, when Robert had first explained all this, because slight ridicule for Robert was her default setting. He supposed they could, in theory, Robert had said doubtfully. But that wasn't really the idea.

Robert, it seemed, was in love with the Lady Melanie, a fairly recent arrival. At different times he had mentioned to

Gina, in a number of fragments which she had pieced together, the evening Melanie had arrived. Gina felt some strong fascination with St Agnes Mount, something she could not quite put her finger on, something which went beyond Robert's descriptions of Sister Agnes ladling out potato and bacon soup for Late Supper, and Robert himself taking his place at the trestle table and being struck by Lady Melanie's mass of silvery-blonde hair, but not daring to smile or speak. The Ladies were often quite traumatised, he said, when they came in; the trip could bring back bad memories of the journey to prison. Sister Agnes had shown the new Lady Melanie her room, and reported back, Robert told Gina, that she had tried the door several times, back and forth, feeling it open and shut as if she could not get over it. Gina found herself imagining what this would feel like, over and over again.

III

It had become customary for Robert's misdeeds and aberrations to be held up to family scrutiny, but Gina was supposed to be the family success, the eldest and most magnificent, Robert's nemesis who could never be imitated or followed. When Gina began to show signs of disintegration, she became more sympathetic to Robert: his inability to plan or to be linear, to get things right, to create a satisfactory narrative.

About a year before Janet issued her summons to Cornwall, Gina was in crisis. Something seemed to be broken, and she feared it might be her. She was making a mess of things at every level, work, love, friendship, the whole sweep. Ironically, she had just bought a new flat, as if everything was going well and this new square of white-painted, shiny-parqueted property somehow proved it. Yet the novel in which she had been living seemed to be drawing to a close somewhere behind her back, when she herself had made no plans to end it. And the problem was that she – she who had spent so much of her time in recent years studying other people's novels – didn't know how to be in another book.

The new flat should have been piece of glorious luck, unlooked for, undreamed of. Gina had received a registered letter from a lawyer's office in Warwickshire, and it had proved to from, of all people, Dr Allingham:

My dear Gina,

I don't know where you will be in your life when you read this, but it is my sincere hope that what I am about to say will come at a time when it will still be useful to you.

My son being well provided for, I have decided to leave a part of my estate to you, in most affectionate remembrance of the times you spent with us (At "us", Gina's stomach flipped). I always felt that you went off to live the life I would have liked to have, but lacked the courage to pursue. You were so brave, my dear, and so determined.

I often think of you in France, pursuing your ideas and, I am sure, making a real contribution. I only ask, if you are still as serious as you always were (which I think must be the case, as we none of us change greatly), that you enjoy yourself a little more.

And then there was a date, and a signature.

Gina bought a flat which faced the small rattling overground metro, towards Passy – that is she was able, after making a very sizeable down payment with Dr Allingham's money, to afford the mortgage and the charges, and to move out of the cramped and makeshift studio near the Gare du Nord which she had bought when she first got her job in Paris on the strength of her doctoral thesis. Among Gina's colleagues and friends, renting out one's flat at Christmas and in the summer and going to stay with family, or finding a live-in job as cat-sitter or home-sitter, was very common, so Gina knew she had been extremely lucky. Janet was not slow to point out her luck either, but Gina avoided too much contact with her parents at this time, keeping things on the polite side of cordial. She needed to go to ground, to sort herself out, and she could not respond to their complaints about Robert's monkery because she herself was no longer in a position to criticise.

Once the bare, white-painted flat had been chosen, the papers notarised and the keys placed in her hand, she realised she did not want to live in it. It would have been convenient to blame this on the long-ago goings-on with Gerry Allingham, to become outraged about his mother trying to buy her silence, but that wasn't really it. There just seemed, in some radical way, to be no point. She found herself wondering what would happen to her stuff when she died: there would be nobody to come for it. She felt something wrench in her solar plexus, and wished, most uncharacteristically, she who had indeed always been so serious in planning her life and mapping her intentions had bought a first class round-the-world ticket instead, stayed in nice hotels and ordered lobster and champagne.

"Rent it out," anyone would have said, and anyone would have been right, especially with the rent she could have commanded in that part of the city, but that was not, or not exactly, the problem. The thing was, Gina did not want to live anywhere, or rather, there was nowhere in particular that she wanted to live. She, who had always known what she wanted, who had set herself goals and run after them single-mindedly, was now drifting. She could no longer remember exactly why she had wanted the life she was stuck inside. seeing herself for the first time unrooted, in what seemed a transient and insubstantial existence, while the people she had relied on to make her real disappeared.

There was Karin, with whom relations had undoubtedly atrophied in the previous year; there was Jean-Louis, her, she supposed, lover of the past three years (he was married to somebody else), whom she no longer wanted to see. But things with more casual friends had also cooled: Maud had gone to Brittany to be a live-in dog-walker and finish her book on medieval poetry so she could rent her flat out for the summer, and it was a month since she had been in touch; Ella, their novel-writing friend whose novels Gina had grown sick of hearing about, no longer phoned. Even Robert, pathetic Robert who had never asked for anything more than to live in Gina's shadow, no longer asked her for anything at all. There was something of the eternal footman about all this: Gina had become the shadow of her capable, bossy older-sister self, the spectre of the person Dr Allingham had believed in. Twice Jean-Louis complained that she woke him in the night, shouting something he didn't catch.

So it was that in the new flat, once she had moved in, Gina did not unpack more than the minimum she needed to function in the short term: the things she had taken from Jean-Louis's apartment, her bedding, clothes and toiletries, a box of basic kitchen equipment, her computer and a few cardboard files. She left stacks of boxes in the middle of each room, coffee tables on top of chests of drawers, legs in the air, and to some extent this kept in check the clammy panic beginning to grip her more and more, the sudden, appalling homesickness which seemed to propagate like fungus.

She didn't even know where home was. She had cut England off, had exiled herself stupidly and needlessly to prove a point, some arcane point she could now barely remember. And now she had done over twenty years; it was more than you got for murder. There was an image which kept playing in her brain, a ten-second meme, herself creeping back to Oak Lodge with her suitcase one crepuscular summer evening: there she was, unlatching the iron gate as the taxi drove away behind her. Up the gravel path, slipping her key – the key she had not had for years – into the front door. And then the house, silent around her, all of them dead, all long gone and Gina years too late.

She was at this time caught up in a ridiculous story of her own making. At heart Gina was a Freudian: the interpretation of dreams and symbols and *actes manqués* was her element. This made it all the more enraging when she, she who was early for every appointment, who was an inveterate writer of lists and kept an engagement diary with a system of colour-coded alerts, managed in a complicated way to miss the deadline for a post for which she had been supposed to apply. It was not just any post: it was a post to which her work of the last decade had been leading, and, more than that, it was the post for which Jean-Louis had carefully prepared the ground. He had power, and influence, and he was very much on Gina's side. And she had duly filled in the application on the internet – qualifications, publications, teaching experience and so on – been over it a number of times, made the final tweaks, and validated it with forty-eight hours to spare. That was a Thursday evening. Confirmation of receipt arrived straight away, she printed it out, and didn't think much of it after that. In retrospect she realised this was strange in itself: she should have been wondering about the progress of her dossier every second; she should have had her ear to the ground.

On the Monday evening, when she arrived at Jean-Louis's apartment (on a graceful, red-brick rise near Gambetta), he shot out of the sitting-room where he had apparently been lying in wait and working himself up and said, without preamble, "I don't understand you, Gina. I just don't get it. The whole thing, more or less set up for you, and you didn't even bother to apply?"

Gina stared at him, uncomprehending. "Well of course I applied – what are you talking about?"

"Here," said Jean-Louis said, picking something up from his desk, "Is the list of candidates. Madame X, Monsieur Y, Madame Z – but no Madame Gina Ellis. There won't be another post like that for years – you do know that, don't you? Do you have any idea how hard I fought to get that profile for you? And now we're going to be interviewing candidates with books on medical literature and Christina Rossetti and listening to them try to explain how their research really is about Contemporary Apocalyptic Literature with particular reference to Old Testament intertexts? You've made me look like an idiot, a complete and utter fool."

Gina sat down at the desk, twirled his laptop to face her, connected to the recruitment interface, and saw, with a lurching stomach but also an uncanny sense of recognition, that candidates were supposed to send in a hard application, as well as an electronic one.

"But how absolutely ridiculous," she said. "Why would they need both? It doesn't make any sense at all."

"What doesn't make any sense," said Jean-Louis, "is you. Because do you know what, Gina? This has got nothing to do with electronic dossiers or paper dossiers. It's got nothing to do with dossiers at all." He swept both away with an exasperated gesture. "What this has to do with is your complete inability to *go through with anything.*"

This, of course, cut Gina to the quick. Her entire existence had been founded on going through with *everything*, with taking on projects of horrible weight and difficulty and unfailingly finishing what she started, so "How dare you?" she shouted now, knowing her face was distorted and ugly with anger and not caring. "What does that even *mean?*"

"It means," Jean-Louis shouted back, banging the papers back on his desk, "That you want to be in, but you want to be out more. You should be meeting people, getting yourself known,"—shouting over her to silence protestations she wasn't sure she wanted to offer— "And instead you spend your whole time sloping off to do God knows what with *God knows who*" (clearly a reference to Karin, although Karin was now out of the picture).

He paused for breath, looking around for something to pick up or throw down and lighting on Gina's apocalypse book, which he tossed onto a leather sofa so that it landed open, face-down, pages askew under its small weight.

"Oh, who gives a fuck," said Gina. "I'm just so sick of the whole thing. It's all so sterile, so completely pointless. Writing things about what other people have written and sitting around talking about it like great big toads puffed up with their own importance. I don't know why I've wasted my life here."

"So go back to your own country!"

"This *is* my country! I've got a French passport, French qualifications, a French career, I pay French tax and I've got French property, we are conducting this ridiculous argument in French, and you still tell me to *go back to my own country?*"

"And in all that list there's no mention of a French boyfriend, is there."

"Why? Because without a *'boyfriend'* I don't exist? That's typically fucking French as well." Probably it wasn't, but she was too angry to care. "Anyway, I don't want a boyfriend.

I'm too old. I'm past boyfriends."

"If you hate it all so much Gina, just piss off."

Pointless to rise to this futile baiting. And besides, they had come to the end of it. Suddenly there was nothing more to be said. Gina gathered up her things, picked up and carefully closed the copy of her book that had been hurled across the room, and left, shutting the door quietly on her way out. Before she was down the first flight of stairs, Jean-Louis opened the door again and shouted after her, "And don't think we're going to hold the post until you get your act together! There are dozens of far better candidates out there."

And she heard herself say, in a steady voice, in spite of her shaking legs, "You know what? I don't want your post." She said it without energy, without bitterness, without, really, much interest, and knew that it was true. And so she was in more trouble than she'd imagined.

*

She met up with Jean-Louis two weeks later. He phoned her and invited her for a drink – a drink, not dinner – on the terrace of an anonymous fake-vintage brasserie near Les Halles. He told her, in what seemed to be a prepared speech, that he would not be spending so much time in Paris any more, that his wife had been diagnosed with a long-term condition which he did not name, that she needed him in Lyon, and that he would be commuting up for days only, spending fewer nights. The apartment in Gambetta would be rented out; when necessary, he would stay in a hotel. He seemed paler, older, sadder.

Gina sipped her drink and gave in to the gnawing within. She saw him look at her with something like pity, and didn't care for it at all.

The thing that hurt most, the thing that gnawed, was that she resented Jean-Louis for taking her away from Karin, who had meant as much to Gina as Jean-Louis. But, worse than this, and more difficult to admit, was that Karin had no longer wanted her anyway. The months before she had moved back to Sweden had been odd and uncomfortable, and had involved a great many rules about food consumption and membership of a meditation group. Karin was moving, she said, because she wanted a baby, and Sweden was a better place for lesbian mothers. Babies seemed to be a very recent feature in her mental landscape, and this in itself created an estrangement, since Gina felt little interest in them; but there had also been a period of gradual and calculated withdrawal, of not phoning, of not wanting to go out, of not, apparently, wanting Gina around.

And this, Gina thought bitterly, was the woman whose life she had saved. Barely a year before Karin announced her decision to leave, Gina had gone round and found her in one of her bad phases – in bed, unfresh, unshowered, not eating; Karin went through this. She had been looking through a holiday brochure on Portugal, which might have seemed like a good sign if she hadn't looked so awful, intense and hollow-eyed. "Suicide tourism," she had said, sounding exhausted and defeated. "Where to go and make it look like an accident." Easier, she said, for beach police to deal with a washed-up, accidentally-drowned body on a surfing beach in Nazaré than for a hotel chambermaid to have to find her with a plastic bag over her head.

In the end they had gone to Portugal together for a week. They had stayed in last-minute cheap hotels in Lisbon and Porto, and had taken a day trip to Nazaré to lay this particular ghost. They had eaten seafood rice with the creatures' claws arranged to look as if they were escaping from the pot, and laughed at the existential angst of it, and ridden the funicular and watched the beach police patrolling the shore to warn off would-be swimmers, and Gina had said, "You see, a dozen policemen, all here to save you." Then when they had got to the top of the hill, and walked around the tourist shops and stopped to stroke a black kitten and admired the church and had a drink, they walked across scrubland to where there was a view of the next beach, where the waves crashed with equal violence, and where there were no police at all.

When Gina had said that, about the maritime police, although it was a feeble joke and they both knew it, they had laughed and Gina had put her arms around Karin and felt her thinness, running her fingers over each of her protruding ribs under her long-sleeved top: Gina was in a sleeveless summer dress, but Karin's sadness made her cold. Then they had kissed, discreetly, in deference to a what was perhaps a more conventional society (honey-taste of her mouth, lips red and soft and full among all that pale thinness).

But now it wasn't only Karin, and it wasn't only Jean-Louis, or even the mix of losing them both. It was more pervasive, more insidious. Gina could no longer pretend that she wanted to go on as she had before. She didn't want to work on her flood-as-apocalypse novels, and she didn't want to live in this flat, supposedly her reward for all these years of exile. In Paris she felt like a ghost, haunting a city she could never truly be part of.

It was all very well to discover, or see at last confirmed, some essential truth about oneself, but what on earth was she to do? She sat on her basket chair in her new flat and stared out of the window until the reflected sliver of the Eiffel Tower on the window of the apartment opposite faded away. She was not to know, at that point, that by Christmas of the same year, everything would have changed, and what felt like home would be somewhere else entirely, four thousand miles away.

Paddington to Falmouth

IV

When Gina travelled to London for the reunion, it was more than a year after that terrible Paris spring. She surfaced at Paddington, and decided she liked English railway stations, enjoyed their cleanness and commercial opportunities. She did not know Paddington, could barely remember the last time she had been there – something to do with a student boyfriend and a late train; he had waited for her for hours, sitting on a luggage-cart, in striped braces. Now this made her smile and think of the sweetness of youth. She nosed towards Marks and Spencer, observed, but purchased nothing from, its bank of ready-mixed cocktails and mini-bottles of wine, then wandered around purchasing newspapers and the chocolate which seemed somehow to come with it. Feeling a little light-headed, she went to sit down at a table outside a café. Exhaustion threatened.

Nonetheless, the Gina of a mere few months before would have been astonished at this return to England, this sense of light and hope, this almost-joy. She took Janet's invitation out of her handbag and examined it afresh, its colourful jauntiness, its promise of sunshine and sailing boats. There was a tramp a few tables away, and she nearly got up to move, but then couldn't be bothered. Gina, who liked things clean and hygienic, tested the air, found it acceptable, although the man was wearing some kind of strange brown canvas garment which suggested mustiness at best. He was slumped on the table, apparently insensate, head on arms, fronds of bushy, formless beard spilling over one arm; suddenly, as Gina sipped her coffee, he reared up in his seat, gave out a horrible noise which was something between a gasp and a roar, let his head fall back onto the table and began to weep noisily. Gina, who had glimpsed his face in profile, struggled up, stumbling over her bags, and lurched not away from but towards him.

"I can't go!" half-shouted the tramp who was her brother. He expressed no surprise at seeing his sister on Paddington Station where they had not arranged to meet, nor any sense of the time which had passed since their previous meeting. They were back to Gina and Robert, big sister and little brother, and it seemed to be her place to clean him up and sort him out, just as it always had been.

"Robert, for goodness sake, pull yourself together," Gina hissed, rooting with one hand for a tissue, arranging her bags on and around a spare chair at his table with the other.

"But I can't, I can't, I can't go." He continued to weep, far too loudly, but made no move to leave, so that Gina wanted, on principle, to say, "Oh well then, never mind, see you some other time," and walk away.

"What do you mean, you can't go?" she made herself ask, although she could imagine the answer well enough to give it herself: seeing Nadège would all be too much, it couldn't be done; dull, unimaginative and insufferable Nadège, who was somehow still hanging on as Robert's wife, and had no more idea of what Robert was or what he needed than if he had been an alien life form; Nadège who, in Gina's opinion, was not really worth caring about.

"I can't, I can't see her," Robert went on, his voice laden with snot and phlegm, Gina's tissue scrunched in one large square hand. People were looking now. Gina stood behind him, stooped, put her arm across his shoulders, not because she wanted to but because in that way their two backs created a barrier of intimacy. But Robert's shoulders were shaking so much she had to take it away. Security would probably arrive any minute, thought Gina, in a little access of bitterness: she disliked the bland, unmeasured, catch-all responses of the modern world. By now Robert was making even more noise: "I can't", had become less of a wail than a chant.

"But Robert," Gina said, in a tone of great reasonableness, "she's nothing. She's just a bore. You don't have to talk to her, not really talk. You can do polite conversation, can't you?" But this set only set off another paroxysm. Gina looked at the clock, caught a few curious glances and glowered back. She only had twenty minutes to get her train, and probably Robert was on the same one. Anyway, in England they had this odd system of not having to take the train you'd reserved your seat on, so whether or not he was planning to take this train in particular, it would be better if he did.

"Get your ticket out," she told her brother, and when he continued to sob, rolling his forehead against his arms on the table, she said, quite loudly and sharply, "Robert! Come on, we're going. Now. Stand up. Wipe your eyes. Blow your nose." She stood and watched while he did these things. "Put it in the bin. The tissue". She wasn't going to touch it. "Right. Pick up your bag. Come on. Quick." Robert never had been quick, he had never been anything other than lumbering and slow. Nonetheless he heaved himself up and did as he was told.

They stood on the concourse, Gina's eyes fixed on the

departure board to see the platform announced, Robert with his face in his hands, upright, and at least functioning to some extent. People were still staring, as well they might, since you didn't see a weeping monk on a station concourse every day of the week. "Oh, Robert," said Gina, as she had said so many times before, "Do try. Do try to pull yourself together," and, as he threatened once more to turn back once they were through the ticket barrier, "Robert. Robert! Will you just get on the damn train!"

The train was the bun-fight she had expected. The luggage racks at the end of the carriage were blocked with suitcases too big for the overhead racks, and there was somebody in her seat. Since they both had the same seat number, there was nothing to be done about it. She finally found a seat which was booked only after Exeter, while Robert seemed to have subsided at the other end of the carriage. If she half stood up, she could see the top of his head. And given that there was no way of moving along the aisle and that there were no other free seats, they would both have to stay where they were, thought Gina, and he would just have to manage on his own.

No part of her body was comfortable, her legs were heavy, her shoulders ached, she needed to stretch and move. The air-conditioning hadn't yet kicked in, there were lurking smells of food and toilets, people talking far too loudly, tinny noise leaking through earbuds – but these days you had to be grateful people were using earbuds at all. Her seat was inadequately padded and rigid in a way that hurt her back... By Reading, she was in a heavy doze, and long before Taunton, fast asleep. Just before Exeter, with someone bumping a jumbo suitcase and a pushchair along the aisle and banging her knees and her neighbour in the window seat trying at the same time to climb over her to get out, she woke confusedly, with a horrible thought trailing through her head like strands of egg in boiling water: it wasn't Nadège all that had been about, the weeping and the not wanting to go. It was Clara.

*

"So," said Gina to her brother. At Plymouth, the train had begun to empty out. She had woken again, gritty-eyed, sorted herself out with a wipe, fresh lipstick and eyeliner, a spritz of perfume, and made her way along the carriage to where Robert sat, surrounded by empty sandwich cartons, badly-folded newspapers and soft-drink cans. She sat down opposite him, eased her shoes off and put her feet up on the seat next to him.

"You look better," said Robert. It was true, she could feel her face somehow plumped up, a better colour, eyes less sunken, some far edge of radiance beginning to be restored. But for Robert, after all that, to tell *her* that she looked better—. She managed to say only, "So, what's the deal with Clara?"

Clara was Robert's daughter. He hadn't seen her for some time, perhaps three years, Gina knew, since Janet was vociferous on this point (and Gordon quietly contemptuous). Gina brought Clara to mind: pale, straight brown hair, quiet, biddable, studious. Gina had not seen her niece for some time either. The problem, or one of the problems, was Nadège. Gina's trips back to England had never been either long or frequent, and travelling to Warwickshire to see her unloved (and unloving) sister-in-law was an effort too far. But that was a different matter: aunts weren't fathers.

"No deal," said Robert. Gina noted with relief that his voice had returned to a more normal resonance and volume.

"She never gets in touch. I should never have had a child. I should never have gone along with it. I wasn't cut out to be a father."

This seemed odd to Gina: whatever his faults, Robert was a born nurturer, patient, kind, encouraging. In Gina's opinion, the problem was not his daughter but his wife (Nadège was still his wife – there had been no divorce). Nothing was right between the couple, so how could looking after their offspring be anything other than tiresome? But it didn't seem the time or the place to pick apart Robert's marriage, so Gina said instead, "Isn't she a bit young to – you know, take the initiative?" Clara was thirteen. Gina didn't really know, whether that was young or old these days. Children now seemed to be at once so knowing and competent about the world and yet so babied, it was hard to tell.

"She only has to write back," said Robert. "That's all."

"What, by post?"

"No, email," Robert went on. "I used to email her every week. Send her photos. Animals and things. She used to like animals. She never replied. Not one single time."

"So you stopped?"

He nodded. Gina did not know what to say to this. You could neither condemn nor condone. She could completely see why one might just stop in such a situation, but at the same time, weren't your children supposed to be your children, no matter what and so on, a whole string of clichés running back to the beginning of the world?— Although family events, over the years, had placed a question mark over all that.

"Oh, *I* don't know," said Gina, with a return to the old exasperated tone. Her brother made no reply, and Gina picked up a crumpled *Evening Standard* somebody had left, glanced through it idly, and then looked out of the window.

England was more beautiful than she remembered. It was years since she'd been down this way, and she was struck by the quality of the early evening light on the meadowland. It was years, also, since she had been anywhere with Robert, probably not since outings with the boys at Crick House, hikes and campfires, the sort of thing Gordon used to cure the boys of their criminal tendencies. Robert had gone often, Gina only occasionally. Gina thought of these things, vaguely, and wondered, for the thousandth time, why Robert had married Nadège.

*

It was almost six o'clock when they arrived at Truro. They had been standing at the end of the carriage for a while, bags lined up, although you no longer had to pull down the window and turn the handle. They had said, inevitably, "Do you remember that man?" When they were children, there had been a horrible incident with a train approaching Ashwick station: a man had pulled the window down and put his head outside, taking the air, or looking at the view, or something – without realising that there was a tunnel coming up. Such things were childhoods made of. But of course they reached the platform without mishap, and there was even a man from Great Western to help with their bags.

Station or no, the air struck Gina as fresh, and cool. So far the journey had been a matter of logistics only – how best to get to where by which day and time – but now, after the view of the green roofs and pale, somehow homely stone of the cathedral, she thought about where she was, and found she knew nothing about it. To such of her entourage as required an explanation she had said Cornwall was "where Brits go on holiday, maybe quite well-heeled Brits. David Cameron has a house down there," but she had not considered what it would look or feel like. She had a vague idea that whatever it was, it had quite recently turned into something it hadn't been before: surfers and celebrity chefs and having to book a year ahead. But the light, she thought, looking up at the pale grey arch above her, the sun about to pierce the clouds. You could come for that alone.

They wheeled their cases along to the Falmouth platform, with its train-set buffers and smell of old British Rail. If it was odd, thought Gina, to be travelling with Robert; it was even odder to be travelling with him towards Gordon and Janet. As a family, they did not see each other a great deal, and never had family reunions, which made this sudden initiative all the more surprising. The last time they had been together – not Susie, of course – had been at a hotel in London for Gordon and Janet's thirtieth wedding anniversary. Public places were safer – they limited what you could say. The last time with Susie had marked no particular occasion. It must have been just some ordinary meal, with Gina and Robert home for the weekend or the holidays. Nobody could quite remember.

In recent years, Gina had seen Gordon and Janet when they were passing through Paris to go on holiday, which they liked to do once or twice in the year, and thought up little enjoyments for them, exhibitions and restaurants. She phoned, she emailed, she enquired about their health and well-being. Along with Robert's more recent defection from any semblance of normal life, the Susie situation forced her into playing the role of satisfactory daughter: it was not just a question of being the one who had *not* removed herself and gravitated to some other orbit, it also meant not causing trouble, compensating, making up. Nonetheless, there was a constraint on both sides, something Gina could never quite put her finger on, but which remained evident and troubling. There were times when Janet seemed to feel some bitterness towards her, and Gina could not work out why, and could not bring herself to ask.

It was true that Gina had once (Only once! – she cried inwardly in her defence) broken her own golden rule concerning the relationships of adult children with their parents: she had said what she thought. It could have been tiredness (she had been hard at her apocalypse book) or it could have been, quite simply, a monumental and inexplicable lack of judgement. But she had said, when Susie had, inevitably, been mentioned and then allowed to drop, that perhaps they would never hear from her again, and that perhaps it was all their own fault – including herself in this – that perhaps they had all been too busy with their own affairs and had let Susie fall through the cracks (she saw her sister in her head, Alice-in-Wonderland small and falling between the floorboards, where she had wandered ever since like an escaped hamster). It could have been taken as an innocent-enough remark in circles where people habitually blamed themselves and went in for self-deprecation, but such were not Janet's circles, and she had pounced. What did Gina mean, too busy? Susie had never lacked for anything. And how dare she talk about affairs! Which affairs did she mean? But it was perfectly clear to all of them which affairs Gina might have meant, had she been referring to extra-marital relations. She hadn't been, as far as she knew – but who knew what anybody ever meant and didn't mean to say on any given occasion? The unsaid was always there, roiling like underground volcanic activity, struggling to burst out like a boiling geyser. And she couldn't be bothered to backtrack and pretend to have no idea what had gone on when everybody knew and had known for decades.

But was it that remark that still riled Janet? Was it to do with Susie at all? Gina could not be sure. There had been various phases of mentioning and not mentioning her. It was hard now to see exactly when they had begun and ended, but the first one had been defined by the belief – it had not been a pretence, at first, it had been real – that whatever Susie was doing, it was simply a temporary aberration, and that she would be back soon, arrangements would be made for her to finish school and then apply to university, and things would go on very much as usual. During this period, Susie was spoken of with rough, familiar and familial disapproval, and what she should and should not do with her life was discussed at length. But as time passed and she did not re-emerge, not in any substantial form, but only with bits and pieces of news, postcards, and later electronic snippets, and as the whole idea of Susie as a normal family member faded away, conversations about her had mutated: they were no longer open, but one-to-one, by phone, or in corners in low voices.

Both Gordon and Janet seemed to suspect Gina of having news she did not want to pass on, and in their different ways they would try to winkle it out. Gordon's approach involved making blanket statements and waiting for a reaction. "How sharper than a serpent's tooth," he would begin, "to have a thankless child." Of course, this was not exactly what he said, but it was more or less what he meant when he said, "You know it's very difficult for your mother and me, what with your sister." To this Gina could only assent. Janet's approach was more straightforward: from time to time, certainly not in every conversation but a couple of times a year, she would demand to be made party to whatever it was she knew. "So, have you heard from that sister of yours?" And Gina would have to say no, or not more than a five-word message some months ago, and then go through all the annoyance and upset of not being sure she had been believed.

But in the last few years there had been a shift. Susie was quite often mentioned, now, as if nothing had happened; incidents from her childhood were brought up quite frequently. If these mentions were uncomfortable – the sudden intrusion of what usually went unsaid – at the same time they seemed to be indicative of some level of recovery. "You remember Sarah, Susie's friend," Gordon might say, telling Gina about some lady he had run into in Sainsbury's in Ashwick and what her daughter was doing now. Of course, what was said raised any number of questions about what was not: would Susie's friend Sarah's mother have asked after Susie, and what would Gordon have said? But still, the Ellises had arrived at some sort of modus operandi. It was noticeable that Janet did less of this mentioning of Susie than anyone else, but there was an overall feeling that they were getting better at knowing how to be, how to deal with it all. They had learnt how to be the relatives of a missing person, how to ignore the jagged tear in the fabric of family life. Otherwise they could not have carried on.

V

Gina did her exercises on the platform as she and Robert waited for the Falmouth train. There were very few people around, and none of them were looking, so she arched her back with her arms stretched in front of her, rotated her neck, her shoulders. To feel more awake, she said. Robert was talking about a painting in Truro cathedral by someone called Craigie Aitchison which Anthony had "strongly advised" him to see, asking if Gina would go with him at some point. Gina said "Why not," and it occurred to her that she had not really thought about how the three days were to be spent.

Gordon was to meet them at the station: go past the town and onto Falmouth Docks, he had said, because it would be easier with luggage, there were not so many stairs. He had probably been thinking of university vacations, both of them hung about with bags and badly-put together packages of all sorts, continental quilts and portable box TVs. Now, having at last learned how to behave acceptably as grown-up children, they arrived with modest wheeled cases. Even Robert had managed this.

Gordon – tall, with grey, still-thick hair, schoolmasterly as ever – was indeed waiting on the only platform. Perhaps he looked a little older, the skin drooping slightly more on his jaw, the beginnings of a stoop, but he seemed happy enough, although his face registered a moment's displeasure at the sight of Robert's habit. Gina noticed that he had the same reaction she had had – checking the air. There was something about this garment that suggested dirt and dankness, but when you got near it smelt very faintly of detergent, or had when they had set out from London.

The light was not exactly fading, not yet, but somehow the sky seemed to hang differently over the earth, and this made Gina ache for a moment. But she was quickly taken over by the buckets-and-spades thrill of it, promised from the invitation, and she sat in the car and answered Gordon's questions about the journey ("Oh yes, the plane was fine, thanks; yes, quite hungry"), and listened as he decried the new luxury student flats springing up all around and the folly of an education system build on debt ("houses on the sand", said Gina, because she didn't want Robert to. Biblical references were one thing if she made them, but she didn't want them from a fully paid-up monk). Gordon drew up after a very short time on a gravelled parking-space in front of a house on a hill, a modest Victorian brick house, semi-detached, but with the quiet and gracious glow of sun-warmed red brick that Gina associated with Oak Lodge, and for which, in the flat in Passy, she had so ardently longed.

Janet, who must have been listening for the car, threw open the front door. There could be a sense of underlying threat with Janet – Gina suspected her mother of harbouring ice-chips in her soul, like insufficiently-churned ice-cream – but now she looked, Gina thought, radiant. She hugged her mother, which she did not usually do, feeling her boniness, different from Gina's own more solid body. It was not their way to go through the rituals of "You're looking well," "You don't look a day older," "You've lost weight, you've done something different with your hair", but Gina noticed as she drew back that Janet, Janet who had spent so much time in rather neutral, shapeless trousers, was wearing a bright and lovely cotton skirt in a petrol and ivory flowered print.

"Seasalt," said Janet, seeing her look, which got rather lost in the convivial confusion of arrival, with Gordon wanting to take the cases upstairs and Robert remembering to stop him and Gina saying she was perfectly capable of taking her own, and Janet wanting to show them to their rooms.

"Three bedrooms," she said, like an estate agent, opening doors one after the other. The carpet on the stairs and landing still smelt new, Gina noticed, and each room had a polished wooden floor which also smelt of newness and wax.

"So this is Airbnb?" she said, ready to be surprised, but Janet was busy explaining that she had put Gina on the top floor, in the third bedroom, where there was an additional bathroom, and that Robert, who was across the landing from his parents, could use whichever bathroom he wanted, which meant she wanted him not to use theirs.

Gina's room upstairs had a sloping wall into which was set two small dormer windows, through which she could see treetops, and beyond them, the gleam of the sea. It might have been the light, or it might have been the length of the journey, or the time of day, but she felt a huge lurch of confusion inside: this, beyond all shadow of a doubt, was the England she had yearned for, the previous year. But now it was too late, or it was supposed not to matter any more.

Janet stood in the doorway, watching Gina discover the room. She had put a jar of wildflowers on the table, a stack of towels arranged invitingly on the bed, as if in a hotel. Gina turned form the window – luckily she had had her back to

Janet, in that fleeting moment of discomfiture – and said, "How beautiful. How lovely. How did you find it?"

"Oh, the internet," said Janet, and then, "I thought we'd go out for fish and chips this evening."

"Oh yes, perfect," said Gina, with a return of the agreeable buckets-and-spades sensation. And it was only then, as Robert came up the stairs to see her room, having at last removed the habit, under which he had a perfectly ordinary pair of chinos and a polo shirt, that she said, with a gasp, "But what about Nadège and Clara?"

"Oh," said Janet, and how wonderful, thought Gina, if she had added, "They couldn't come, in the end," or "I didn't feel like inviting them." But she said instead, "Well, you know, there are only the three bedrooms, so we've put them up at a guest house in the town. They came round for tea, but they had other plans for tonight. They'll be round in the morning."

"What do you mean, other plans?" said Gina, sharply, at the same time catching Robert's eye as he sat down on her bed – she rather wished he wouldn't do that. "How can they have 'other plans' when they're only here for three days?"

"Nadège says Falmouth isn't really a holiday place and we should have gone somewhere better," said Janet, very neutral. "So she's taking Clara to a 'proper beach' tonight." Janet returned Gina's verbal inverted commas in a way which was not entirely comfortable.

Gina did not comment on this: it was perfectly obvious, in her opinion, why this was happening in Falmouth and not in some remote coastal village: Falmouth had a station. In fact, it had two. There was nothing to prevent anyone from getting out. But Nadège had never understood Gina and Robert's propensity to see trains as the default method of transport.

Robert had never learnt to drive, to Nadège's annoyance, while Gina had always maintained that she couldn't drive on the wrong side of the road.

Probably it was all very unfair on Clara: it wasn't just that most children, in Gina's opinion, would enjoy fish and chips, looking out over the harbour, in a restaurant which turned out to be rather agreeable ("It's won awards," said Janet), but also that the child was being cheated out of what she had been asked here for, which was to see her family, and however disappointing or inadequate they all were, they were at least not more Nadège. But Gina had mixed feelings about Clara. She had tried to play the game, act as some sort of functional aunt, had sent birthday and Christmas cards and presents. Phone calls, even when Robert and Nadège had still been together, had not been successful, with Clara shy, and Nadège listening. Once the couple had separated, phoning Clara meant talking to Nadège, so Gina had stopped. She had not seen Clara in the flesh since she was a little girl. Now she was thirteen, Gina felt slightly scared of her, worried that she would be the sort of thirteen-year-old Gina had never been herself and no longer recognised, all long glossy hair and thick make-up. Gina was not heedless of her own appearance: she kept her hair long and well-cut, she used make-up, she was reasonably interested in clothes, but she could not relate to being "camera-ready", as they said now. The only camera-ready thing Gina knew was copy, for publishers too mean to pay copy-editors, of which she had experienced one or two.

Besides, it was more than odd to think of Clara reliving their lives at Coombe's, not, admittedly, on the private side of a house, but nonetheless in staff accommodation, which was probably worse – a row of terraced houses converted into flats on the edge of the town, so that everyone knew your business but you did not even have the pleasure of being at the centre of things. Or so Gina imagined.

Clara was going to be a Girl, in September: the school had seen another generation of changes, "reinvented itself", as the new, sharp-suited, business-educated headmaster said (Gordon still reported back on these things). His glottal stops and bad grammar and plebeian name (Smyth, and pronounced Smith, not Smythe) had made the old guard wince, but his "business plan" had saved Coombe's from disaster. Boarding schools, particularly boys' boarding schools, were falling out of fashion. Token girls in the sixth-form no longer cut much ice, and Smith had summoned the staff and given a slick PowerPoint presentation with graphs and numbers, the main import of which seemed to be that the future was both coeducational and international. Girls would arrive at thirteen rather than sixteen, chapel would lose prominence, and there would be more emphasis on "diversity" ("That means Muslims," said Mr Daniels, Physics, who had been there forever, but in practice it meant rich Chinese and Africans of all religions and none).

This year the school website, recently and unctuously PR'd, teemed with child geniuses and prodigies of all kinds – chess champions, would-be concert pianists, Olympic pole-vault hopes. A scholarship had been made available to Clara, with emphasis laid on the "family connections" with the school, which apparently trumped her "adequate" performance at the entrance exam and her general ordinariness. But thirteen-year-old girls were the new guinea-pigs, numbers were short, and Clara was sufficiently eager and bright-eyed. Gina, when she had heard about the "adequate" remark, had felt a stab of deep class anger: what were they, villagers needing favours done by the people at the big house? And after everything Gordon had done? Now, over the fish (haddock so fresh it almost seemed to melt off one's fork) Gina asked, "Might it just be lack of polish, with Clara?" Gordon said he thought it might well be. He said she hadn't been prepared to write proper essays, and that was what Coombe's wanted, and that her French was poor.

"How can Clara's French be poor when her mother's French?" Gina asked, exasperated as ever by the very mention of her sister-in-law, and Gordon said it seemed that Nadège had some idea that while it was all right to speak French to Clara it was not advisable to teach her how to write it. "Because she's not a teacher," said Gordon, offering no other comment, as was his habit when things were particularly stupid or absurd, while Janet let loose a "How ridiculous! What can she be thinking? Her own daughter! I taught you two to read and write – teacher indeed," and so on. Janet liked to proceed in little volleys of condemnation or delight. Gina looked out of the window, watched a rather sleek and expensive-looking boat come in to dock, and said nothing.

"Did you notice?" was the first thing Gina said to Robert, at a table outside the pub on the harbour to which they had repaired after the meal. Gordon and Janet were going for a walk, they said, and then back to the house. Janet had said they were rather tired from the drive down, and given Gina a spare key.

"Notice what?"

"Two. You two. I taught you two to read and write."

"That's true, isn't it?"

"*Two*," said Gina, more insistently. "Two, not three. As if Susie didn't count any more. As if she really had disappeared. It's as if she, Mum I mean, has got on to some new stage." She heard her own voice tighten and darken.

"Do you remember," said Robert, surprisingly, "Susie, and that wave?"

Gina didn't.

"I'll go and get the drinks," said Robert. "What are you having?"

Gina said she would have a beer, at which Robert looked mildly astonished.

"Bottled? Draft?"

"Bottled," she said. "Something craft. Not too hoppy. You know."

She wondered, as she watched seagulls circle high up, riding the breeze, which wave he had meant, but then fell to contemplating what might be termed the New Robert. He had certainly improved, she thought, as she watched him make his way indoors and up to the bar, in spite of all the business at Paddington. Being in love with Melanie (this was not the term Robert used, but it was surely what it came down to) must be doing him good. He was less gruff than he had been – what are you having, not what do you want – and he looked less hopeless and shuffling now. Doughy, yes, but she saw him smile and exchange a word with a young woman as he went past, saw the woman react as if this and he were perfectly normal. He was not unattractive, although getting that beard trimmed would certainly be an improvement. In fact he looked somewhat more urbane than in times past, which was incongruous for a man who had recently entered a monastery: oddly, this seemed to have done more for his social polish than several years of marriage.

Robert came back – the queue at the bar was not too bad, for this time of year – and set a bottle of beer in front of her with a glass. "Cornish craft," he said. 'Proper Job', it said on the label. Gina drank from the bottle, ignoring the glass, and, as Robert looked at her in surprise, said, "So?" and then, "Which wave— ?"

"I don't think it was that far from here," he said. "Somewhere in Devon, I think. You must remember." And now that he had mentioned it, of course she did. It had been a similar English, donkeys-on-the-beach and ice-creams kind of holiday, in fact the only holiday of that kind they had taken together as a family that Gina could remember, Gordon and Janet's tastes tending more towards camping in the French or German countryside and learning to do useful things, speaking French and German among them.

"Why did we go to Devon? We never did things like that."

"Because of the new job, I think," said Robert. "Moving to Crick House. No money to go abroad. Auntie Jenny lent us her house while she was in Spain."

Auntie Jenny was in fact a great-aunt on Janet's side they had hardly known, but it was coming back to Gina now: the house so much more comfortable that their own, although "vulgar", as Janet said, with faux leather sofas and carpeted bathrooms, double beds covered with cushions even in the children's rooms and a bar in the lounge *("sitting-room"*, said Janet). They had gone to the beach, walked along the promenade in the evenings, gone for ice-creams and sometimes fish and chips, but otherwise done things which hadn't cost much money or any at all, although that had not struck Gina at the time. After two or three days, once they knew their way around, Gordon and Janet had left the children to it, taking the car and going on long afternoons out – the children, they said, were quite happy on the beach, and that was so: it was their first experience of a beach that was not "unspoilt", a beach with ice-creams and plenty going on. Gina would read her book between forays into the sea;

Robert and Susie would build increasingly elaborate sandcastles or bury each other up to their necks. Sometimes Susie would go looking for shells: there were particular ones she prized, intact razors and anything with a whorl. The rules were that none of them was to go into the sea alone and that Gina, as eldest, should always know where the other two were, and it worked well enough.

On the day of the wave, however, the uninterrupted sunshine and frivolity gave way, quite early in the afternoon, to cloud and a creeping coolness. Families began to leave the beach. Gina pulled a sweatshirt on over her swimsuit, legs long and bare, and carried on reading, but when next she looked up Robert and Susie were dressed, their bathing things and tea things packed neatly in the beach bag, and clearly waiting for her to get up from where she lay on her towel. She complained that she was quite happy where she was, but her legs were cold and the wind was getting up, so she struggled into her shorts and shook the sand out of her towel.

They straggled up the steps, aiming for the promenade, stopping when they reached the carpark, not quite sure what to do with themselves. In the end they sat on a bench at the back of the carpark, looking out over the sea, slightly sheltered from the wind which was now quite cool. And it had been then, the wave.

"I do remember," said Gina now. "I do remember now." She could feel something stirring, preparing to surface, under the skin of consciousness. How very monkish of Robert to bring this up now, answering her in parables. What was the idea of this one?

At the time the trouble was that it didn't look like a wave: it didn't "look like" anything, because they had no idea what they were looking at. Tidal waves were not much spoken of in those days, they were not in any way within the children's experience. There had seemed to be some disturbance on the horizon, something you could not really make out, some grey-blue mass you had no way of interpreting or understanding, and then there was Susie, bored and chilly, running towards it to warm herself up and try to see what it could be.

They had sat there, Gina and Robert, until it was a moment too late for fear – and then each could hear the other shouting and they were both running towards her, towards the place where Susie had been, between the bonnet of a car and the railings at the edge of the car park. Gina realised now that she had always had an image of these railings in her head, that they had never gone away: a pattern of fat, horizontal metal tubes and spheres, three bars to a section, turquoise paint peeling, and patches of rusting iron underneath. What she had forgotten in the meantime, and remembered now, was the great wall that had slammed into them from the sea, and, when it sucked away, the sudden sight of a soaked blond pony-tail and a rainbow-striped Clothkits sweatshirt which meant Susie. She was trapped, mercifully, between the railings and a car bonnet, and she was crying and breathing in appalled, laboured pants, but breathing all the same, and not only breathing, but, oh joy, managing, as they put their arms round her and helped her back to the bench – Susie, their little sister! – to speak. "I wanted to see," she was trying to say, through chattering teeth, "I wanted to see what it was!"

"Did people help?" said Gina to Robert, three decades on. "Did anyone come and help us?" She had no memory of what happened next: they must have got her dry, she thought, they must have given her tea from the flask Janet always made up for them – this was before bottled water, and fizzy drinks were strictly rationed.

"There was a family," said Robert. "Don't you remember? A couple, with a spaniel and a baby. They made us get in their car and you thought they were going to kidnap us."

"Presumably they didn't."

"They drove us back to the house and we gave Susie a bath. With Matey."

"Matey?" Gina remembered Matey, bubble bath in a slightly conical tube made to look like a funny sailor, but she had no recall whatsoever of this particular bath. Her mind was running on a different track.

"We didn't tell them, did we?" she said. "We didn't tell Gordon and Janet." She was surprised to hear herself referring to her parents by their Christian names.

"Because if we had," said Robert, "It would have been the end of going to the beach on our own. Even Susie could see that."

"Yes, I suppose so," said Gina. She had a sudden vision in her head of an adult Susie, waving – waving, maybe, to say yes, I'm still here, waving to say, no, I haven't disappeared, there are still three, three not two. Or perhaps it was only a meaningless spin-off, her brain making connections that weren't there. She was tired. The alcohol wasn't helping.

"Anyway," said Robert, as Gina shredded a beer-mat absently. "What's going on with you?"

"What do you mean?" said, Gina, panicked.

"You look... different. And what's with the beer?"

"Beer?" But she knew there was no point hedging: it wasn't just the beer. And since she had been in more regular contact with Robert in the past few months than ever in their adult lives, which was how she knew about St Agnes Mount, and Anthony and Melanie and Sister Agnes, at some level she probably wanted to tell him. She sighed, because it was a long time since her journey had begun the previous day, but withholding suddenly seemed more tiring than answering the question. But there was the difficulty of knowing where to start, as the wavelets lapped in the harbour and the pink and purple sky began to darken. "Come for a walk," she said, "And I'll tell you." It might be easier if she didn't have to sit and watch his face.

VI

Where, where to begin? Gina had not come from Paris. That is to say, she had come from Charles de Gaulle on a tiny, insectile plane, with propellers over the wings you could see from your seat if you looked up, which was most odd, but she had not come only from Paris. Prior to that plane, she had been on a much larger plane for the best part of nine hours, and where it has flown from was Chicago.

"Chicago?"

"Yes. It's sort of where I live now."

"You live in America?"

"Yes. Sort of. Pretty much. But not Chicago. I live in Waldo, Michigan." How American, to give the town, then the state. She heard herself do it as her eyes raked over the window display of the independent bookshop, filing it away to be explored next day.

It had started in Paris, a few days after her last meeting with Jean-Louis, when he was up from Lyon and the thing was clearly over. There had been a conference, as there were always conferences, and Gina had been doing her usual apocalypse thing, speaking, specifically, about the Noah myth as intertext in nuclear novels, with the flood as stand-in for the bomb, or the reverse, depending how you wanted to read.

She was a little removed, a little elsewhere; she was, in short, past caring. She had by this time been living in the new flat for a few weeks, boxes still unpacked, and one of the things she had stopped doing to a great extent was eating, or at any rate eating at home (if the flat could be described as home, since it was more of a depot). She would buy bits of things from Monop or Marks and Spencer, salads and packaged fruit, and eat on benches in the street. So by the day of the conference she felt lighter, but also somewhat weak. She was thinking about seeing Jean-Louis, and how she didn't really want to, though she didn't care very much either, but once she was on the dais and beginning, eyes sweeping over the audience, trying to gather her authority and salvage her sense of self, it was not Jean-Louis's face that drew her eye but a different face altogether.

It was – how to make Robert understand this? – a very interesting face. It had a pronounced bone structure, a square, un-European bone structure which could have been severe, but was softened by fine, very arched eyebrows, large brown eyes, a flattened nose, and by an expression of the most courteous attention, which was unusual now that it had somehow become acceptable for conference-goers to openly spend their time fiddling with their phones and laptops, like students in a lecture. Seeing this face, and the expression on it, had immediately made her paper much better: not what she intended to say – it was too late for that – but the conviction with which she said it. Once, at an important point in her demonstration, she looked up at this face in particular, discounting anyone else in the room, and saw it gently nod.

When she went back to her place, she perused the programme and wondered if the owner of the face might possibly be one Professor Edward G. Almeida da Silva, of

University of Waldo, Michigan (North America), who had spoken, the previous day, about Foucault and post-structuralism, when Gina had not bothered to show up. But when the session broke up, the man who may or may not have been the owner of this name was at the centre of a little group of people Gina did not want to see, so she left, and that should have been that. However, two days later she had found herself on the metro, on line four. She had been to Les Halles, looked round the shops a little, intended to go back home, taken the metro the wrong way by mistake, as she sometimes did at that time – it was part of her ghostly wandering around, her haunting of her own life. The train was joggling along in its hot, slow, uneven way, and the window at the end of the carriage was pulled down, so Gina went and sat by it, to get some air. Something made her look up as the train rounded a slight bend and improved her line of vision into the next carriage – and there it was again, that face. And the owner of the face must have sensed and then seen her looking, because just after the next stop, he suddenly appeared at her side, and said, not as a question, but as a statement, "Gina," and she heard herself say "yes", in response to she knew not what.

He sat down beside her, steadying his suitcase between his knees. They talked, as academics do when they need to substitute social interaction, about the papers at the conference, and he said he had enjoyed hers and that she would probably be interested to meet the people in his department back home who were working on climate-change literature, and she had asked where home was; he had said Michigan now, but he was, originally from Brazil, and that his first name was Edward Green. And by this time, which couldn't have been more than ten minutes, it no longer felt as if they were substituting conversation. Gina had an uncanny sense that they had things to say to each other, real things.

"Edward Green?" said Robert, as they walked up a side street towards museum and library. "Why Edward Green?"

"Because," said Gina, who had learnt this some time later, "It was the name of a man in his parents' town, an Englishman, a missionary between the wars – very much respected, it seems. So they called their eldest son Edward Green." He was Edward Green, E.G., and she was Gina Ellis, G.E, they mirrored one another. She liked the symmetry of this, the arbitrary rightness.

"They called him that as a first name?"

"Yes, as a first name."

"With a hyphen?"

"No, of course not with a hyphen, that would put the word stress in the wrong place," said pedantic Gina. "The point is, that's his name. Edward Green."

"And that's what people call him?"

"No, they call him Ed."

Gina did not call him Ed, she called him Eduardo, and he called her Georgina, because he said it was a pity to waste a beautiful name, but she was not yet ready to explain all this to Robert. Suddenly her lover's face flashed across her mind, his Snoopy-face, his intimate face, looking at her quizzically, and something inside her hurt, simply because she was away from him. Talking about him was next best to being with him.

What had happened, said Gina, was that they had arrived at the Gare du Nord, where Eduardo needed to change line and get the RER to Charles de Gaulle, and Gina had found herself following him. They had stood in front of the ticket barrier to the RER for some minutes, still talking, as people rushed and pushed, and then when a particularly aggressive elbow went by Eduardo had said perhaps they could get Gina a ticket to the airport and they could go on talking in the train. And once at the airport, she had gone through to departures with him, and then it has transpired that his plane to Chicago was delayed by two hours. The chance of it, the sheer happenstance, seemed dizzying to Gina, even now – not only that she had gone to the conference when she had thought of not going, that they had met again in the train, that his plane had been delayed, but that Eduardo, born in Sao Paulo, six thousand miles away from Paris, should have been there in the audience at all.

"So – what did you talk about?" Robert asked. Robert was not always a satisfactory conversational partner as he missed cues, missed the point, but he seemed to be making an effort. What he meant, or at least what anyone else would have meant, was, "What did you talk about for two hours at an airport that means you now live in America?" And although Gina felt like talking, suddenly felt like kicking in the dam against what was unsaid, it was hard to remember exactly how it had gone. It hadn't been *exactly*, or it hadn't been just, what they had talked about: it had been the sound of his voice, the smell of his skin, the oddest sense that there was something in this man that had always been missing in her. They sat and talked at a table in front of a café, and he said again that she should come to Waldo because of her interest in floods in literature, and he had not only said this but added, "So when are you going to come? Christmas?" And then he had said, "Have you got an ESTA?"

It was this practicality, this concreteness, that swung it. He had told her to bring snowboots and a fleece and a warm coat, a hat and two pairs of gloves, one to wear inside the other, and asked her what date she would need to be back for her second semester. It hadn't been, Come if you feel like it, come

71

out sometime. It had been, Come from this date to that date, he would pick her up at O'Hare. It had been, Come and work on your papers, come and use the library, come and meet my colleagues. There was an interdepartmental interest in floods, he said, because of the Great Lakes.

When his flight was finally called – the two hours had extended to two and a half – he stood up, gathered his things together, and kissed her on the forehead. What did he see, wondered Gina, what did he see when he looked at her that made him want to kiss her with such tenderness?

Robert said, "And you did? You did go? That's what you did last Christmas? You never even mentioned it."

It was true, she had not mentioned it. Family Christmases were now so far in the past that that her absence would not have registered, but it had all been too fragile and precious to mention, to anyone.

Through the eleven weeks of the semester between Eduardo's trip to Paris and Gina's visit to Michigan, they had Skyped and emailed. As time went on, he picked up his laptop and showed her around his house – his very homely house surrounded by trees, lime and dogwood – the dogwood, he said, would be beautiful for about two weeks in the spring, then he would spend two months clearing up the dead petals. The house seemed to have an extraordinary number of rooms and an excess of undesignated space. In Paris, at least the part of Paris where Gina lived, there were a few aggressively coppiced trees, but no houses. People lived stacked up tight and high, like books in a library. Gina could hear the neighbour's keys in the lock, their footsteps, and their conversations over dinner. The sheer amount of space in and around this house astonished her.

One of the upstairs rooms was to be hers, for her stay. It

contained only a divan, a desk and a chest of drawers in cherry wood (everything was cherry wood in Michigan, he said), but its bareness seemed welcoming rather than bleak: the emptiness contained possibility. As the weeks went on, he added small touches to it and showed them to her – there was a set of new bed linen in bright candy stripes – a lot of sunshine yellow – and the selection of books on the shelf changed as he thought of things she might like to read. On one occasion there was a large black cat stretched on the bed, sleek and pleased with himself. "Oh, don't mind him," said Eduardo, as if she was already there. "That's just Pete. If you're allergic to him I'll wash the sheets again." So he had already washed them before he put them on the bed, Gina noted.

"You never said you had a cat," said Gina, to whom this was one more boon.

"No, no, I haven't. He belongs to Kelly. My neighbour, behind,"—as Gina's heart missed a beat. "It's a cat circle. We keep an eye on each other's houses when we're gone. You don't have to have your own cat but you have to feed other people's." He moved the webcam so that she got a good this cat, who looked lustrous and well-looked after, and stretched a front paw languorously, as if in acknowledgement of being admired.

"Why's he called Pete?"

"Short for Jupiter," said Eduardo. "I'm not going to call a cat Jehovah. I've known him from a kitten." And this was the way they went on, on the phone, as Gina was drawn into the domestic life of this house in a town she had never heard of in a country she had barely visited.

In return, Gina showed Eduardo her reflected glimpse of the Eiffel Tower, but not much else. She did not want to show

73

him the boxes, which were still piled up, unpacked. It might have looked as if she had been waiting to be scooped up into some different kind of life, all packed and ready to go, portable, available, and that wasn't it, said Gina's pride and independence: that wasn't it at all.

She had flown out on 21st December, the shortest day, although the journey had felt infinitely long. There was fog, and they sat on the runway for some time before take-off, getting in hours late. She had not wanted Eduardo to pick her up at O'Hare: she got the blue line into the city, although in the end she still had to get a taxi to the hotel, defeated by the slush on the pavements and the cold and damp. She had booked herself into what was advertised as a boutique hotel, near the Hancock Tower. It had a wood-panelled lobby, elevators with brass fittings and antique, fly-spotted mirrors. She had not wanted to arrive in Waldo gritty and grubby and exhausted from the trip, with her semester only just over. She wanted time to recover, and some sort of buffer zone to try to come to terms with the enormity of what she seemed to have started. So she ordered room service, took a very hot bath, and then collapsed into the bed, which was immensely wide and high, like an island she just needed to row a few last strokes to land on.

Next day she took the train to Waldo. "This is America," Eduardo had said, when they had Skyped. "Nobody takes the train." But train-taking was Gina's way, although she was confused by the whole business of this one: being filtered through different waiting rooms at Union Station – no gathering on the platform – and then the strange slowness of it: "C'est le TPV," Eduardo had said, "Le train à petite vitesse". She was, however, charmed by the romance of the musical blaring of the horn, the clanging bell at every level crossing. And when they finally arrived in Waldo, again hours late – the weather was not favourable, there was more fog, so she had not seen a great deal of Michigan as she went past – there on the platform, in a big navy winter jacket and crimson scarf pulled up high and dark woolly hat pulled down low, which made his face all big brown eyes, was Eduardo. She fell into his arms, and then thought how strange it was that this was the first time they had ever hugged.

It went on for a while, the strangeness, as how could it not. She was staying in the house of a man with whom she had only ever spent some three hours, and that by complete chance. Nonetheless, arrival had been encouraging: as well as what Eduardo had shown her of the inside, she had seen the outside of his clapboard gabled house online, painted midnight blue, so she knew what to expect, but what she could not have anticipated was the wash of homeliness as she went in, the sheer him-ness that somehow emanated from the colours, the fabrics, the designs, and the smell, the light, pleasant, unique smell of him. The evening she arrived he had roasted a chicken, and they had it with wine, brought by Gina as a present for a host rather than a lover, and then an apple pie, which almost made her cry for some reason. And later, when she had had a long bath, he came into her room, and circled around her a bit, before settling beside her, in what she thought was a very feline way. Gina pulled the quilt off her own body, pulled it back over both of them, and, as they made love, she felt in him something very ancient, again very home-like, something completely acceptable to her. There was no resistance, nothing to fight against; she felt herself, for the first time in a long time, undivided, and also for the first time, except perhaps long ago with Karin, sex had not felt like some parallel activity. It was part of it, part of how they would know each other.

This part she skated over with Robert. She went on to how odd it was to be suddenly in such close quarters with a man she barely knew. They were still at the stage of being polite with one another. They smiled at each other a lot, like people who didn't share a common language. But sometimes it was like being in a play where the scenery and costumes and actors were all set up but – sudden, nightmare lurch – somebody had forgotten to write the script. She was a dinner guest from Buñuel, abruptly and appallingly on stage. Perhaps Eduardo felt the same, but being on home territory, he had the advantage.

He had arranged drinks, and dinners, and introductions to people in the philosophy, literature and language departments. He also made sure they went to the theatre, and concerts, and talks: in other words, he legitimised her, which was, she thought, very nice of him. He was giving her something to belong to, something to hold on to, other than himself, so she could escape with her dignity intact if it came to it.

Gina found she could not imagine it not working out, but sometimes it felt like being – not a mail-order bride, that would be ridiculous (something like Mary, thought Gina, a quick, grim flicker from the past. Mary had had that kind of life). But it was like being tried out for a job, or auditioning for a role, demonstrating skills in improvisation, something Gina had never done. How to be, what to do? She would come down in the morning and they would kiss in what she experienced as a little whoosh of joy, just to see each other – but how to go on?

Jupiter proved to be a most useful prop: he could be attended to in one way or another when you didn't know what to say. His doings – forbidden leaps onto the breakfast table, miaows of greeting which sounded uncannily like a civil good morning or evening, prolonged gazing at the squirrels Eduardo fed on the deck outside the kitchen – provided something to comment on. He was a mascot, a benign presence, helping them on. Kelly fulfilled this last role also: she had been over with banana bread, a thank you for Eduardo's last bout of looking after Jupiter, and, midway through a spirited description of her trip to see her mother in Florida, in nothing more than a slightly raised eyebrow as she contemplated Gina drinking tea in Eduardo's kitchen she had seemed to bring her into their circle.

A few days in, it was already easier: Gina and Eduardo would sit on the sofa in front of the evening news – he watched French TV, with a laptop hooked up to a big screen – and gradually, with neither of them really seeming to move, they would become closer, and his arm would go round her, and her head would sink onto his shoulder. They did not comment on any of these things – it was too soon for analysis.

"So why does he watch the French news if he's Brazilian?" said Robert, passing over the little gradations of acquaintance Gina was trying to convey.

"Because he spent a long time in France. Nearly ten years. He did his PhD there." Eduardo was a French national. "But for me too, I think."

"To remind you of home?" But this was a very complex question, which Gina could not go into at the moment, not with Robert. There was the utterly unexpected homeliness of Waldo: A-frame houses and tree-lined streets; porches and going places in cars; chicken pot pies and craft beer. Then there was the pleasure-pain of being in England, which had somehow distilled into a grassy rise, glimpsed from the train: poppies against a grey sky on the very verge of opening into light. And there was also the unexpected stab to her soul of coming back to France only to leave again. She had never felt so French as in this last day or two. Her life in France, it seemed to her now, had always been about working on her own sense of alienation, and she had grown sick of it. Yet the very place to which she had fled thinking, "What has this to do with me?" now threatened to wrap around her heart and refuse to let her go.

So she said now to Robert, "I do feel very French, in Waldo. It's *La Nouvelle France*."

"What?"

"You know. Where the French settled. Up into Canada and right across to Detroit. It's full of French people." What she meant was partly-French people, and nearly-French people, and historically French people, and people she could feel at home with, since apparently this was beyond her with actual French people, in France.

"But still – Waldo's where you live now? No more actual France, no more *vieille France*?"

"No. I mean of course I still have to go back to France. It's where I work." But Gina had it in mind to do all her classes on one semester, every year for the foreseeable future, and, if this could not be arranged, to take unpaid leave and try to get a visa which would allow her to work in America, supposing she could find a job. For all the sight of French fields spread beneath the plane had brought tears to her eyes, she was champing at the bit. She had had enough; she needed to leave.

During that first sojourn in Waldo, she had ended up putting her return date back, not forward, travelling on Valentine's Day, wearing a Victorian silver heart-shaped pendant Eduardo had given her, a solid and beautiful thing, something between an amulet and metaphorical armour against the separation. By this time she had already bought another ticket back, for the end of April, and applied for a tourist visa which would allow her to stay for six months. There were ten weeks of the semester to get through, then one week of exams, but she saw this as parenthesis only. She moved between protective brackets; she wasn't really there. By the time the day came to fly back to Chicago, she had placed her flat with a rental agency, furnished, to maximise short and lucrative lets, had put some of her possessions into storage, and had others, clothes, books, her desktop computer, shipped to Waldo, at great expense.

Now it was getting late and Gina's fingers were closing around the key Janet had given her. "Time to turn in", she said, which was Gordon's phrase, and still made them giggle, and they began to head back along the deserted main street. It was only when they were practically in front of the door that Gina turned to Robert and said, in a threatening, older-sister hiss, "Don't say *anything*. To *anyone*." And then, more quietly, "I'm just not ready. Not yet."

*

While she was in the shower, it suddenly occurred to Gina that she had not asked Robert anything in return, about how it was going with Melanie. She had monopolised the conversation, made her own story the main narrative with Robert's a very minor subplot, and Melanie's nowhere at all.

Once in bed, in the high room with its view of treetops raked by a slow breeze against the not-quite-dark, she gave herself over to inventing Melanie. She took things that Robert had said and found herself embroidering around them, but it was more than that: she somehow saw her from the inside, felt her, became her in imagination. She could pull her on like a glove, tune into her, feel her loss of her sense of self, the new vacancy in her eyes. There were moments clearly imprinted on Gina's mind, as if in memory, except that the memory was not hers: the high arch of a late summer evening as she was driven up the backbone of England from prison to St Agnes Mount, the fields of yellow rapeseed, on and on, the light just beginning to fade. She could feel Melanie thinking about her suitcase in the boot, about the possessions she has suddenly been allowed to need again, to be defined by. She could imagine her imagining the nursery and the market garden at St Agnes, where she would be put to work, and wondering if she would give way to vacancy or craziness and lie down and cover herself with earth and weeds and wait for it to end.

What it was, perhaps, Gina thought confusedly, as sleep began to seem, at last, possible, was that they were the same. She had seen a French film, long ago, in which the heroine sat in a café spooning espresso poured over vanilla ice cream and said, "I used to be someone, and now I'm somebody else". And that was entirely it, this was where Gina and Melanie joined. "Under sleep, where all the waters meet," she thought, and then thought no more.

Day one

VII

Gina slept for nine solid hours, and woke up next day to the smell of frying bacon. She rooted out the kimono she had been too tired to find the previous night, shook out her hair, and made her way downstairs to the kitchen, where Janet stood at the stove with her back to her preparing what looked like a traditional English breakfast; not a thing she had ever done in the old days. A half-full cafetière stood on the table and Gina moved towards it, but her bleary, grateful greeting came out wrong because there at the table sat Nadège, Nadège with her mousey hair and her beige name and her air of dispassionate chic and reproach. So what Gina said was "Good morning," rather stiffly, while she looked around for someone to absorb her sister-in-law so she herself could tuck into breakfast. Nadège had always been very odd about manners: for two French women, more, two French female relatives to meet without kissing was bizarre, and Nadège knew it: but she had some sort of thing, one on the list of her many *things*, about not behaving in an ostentatiously French way in England. And if Nadège wasn't going to behave normally, it wasn't for Gina to make the effort.

Then she spotted another mousey head in the garden. When she had loaded her plate, thinking that fish and chips and bacon sandwiches might be best followed up by a salad later in the day, she wandered outside and sat on a wooden bench which had been set against the kitchen wall. After a minute or two of inspecting plants in the flower-bed as if unaware of her presence, the child who must be Clara came over and stood in front of her. If she had been a cat she would have been asking to be stroked or picked up. Mouth full, Gina patted the seat beside her, and her niece sat down. She said, as Gina cast around for some suitable opening gambit and failed to find one, "I like your bathrobe."

"Thanks. I like your jeans," said Gina back, and she did look rather sweet and nicely-dressed, this niece: not all like a reality-TV star. She had her mother's chic without the annoyingness, and her jeans were three-quarter skinnies in a dusky pink. Her hair, which though mousey was more plentiful than her mother's (Robert's genes, so evident in his abundant beard, must have prevailed), was gathered in a pony-tail at the nape of the neck. She seemed quiet, and serious, and altogether more appealing than Gina had dared to imagine. But what, thought Gina, beginning to wake up properly now, what on earth were they supposed to do about Robert – Robert who had not seen or heard from his only daughter for the last three years? *Keep out of it, keep out of it*, said a voice inside her head, but it was too late; she could hear her brother's voice in the hall, talking to Gordon over one shoulder, something about gardens, and now he was pouring coffee, and now—

"Hi Robert," said Gina. And here was the Robert of Paddington Station, standing with his mouth opening and closing silently, looking slapped and bewildered. And how could this be, thought Gina, with a flash of yesterday's annoyance – he knew perfectly well this was going to happen, he must have prepared himself for it at some level. The important thing now the only thing, was that Robert should not, in front of his daughter, weep.

"So here she is," she said, standing up, putting her arm around Clara's shoulders in some sort of gesture of protection. "Here's Clara. Good old Clara."

Good old Clara? She was wittering, she did not know what she was saying. She gathered her plate and her mug, glided through the kitchen in her kimono, and made away upstairs. By now both Janet and Gordon were in place, Janet with her arms folded, waiting to see what Robert would do next, Gordon hovering with a bothered expression.

"Hello, Clara," Gina heard Robert say in a just-acceptably firm voice. And he would just have to take it from there.

*

Gina, smoothing down her ruffled feathers upstairs, felt a little sorry for Robert, with both parents and his older sister acting as audience to this awkward encounter with his daughter. There was always the suspicion that he could not manage, would, to put it in her new American way, screw up. It was as if he had been propelled into a corner in disgrace and had never been able to manoeuvre himself out of it. It seemed to be a given that something had gone wrong with Robert, or had always been wrong with Robert. Janet was in the habit of saying, in relation to her son, "As it was my fault!", or even "It's entirely your father's fault," which probably meant, as Eduardo had once pointed out to Gina, she felt guilty. Gina had conceded that this was perhaps so, but when she thought about it, she couldn't really see what Janet had to feel guilty about, unless it was just being herself, and you couldn't really expect guilt for that.

85

Gina was probably right to see the shunting of Robert into the place marked out for unsatisfactory children as unfair. He had attended Coombe's: a scholarship had been found for him there, although it had been made just as clear to Robert as it would be to Clara later on that this was granted as a favour to Gordon rather than to reward any natural brilliance on his own part (it was recalled, more than once and in front of Robert, that Gina had got in on her own merits). He went as a day boy: Coombe's by then had changed its mind about boarding requirements, since the day girl market was proving lucrative, and had converted an old block of garages at minimal cost to create studies, common rooms, and a dining room for them (lunch only, and the lunches involved a lot of potatoes and tinned tomatoes), calling it New House, a name nicely calibrated to celebrate change while ensuring that the day boys didn't get above themselves.

Robert never rose above academic mediocrity, but with his gentle good nature and imperviousness to the nastier kind of teasing, which he noticed but disregarded, he was considered a stabilising influence. He never acquired a nickname, never became Rob or Robbie, as later on he would never be Bob or Bo. From mid-adolescence, Robert had developed oddly middle-aged looks, accentuated when he was able to grow his beard, and he seemed in some ways older than the others. But above all he was kind; and kindness was in short supply. The virtue of it in schools like Coombe's was just beginning to be felt. A pleasant, family ethos was a selling-point like any other, and it could be used to distinguish Coombe's from bigger, older, more impressive schools. Robert also had a gift for crafts – pottery and silk-screening and silver-smithing, which had been brought in as an attraction for prospective parents, so he could be showcased or explained away, as necessary.

He had also been good, more than good, with the Crick House boys. In fact, there had been a period when he been a real source of strength to Gordon, someone he could count on, not to take initiatives or come up with ideas – this was neither Robert's style nor his place – but simply to understand what Gordon was trying to do and co-operate in it. At this time, Gordon, much concerned with the nuclear threat, had brought in a "module" (new educational jargon at the time) about survival. This he had inaugurated with a showing of the *Protect and Survive* films on a Friday evening. The point had been to get the boys to understand that there might come a time when water might not come out of taps, when food might not be found in shops. He had meant it to be a positive thing, to show the boys how they could help themselves and others, but it had not gone down well.

"We don't want to see this shit, Sir."

"What's the point? Russians drop a bomb on us, ain't nobody gonna survive."

"I'd rather be dead anyway. Just get on wiv it."

And so on. Mary hadn't helped, what with "Won't be long, now", and "World destroyed by fire next time, just you read the Revelation." It seemed she had been involved with some fundamentalist church which she no longer frequented, but to which, if Gordon understood correctly, efforts were being made to lure her back. Then she had started on pregnant women being ripped open and the moon turning to blood, and one of the boys had told her to fuck off back to where she came from, which was a perfect example, Gordon hastened to interject, of knee-jerk racism caused by social ills, and that what they probably meant now was that what Mary had said had disturbed them, not that they wanted her to leave. He had said all this before, or a lot like it, on a number of occasions, and some of the boys had admitted that he had a point, but now it was "I don't want to listen to this crap," and "Stupid Paki bitch" (whatever Mary's origins, they were not Pakistani), and "What's the point of all this blah blah blah *shit*? Bloody nuclear bomb's coming!" Gordon had said, "I'm so sorry, Mary, and Damon will apologise to you in the morning when he's had time to think it over." But he had to admit, at least to himself, she hadn't helped.

Later on there had been what Harry Binley, the most senior night-supervisor, put down in the logbook as "unrest", which probably meant fighting in the dormitories, so Gordon had decided to change tack: he arranged a whole spring and summer programme based on survival, which meant, Janet said, "rough camping". The boys did not have holidays as such (a substitute was brought in to allow Gordon and Janet to go away for a fortnight in August), but Gordon wanted to make these times in some way holiday-like, so he shifted the emphasis from fear, edging cautiously towards the idea of "fun". Learning how to do things might be more acceptable to them than being threatened with annihilation. After all, he argued with himself, the resulting skills would be the same.

Robert had proved invaluable on these trips. He was not only willing, or at least uncomplaining, but competent and reliable in his slow and stolid way, fishing, trapping and skinning rabbits, identifying edible fruits, building makeshift ovens, filtering drinking water, improvising showers with hoses and warmed-up rainwater, digging holes for latrines. "Rich boy," the Crick House boys jeered, to mark him out as not one of them, and because he was at Coombe's, but he was so obviously not rich and not likely to go to *Oxford University*, said with scorn, that soon it was for form only. Robert got on with things, and he never had much to say, and this seemed to go down well.

Gordon came home from the first trip full of his son's survival skills. "But he needs to do more than survive, doesn't he?" said Janet. "He's got no sense of a trajectory. There's nothing he wants to do!" And it was true that Robert seemed to show no ambition, no desire to shine, and had no real idea what he wanted out of life. In spite of his success with the Crick House boys, he showed no signs of wanting to be any kind of educator. He didn't have the backbone, Janet said, and while Gordon thought this unkind, he had to concede that it was pretty much the case. Meanwhile, Gina was at Durham – Durham not Cambridge, in the end, but she was obviously a thriver and a striver and the star of her year, with her nose, as Janet said, constantly in a book, and all sorts of ideas about MAs and doctorates and heaven knew what. Robert had no chance of any of that, but he thought he might like to read French, like his sister, as he had chosen French for one of his A-levels, apparently for lack of other ideas. In the end, after Coombe's, he had got a place at what was known as a "new university", and come out with a 2:2 ("Oh honestly, what's the point?" said Janet).

It was true, Gina thought, thinking about all this as she took her shower, that Robert had not been brilliant, had shown signs of drifting, had had no real idea of what he wanted to do. It hadn't been the best start to adult life, but surely not that unusual. At the time, she had not seen it like that; she had been annoyed by him, because having nothing he wanted to do he had followed her. At this time, she was in Strasbourg, busy with her PhD, and she could have done without him sleeping on her sofa and limping along in her shadow.

Gordon had warned Robert: "Gina's very busy. Don't put

her off." But Gina was not to be put off, not at any price. She had her eye firmly on the prize, as she saw it then, and Robert's various misadventures with finding lodgings and teaching hours – "Are you sure you can teach?" said Gina – interested her little. Why in heaven's name, she wondered, didn't he go somewhere else and do his own thing? Why did he need to try to do hers, or some watered-down version of it? It didn't work out anyway, it was doomed from the start. It was the wrong time of year, and Robert's French was business French, and he had no idea how to analyse grammar or provide commentaries on translation or literature. All that was left for him, said Gina, was giving language classes in companies at an hourly rate, or being some lifelong sessional clinging to the underside of academia.

"You didn't do English literature," he said, frustrated, but she said, "I did subsid English Literature, I have a degree in French literature, an MA in comparative literature, and I'm finishing a PhD in English literature". She fired all this off like bullets from a gun, and watched Robert die. But the Gina of the time didn't care. She had set her heart and chosen her destiny and she looked neither to the right nor to the left. Four days a week she worked on her thesis from two in the afternoon to midnight. One day she devoted to preparing her classes, one day to teaching them, one to other business. She was like a machine. Having Robert sleeping on the bed-settee in her tiny sitting-room/study was an annoyance and a distraction, and she could not understand why he was there anyway, hanging on.

"I need to get on with my work!" she would cry (she was insufferable). Robert would go out and sit around in cafés or see films or whatever it was he did. He tried to propitiate her, prepared food and hoovered the carpet, and came in one day saying, "I've got a job."

"What sort of job?" said Gina, looking up from her card index, assuming it was going to be one more zero-hours tutoring contract. But, "Making dolls," said Robert.

"Dolls?" She pictured wooden spoons dressed in Alsatian bonnets and costumes, done up to be sold on the market. She was not to find out what kind of dolls these were until she went to visit, some time later, and by then, there was other news.

*

When Gina came down to the Falmouth kitchen, dressed and ready for the day, chairs had been brought outside and everyone was drinking tea. "But nobody's said," said Janet, suddenly anxious and peevish, "What we're going to do for the rest of the day. Has nobody got any plans?"

"We weren't sure," said Gina. "We didn't know if we were supposed to make any. I mean," because now get out of that, "We weren't sure if you'd already decided what you wanted to do."

"Didn't you bother to find out *anything* about Cornwall?" said Janet, sounding vexed.

"Well, I did wonder about the Eden Project," said Gina. "Apparently there are these two huge domes—"

"I know what it is," snapped Janet. "It will be overrun with children and it's very expensive".

Gina concentrated hard on saying nothing.

What was decided was to go to St Ives, probably because everyone had heard of it. Janet disappeared back into the kitchen to make a picnic lunch, and Nadège followed Gina in when she went to help, which meant that conversation was limited to, "Cherry tomatoes or gherkins?", "Shall I put in a few oatcakes?" and so on. See it as restful, Gina instructed herself – her own conversations with Janet could come later. But it was still annoying, because Janet saw a lot of Nadège at home so there was no need, thought Gina, for her to hang around the kitchen here too. In fact, it had long been Janet's complaint that Robert's desertion had left her with the widows and orphans, a card Nadège played pretty well. It was not so much that she imposed, said Janet, or that she made it clear that family meals including herself as well as her daughter should be a regular occurrence: it was the waves of disapproval and indignation that somehow, and silently, emanated from her.

VIII

Robert's job with the dolls turned out to be way out in the Vosges, the boonies of eastern France, and the salary was ridiculously low. This was because it came with bed and board – which who but Robert could possibly want in that rather grey, rather grubby, rather bleak little place, the back of beyond, with its morning and evening buses in and out, and no hope for Robert of affording a car?

In fact there were two others who wanted it, or put up with it: these were Robert's colleagues, Marcel and René. They lived in too, on the upper floor of the family home of the Schmitts, the couple who owned the doll factory. Both these men must have been in their fifties, and René, in an unclean white singlet, seemed a little on the slow side. What on earth did Robert find to talk to them about? wondered Gina. But his French had certainly come on by the time she visited him there.

There was only one bathroom for all five occupants of the house, and an outside toilet (Gina stayed in a hotel, which was not much better, a locked shower room which you had to ask permission to use, with each shower added to your bill). The mountain ridges in the distance were blue and striated and beautiful, but the houses spread along the main road in a line were made of something harsh and colourless. Gina looked around when she saw the place and felt one desire only: to run away.

But the dolls were certainly a surprise, and could not be written off in the same way. Robert took the keys – it was a Sunday – and showed Gina around the factory. In the first room was a long work-bench, part of which was piled high with bolts of fabric. Next to this part lay the legless torso of a woman, life-sized. She had white-blonde, shoulder-length hair, and was clad in what was apparently shaping up to be a traditional Alsatian costume – black dress with red and green trimmings, white apron, high hat.

"Oh, I see," said Gina, thinking, Oh, how dull. "What are they for? Museums?"

"This one's for a restaurant," said Robert, but he was moving her on, into the next room, and easing the lid off a crate, then off a large, glossy cardboard box, and she realised she had not seen at all.

This second doll was apparently ready to ship. She was in a sitting position, her arms hugging her knees, "Because we don't want it to look like a coffin," said Robert. She was dark-haired, with the figure of a catwalk model, and wore a peach lace negligée.

"I did the face," said Robert. "Look, I'll show you the photo."

"The photo of what?"

"It was his wife. The client's wife. She committed suicide."

"What?" Gina's eyes flitted back and forth between the artificial face – somehow velvety, not shiny, it must be some special kind of plastic – and the photo. She said, "But... *why?* Why would anyone—" She couldn't formulate it.

"It's a grief thing," said Robert.

"But do they – do they have – ." She could not get out what she wanted to say. It was unusual for her to be at such a disadvantage, with Robert.

"They can," said Robert. "But they don't always. This one isn't for that. The guy just wants her to sit on a chair in the bedroom. So she's there while he sleeps."

"Sleeps!" Beyond this Gina was lost for words.

"And these are the ones that come in for repair," said Robert, leading her to the other end of the room, where more benches were set up, with various pipes and bottles, and protective goggles and masks. He drew back a fleece blanket which had been placed over something that looked now horribly like a corpse.

"She got broken," he said, and, as Gina recoiled, "The guy takes her out in the car, moves her around a lot."

"How?" said Gina.

"In a wheelchair. Because this one's weighted, to make her feel real."

"You're telling me this man pushes a giant doll around in a wheelchair? That's completely sick! I bet people feel sorry for him!"

"I suppose he doesn't see it as a doll," he said. "He probably sees it as his wife. Or his sister, or his mother."

"His *mother!*"

Robert shrugged. He was opening another crate.

"This one"— he indicated a woman whose head lolled back at a horrible angle— "The joint must have gone." He closed it up, opened another. "I haven't started on this one yet, but we're supposed to make her look older. Grey hairs, a few wrinkles a the corners of the eyes." He picked up a piece of paper from within, straightened it out. "Light touch", he deciphered. "Older but not post-menopausal. What does that mean exactly?"

"The waist?" hazarded Gina. "Keep the waist narrow?" Robert found a pencil, scribbled something on the paper, slipped it back under the woman's armpit, patted her hand and murmured something as he closed the lid. "We're always very respectful," he explained, but Gina was off on another track: "How odd, to want it older. You'd think—"

"It makes it more real," said Robert. "If he's getting older, she has to as well."

"Does she?" Gina was beyond amazement. "Why not just get a new doll? If it's dolls you want, just get a new one!"

She was looking at the photos on the wall – she could not stop. These were chrome-framed, with ivory surrounds. If you'd called it a disturbing new exhibition and put it in the Musée d'Orsay or the Orangerie, people would have flocked, thought Gina. She was beginning to feel uncomfortable, also, in a different way: to suspect that this was how Robert must have felt, for so long, with her – being confronted with things he couldn't imagine or handle. She tried to pull herself together.

"And do you – do you have to meet these… these people?"

"The clients? Not that often. Monsieur Schmitt does that. But sometimes they do want to stay with them when they're, er, being mended." Be there when they come round from the anaesthetic, thought Gina. It was the craziest, the most troubling, thing she had ever seen, but it stayed there, in a corner of her mind, always, so that when Robert talked later about the Ladies arriving at St Agnes Mount, that was how she saw them: in crates, in need of mending, before they were sent back out into the world. And she saw Robert watch their broken dance, and be the one who tried to mend them. Sometimes, they were Susie.

The reason Gina had been invited out to the Vosges,

suddenly and pressingly – Robert, talking nervously from a phone box, outside the village's one bar – was to meet his "fiancée". Gina greeted this news with the tactless incredulity of youth: "What d'you mean, *engaged?* Don't be ridiculous." She herself had been finding out some interesting things about love at that time: she had become what Janet would have called "involved" with a Lebanese man, a maronite, a year or two younger than her, who was studying engineering in Strasbourg, but was a poet on the side and who would sometimes recite to her in Arabic, in bed. This man had made it very clear all along that the sole aim of his studies was to get a good job in Beirut, and that some time after this, when he was "about thirty-five," he would marry a Lebanese woman and settle down. Since this had been clear from the start and accepted on both sides, Gina had been unprepared for what she had felt when she had seen him out of her flat for the last time: an emptiness, a brief devastation, followed by the realisation that this was at last a truly adult affair. She had felt herself grow up years in a few minutes, and she was proud of this, proud of herself. She had reached a new stage, assimilated new knowledge, knowledge of a different kind from her apocalypse thesis. So for Robert to announce that he was getting engaged, and not as a long, indeterminate state, but as a clear prelude to marriage (the date was already fixed) seemed to Gina at once bizarrely backward – how old-fashioned to actually *marry* the girl – and annoyingly forward: it was uncomfortable and altogether inconsiderate for Robert to reach this milestone before she herself had even thought about it.

She went back for what was to be the engagement dinner, taking two trains then two buses, with her dress and high heeled sandals in her overnight bag and a good supply of reading-matter. The dinner, at a hotel restaurant in the next village (dark timbered dining room, geraniums on the windowsills, silent waiters) was not exactly grim, but was certainly very odd. Nadège, the bride-to-be, came with her mother. Gina saw that Nadège was slightly built, her thin hair cut in a fringe high across her forehead, and that she had perfect skin. She wore no make-up, then or ever. For jewellery, she wore a discreet silver chain with a tiny pendant in the shape of an "N", and small diamanté stud earrings. She had on a pair of beige three-quarter trousers, fashionably cut, a white blouse, and a pair of espadrilles. There was nothing wrong with any of these things, indeed, Gina could quite see her prospective sister-in-law's attractions, but there was something in her appearance which made it apparent that she was completely hermetic to Gina, and that the two women had nothing to say to each other.

Nadège, meditated Gina. It was one of those untranslatable, unassimilable names, like Bérangère or Séverine, but unlike those names it called to mind beige, grège, neige. Nothing colourful and nothing warm. This evening Gina was wearing a cotton dress, "aubergine," claimed the lady in the shop, long, narrow and cut to show her shoulders. Her hair, of which there was a considerable amount at that time, was piled up; she wore pale moonstone earrings, and a number of silver and bead bracelets, one wide, the rest narrow, on her left wrist, so that they clinked a little when she moved. She had used quite a lot of eyeliner and mascara. If anyone looked as if she was getting engaged, it was Gina, not Nadège. She considered herself through Nadège's eyes: she was not indiscreetly dressed, not flawed, not large – but Nadège made her feel all these things, when usually she was sufficiently pleased with her own appearance not to question it too deeply.

The mother simply looked like an older version of Nadège,

with still less hair. The other members of the party were Monsieur and Madame Schmitt, apparently *in loco parentis* to Robert, and Gina herself. Marcel and René had been invited for an aperitif, back at the house, but not to the dinner. Conversation, Gina found with relief, turned on mutual acquaintances of the Schmitts and Nadège's mother, and the three young people were not expected to say a great deal to the company at large. Gina tried to chat to Nadège, but found herself up against something which could have been hostility or just shyness, or simply a lack of animation, like one of Robert's dolls, as if someone needed to pull a string to make her talk. She answered direct questions – yes, she had finished her studies; yes, she had a job as a secretary for an agricultural firm; yes, she spoke English – but did not return them. Gina was by this time aware that her own go-getting-ness, her absolute certainty about what she wanted to do, and also that she could and would do it, seemed to be less well accepted in France than it had been in the circles she had moved in in England, and so made allowances accordingly, toning herself down. Nonetheless, she was mystified by Nadège's apparent absence from this milestone in her own life. Gina ended up having a more or less sotto voce conversation with Robert, whom she had not been able to phone back: where were they planning to live? Did he intend to go on working for the Schmitts in the long term? Had he told Gordon and Janet? (This last louder, more insistent).

"I've invited them to the wedding," he said. The date was barely two months away.

Janet had, or course, threatened not to come, and then not to stay long, and then not to wear a hat, but in the event both parents had been there, as had Gina. Susie at this point was in Italy and did not make the trip. Nadège wore what was in

Gina's opinion a hideous polyester dress, with long sleeves, a high neck, a full skirt and frills. This garment completely drowned her, when she could have worn a narrow shift or a mini-dress and looked stunning. Robert wore a suit he had come back to Strasbourg to buy, at Marks and Spencer, with advice from Gina. The thirty guests were mostly relatives and neighbours of Nadège's mother's, with a few of Nadège's own friends and colleagues. None of these people seemed at all interested in Robert or his family. But at least it was not an expensive affair, and neither was it long; lunch was at the same village restaurant, and was over by mid-afternoon.

There was to be no honeymoon, since neither Robert nor Nadège had any money, so Gordon and Janet had invited the young couple to stay with them: in other words, Robert went home, although by this time Oak Lodge as home was almost over, and Fairfields was beginning to loom on the horizon. Janet was afraid that she would get stuck with them, that they would never leave, so they specified two weeks. During these two weeks, meals would be cooked, laundry and ironing done, trips out organised, and goodwill would reign. But after that, they were on their own. There was a sense of "You've made your bed, now lie in it" about Janet's invitation.

Nadège was clearly not the sort of daughter-in-law Janet had wished for, if Robert must get married. What was needed, Janet said, was someone to sort him out and jolly him along, "someone a bit older." Nadège looked like a girl, barely finished, barely grown up, and her passivity was a severe and constant provocation to her new mother-in-law. A weak and woolly couple, Janet said, and then claimed she hadn't. And thus it was that the newlyweds found themselves back, or at least in Robert's case back, at Coombe's.

Coombe's published its Posts Vacant in the local paper,

and all Robert had had to do was peruse it when it came through the letterbox. He applied for a job as gardener ("of all things", said Janet), but ended up with a position as bookshop manager, which had not yet been advertised but for which there was nonetheless an opening, as the previous incumbent was moving on to the new Waterstones in Birmingham. The school's bookshop was open to the public, and did a reasonably good trade, but the job involved a lot of collecting and mending and effacing marks from textbooks, and buying used books back from the pupils. Also, sets of books had to be boxed up and taken here and there around the school on a wheeled trolley. Gordon felt shame. If his son had to go back to Coombe's (and there was a world out there; why could he not be like Gina and go and conquer it?) it should be as a master, and a better-qualified master than Gordon himself had been. Coming back to do what was to a great extent a manual job was a humiliation, not just for Robert himself but also for Gordon.

A job as assistant matron was found for Nadège. She applied for nothing on her own account, made no moves, she simply let things be arranged for her, as if she was a package in transit. "Like Mary," Gina had said when she was told, except that Mary couldn't help it. In fact, the two situations were not really comparable – there would be no cleaning or cooking for Nadège. Still, "Assistant matron!" said Janet. "And not even in a House. You know what it will be? Ironing and mending and chasing around after those boys. One up from being a servant." Janet, of course, knew this only too well.

"Girls, now, too," said Gordon, because he wanted to say something that might be in some way positive, and that, perhaps, could be looked on as some sort of achievement or progress, for the school if not for his family. But the truth was that he felt tired and flat and disappointed.

With both Robert and Nadège working at the school, they were given a flat in the row of houses on the edge of the town which had been converted for single masters or those married without children, one of which stood empty. Much later, Robert said to Gina, "I couldn't look for a house with Nadège. I couldn't look for a proper job. I always had this feeling everything was going to fall apart."

"Fall apart?"

"From one minute to another. As if it was all going to just disintegrate. Just disappear."

"Oh," said Gina, who spent so much of her time contemplating worlds suddenly swept away without warning, yet had never considered that this might be a preoccupation of her brother's.

IX

Various question marks hung over the trip to St Ives. Nadège had once more taken Clara off somewhere – they would be back, she had said, in half an hour, with the implication that by then the others had better have their act together or else. But Robert still sat on the garden bench, looking subdued and unhappy. He wasn't weeping, but he looked as if he might. Gina sat by him, wishing she didn't feel as if she had to, because she had nothing to say. There was no point saying "Never mind," or "It will be all right", because for all she knew, it wouldn't. Nothing with Robert ever really had been, up to now.

Then there was the problem of who was to go in which car. Gina ran through the possible permutations in her head: Gordon, Janet, Robert; Nadège, Clara, Gina... no, just no; Gordon, Janet, Robert, Gina— equally, no. She couldn't expose Robert to their parents by himself but she didn't want to have to act as his protector either. The half-hour decreed by Nadège was ticking to an end (Gina, who was naturally punctual, had an eye on her watch). When Janet came out and crossed the garden, carrying the picnic bag, Gina politely took it from her and stowed it in the boot, saying, "We'll go on the train. Robert and me." She removed two packages of sandwiches and two bags of fruit from the bag.

"The train?" said Janet. "You'll have to change twice. It will take all day to get there." She managed to sound personally affronted.

"It'll be fine," said Gina, in the firm but slightly distant tone which was the best way to deal with Janet on those occasions when she needed dealing with. "Tell us where you'll be and we'll meet you there. What's the plan?"

"Well," said Janet, with an air of great concession, "We were going to have lunch on the beach, then go to the Tate. But it closes at five."

"Right," said Gina. "We should be there by two." It was not yet eleven. "We'll meet in front of the Tate at two thirty."

"If that's what you want to do," said Janet, suddenly sanguine. Gina went to chivvy Robert.

*

Change at Truro, change at St Erth. At Truro Gina bought a silly and expensive magazine and buried herself in it. St Erth had a vast carpark, which was presumably why it was endowed with a tea-room with things to buy, retro prints and fridge magnets. She bought a magnet for Eduardo, and felt her heart butterfly as she thought of him, still no doubt asleep, as the new day in Waldo would barely have begun. There was still quite some time to wait after this for the shuttle train to St Ives, and Gina and Robert found a wooden bench and ate their picnic lunch. Gina felt obliged to say something about Clara. "It might be easier to talk to Clara without Nadège," she tried. "If you want," she added heroically, "I can get rid of her while you take Clara for an ice-cream."

No answer, and then, "Can you come with me? I can't do it on my own."

"Well, I *can*," said Gina, "If you want me to." Why not? She could always fade out discreetly, once they got going. She wondered why it was that since being in Michigan she was less inclined to jump down Robert's throat, tell him how hopeless he was: was it the prevailing pleasantness in social relations in the Midwest? Or was it simply the way the world had grown softer, because of Edward Green? She asked, not only to cheer Robert up, "How's Melanie?" As Robert had not heard from her since he had left, there was not much to add that Gina did not already know, but she let him talk on about St Agnes Mount, to take his mind off things.

*

Robert did not tell things well: he forgot to explain who people were or how things worked or what the group dynamics were, but the thrust of what he said seemed to be that the future of St Agnes was in need of urgent discussion. Guidance, Robert explained, had to be accepted in whatever form it came. Anthony had been in consultation, material and virtual, with a number of charitable foundations, possible investors and other bodies, but the long and the short of it was that if they were to survive, they would need to change direction completely. He had called a meeting of the Sisters to explain, and, being Anthony, to placate, but above all to maintain control of the situation. The Brothers had been consulted separately, which upset nobody, since the male and female communities existed in parallel rather than together. Anthony reported back and forth on who had said what.

"So you're going to turn us into a holiday resort?" Sister Philomène said, after listening to what he called his presentation.

"Holiday resort!" snorted Sister Agnes. "With a pool and a spa!"

Anthony had said, very patiently – he was good at patience – that the point he had been trying to get across was, precisely, that they had what many people wanted in the modern world. "Peace, quiet, a working religious community, contact with nature. After all, we already have the lay Brothers. Think of this as an extension of their presence."

Sister Bénédicte was the most overtly political of the nuns, and she had an instructive voice, which often clashed with Anthony's more supplicative style. "What worries me," she said, "Is that you're opening up opportunities for voyeurism." She paused to let the word rest, but Sister Agnes rushed in with another snort. "Voyeurism!" She looked around the circle, pausing significantly on Sister Philomène, the only Sister, with her black skin, long legs and tiny waist, likely to excite lust.

"What I mean," said Sister Bénédicte, who found Sister Agnes's vulgarity trying, and often wished she would think more and speak less, "Is that we don't want the Ladies turned into objects of curiosity. We can't have people coming here and worming their stories out of them and for all we know selling them on to the tabloids. This is supposed to be a place of peace and refuge. If you open it up to anyone and everyone, you'll lose its very essence."

Sister Agnes nodded at this. She knew a well-turned phrase when she heard one. Sister Maria, as often, sat and said nothing, which was better on the whole than when she spoke.

"The bottom line," said Anthony, suddenly rather bleak, his natural optimism and bonhomie in abeyance, "Is that if we don't do this, we'll go under. I may as well sell to a developer. Then there'll be a pool and a spa *and* a Michelin-starred restaurant."

Cynicism was so alien to Anthony's nature that this gave

the sisters pause in a way that cold reason could not. And from there it had been a matter of thrashing out the details.

*

"So," said Gina cautiously to Robert as they waited for the St Ives train, "Is that good, for you? Or not?" She meant the general thrust of Anthony's plans.

"It makes it more of a job," said Robert. "Less of a vocation." Gina could have repeated her question, since he hadn't answered it, but did not.

"And how exactly... how's it going to work?"

"There are going to be several different programmes, it seems." 'Programmes' sounded like an Anthony word. "Retreats from city life, themed retreats—"

"What sort of themes?"

"Oh, you know, Christianity for the modern world, that sort of stuff. And then activities. Bee-keeping. Artisan mead-making." Gina wondered if there was any other kind.

"And what will you be doing?" She made this sound sceptical and slightly aggressive because the alternative was condescending.

"Well. Feasibility studies, for the moment. And then, we hope, a course in event management."

She remembered that Robert had a degree in Business Studies, although that had been some time ago.

"Melanie might be able to get a job there," he said, as if the main thing were to study the feasibility of this. "Some of the Ladies do stay on."

Ah, the Ladies, thought Gina. She was greatly interested not only in Melanie, but in those other refugees from normal family life. She was not at all surprised that they stayed on, given that they had pretty much trashed anything there might have been go back to, which was perhaps where Gina's interest in them lay: she recognised something both of Robert and herself. They both seemed, in their different ways, to be natural boat-burners (and if they were, how much more so was Susie?)

Among the polite murderers, apart from Melanie, there were Lady Tilly and Lady Phyllis. Melanie had helped her elderly mother to die; so had Tilly, who was Indian and was named Tilika, but preferred Tilly. ("Do they have to be Christian?" Gina had asked, and Robert had said no, but they had to want to be there, they had to be a good fit – and that actually, Tilly was, there were various Indian traditions of Christianity). Phyllis had "helped" a good friend. One of the Lay Brothers, Nathan, was writing a thesis on legalising euthanasia. While they were waiting for him to finish and present his findings not only to his university but to some committee, they had prayer meetings to try to change the law.

The crimes of Lady Jane, Lady Margaret and Lady Tanya involved their children. Jane, who was divorced, had walked out on her four-year-old son, simply driven off in her car with her clothes in a suitcase and left him in the house, alone. She had told social services she had changed her mind about having a child, which had not gone down well, and after a trial for neglect, she had ended up in prison. Margaret had abandoned her children too, but later on: they were thirteen and ten, and didn't have a father. (Margaret's first name was Tracey, but she said Lady Tracey sounded ridiculous and so she would rather be Margaret, which was her second name, if she was to be a Lady.) Tanya had consistently refused to pay child support, even when ordered by a judge to do so. Jane was the only one who had contact with her son, once a month, in a supervised meeting.

"But *how* do they 'stay on'?" asked Gina. It sounded like leaving school or going on to the sixth form. "Where do they go? Presumably they can't just stay at St Agnes indefinitely."

"There's a house, in the village," said Robert. "One of them, Kate, rented it a while back when she got out, and some of the others have moved in. They have this little community going."

St Agnes Mount without St Agnes Mount, thought Gina. Maybe they couldn't just go out into the world and pretend to be competent in the arts of family life. Maybe it was easier to stay together.

"But – would Melanie want to do that?" As Gina understood it, Melanie had inherited her mother's house. She could quite see she wouldn't want to live in it, but she might sell it and buy a place of her own.

"Well," said Robert. "She might. You know." Gina didn't. "If it works out."

"If...?"

"If the business works out. Anthony's talking about taking me on as manager."

"And...?" You got further by not saying much.

"We could live. Once Melanie's finished. We could live together."

"So you'd have a salary?"

"I don't know. I'm not sure. We'll have to see."

And since this was Robert all over, Gina pressed no further.

*

Melanie, who did after all have an existence outside of Gina's imagination, and indeed outside of Robert's, was at that moment standing by a mossy iron table pushed against an outside wall of the largest greenhouse at St Agnes Mount, drinking tea, taking a break from potting the plants which were brought up by wheelbarrow by the Brothers and, now, in the summer, the Community Helpers (a new kind of paying guest), for sale.

She was contemplating both her earthy fingernails and a vision of herself she had had early on in her stay, shovelling earth and seedlings into her handbag. Getting back her bag, an old and bashed but capacious leather affair, had been almost the best part of being released from prison, or at least, the most distilled moment of joy. The other business, she thought, probably had to do with childlessness, and the threat of insanity brought on by this whole thing, and being at that peculiar age, in this not disagreeable but somewhat peculiar place... She turned her mind to Robert, wondering how he was getting on. There was an emptiness, without him.

The previous evening there had been a certain amount of raillery. Meals at St Agnes Mount were eaten in silence, apart from the notices which were read out after grace, since this was what Anthony had decreed, but when work and dinner and the last devotions were over, the sisters and the ladies had sat round the refectory table nearest the kitchen, as they often did.

"Take a shower, Robert," said Sister Agnes, starting it (this was the first evening, when Robert had been eating fish and chips by the harbour – not noticeably unclean.) "I heard him say it. 'Take a shower'". She made her voice go American because she meant Anthony, who had indeed been heard to make such remarks to Robert before. Her expression combined self-satisfaction and a malicious amusement.

"He had a shower before he went," said Sister Angélique. "He was all right," whether from nunnish goodness or from some tenderness for Robert was unclear. While Sister Angélique would not allow herself, which was one of her phrases, to look on Sister Agnes with disapproval, she often issued these gentle corrections to the tone of the conversation.

"Still went off in his habit, though," said Sister Agnes, unbowed. Anthony had told him not to do that, too.

Melanie had felt uncomfortably that she was being scrutinised for a reaction, and so looked out of the window at nothing in particular. Sister Agnes enjoyed a confrontation. What she wanted was for Melanie to stick up for Robert so she could keep it going, but Melanie said nothing. Like most of the Ladies who passed through St Agnes Mount, she was good at saying nothing, even outside the times of silence. They were chosen in part for this quality.

As it happened, Melanie had had a text from Robert – "Hope Sam fine", which had puzzled her for a while, as the only Sam she knew was her mother's labrador, who, in the nature of things, had had to be dispatched to neighbours. She didn't know whether these people would have kept him, but hoped they had: she didn't like to think of that patient and good-natured creature being sent off somewhere he didn't know, or worse, put down, but she didn't recall mentioning the dog to Robert. Then, dibbing at a tray of earth in the nursery, planting seedlings, she had realised Sam meant S.A.M, St Agnes Mount, and had pondered his avoidance of "you": he had not said "Hope you're fine". She wondered whether he knew that sudden intimacy, for her, now, could feel like an aggression after the excruciating scrutiny of her days and ways at the trial, or whether he could not bring himself to say it on his own account. They were not in the habit of exchanging texts. Mobile phones existed at St Agnes, but were not a great feature of daily life.

She pulled her mind back to Sister Agnes, still going on about what Anthony had said to Robert. At it happened, Robert, on those occasions when he appeared in the nursery or near to Melanie at the refectory or in the chapel, seemed to be pretty much always showered, at least when you would expect him to be so – not half way through the working day… Not that this was the point. You got used to dirt, in prison. But she didn't want to think about the rest. Yes, she liked him. Yes, she looked forward to seeing him as she had imagined she would never look forward to anything again. But she had no conception, at all, of how life would unfold in three months, six months, a year.

"You've got time in front of you to think," Anthony had said at his reception interview with the Lady Melanie, in which she had felt much like a new pupil being brought before the headmaster. "Time to heal. That's the great advantage of this system. Day by day you can pray for guidance"—praying was taken as a universal in the community—"and find out what the future holds".

This Melanie would have dismissed as new-age American pseudo-religious crap, if she had had the energy, but the stuffing had been knocked out of her, which was also more or less a requirement to be a Lady at St Agnes Mount. And so she had just smiled weakly.

X

On the St Ives train, Gina and Robert gazed, wordless, at the view, cove after cove opening up, and the strange, un-English turquoise of the sea. There was something euphoric about it, something that made you think of the exultation of an inland soul, even only from the train, without the need to go to sea.

Walking down from the station, they found St Ives sunny and warm in a way that Falmouth had not been, quite. There was a microclimate, Janet had said. They had no real plan – in the end they had arrived too early to go straight to the Tate. But it turned out there was no need to plan anything, because on the first beach they came to, they found themselves looking down on Gordon, Janet and Clara, spread out on beach towels, with a parasol, and the picnic bag zipped up against marauding seagulls. Gina regretted not bringing her own bathing things, but Janet – waves, shouts, they had been spotted – had brought spare towels and swimming gear for both sexes, as she had not known, she said, who had what.

Time was getting on, said Janet, and if they wanted to bathe, they had better look sharp about it. "Go on, Clara," she said, nodding at her granddaughter, who gathered up her long slim limbs and rushed seawards. Robert paused a moment before remembering his duties and springing heavily after her. Gina edged in, slowly, braving the painful creep of cold water up her back, working up to the shock and delight of actually being in.

"When did you last go swimming in the sea?" said Clara to Gina, treading water, smiling. There was a sweetness in this child.

"The sea? Let me think."

It hadn't been the sea, or not exactly: it had been Lake Huron, two or three weeks previously, on one of Gina's little trips to get to see her new state (she liked the possibilities of the word "state"). There had been fish leaping in the evening sunlight, a squat lighthouse, a huge steel roadbridge into Canada, and an immensely long goods train at the station which had taken endless minutes to draw out so she could cross the track and get into her taxi. Pebbles on the beach hurting her feet, the water clear and cold with waves, almost like the sea, which had surprised her – were they tidal, or from the shipping canal? At all events, as bathes went it had been quick and exhilarating but in quite a different way from now. But in reply to Clara she said, "Oh, it must have been last year, near Lisbon." Portugal, with Karin, had been two years ago, but never mind. "How about you?"

"Last night," said Clara, with another smile. "Mum took me to Perranporth."

"And did you enjoy yourself?"

Gina wished she could be less vacuous, but Clara looked friendly and amenable and straightforward. "Yes", she said. "It was brilliant. We did belly-surfing."

So at least someone had a good time with Nadège.

"What about you?" Clara said, shyly, politely, turning to Robert as if he were an exchange student or the au pair and she was anxious not to leave him out of the conversation.

114

"Oh," said Robert, echoing his sister's tic of language, but sounding encouraged, and probably he shouldn't sound like that, thought Gina. Probably he should sound natural, although she was not sure how this was to be achieved. "Cullercoats. Last summer when we had the heatwave. It's, er," he cast around for how to explain, "It's about twenty miles from St Agnes Mount. Where I am, where I live, now. I sent you a photo, actually."

"What photo?" said Clara. "I didn't get a photo."

Robert reverted to looking speechless and upset.

"I used to swim on that coast sometimes," said Gina, to help Robert out. "When I was at Durham. I used to get the train to Newcastle and then the metro out to the coast." It had been a Saturday afternoon thing, in those in-between times when the whole business of being a student seemed oddly artificial and the pressure of the constant flow of hopes and expectations and disappointments just too much. Sometimes you wanted to be somewhere people went with families and dogs. Not many other people swam.

They separated and splashed around pleasantly, although not for long as the water soon began to feel cold, and besides, Janet was standing up, now, waving in a determined way which meant she wouldn't stop until they got out. Coming up the beach, Gina said they didn't really need to go to the Tate now that they had all met up, that they could phone Nadège – she had forgotten to ask where she was – and say there was a change of plan. Although perhaps it might be nice to see it, in a touristy, ticking-it-off-the-list sort of way.

"Oh yes, I think we ought to. Your father and I haven't seen it yet," said Janet, as Gina towel-dried herself, while Gordon politely turned the other way and studied his road atlas.

So they bought ice creams, and arrived in front of the gallery a little sticky, a little salty, suddenly a happy family at the beach in a Sunday-paper lifestyle article about three-generational mini-breaks. Nadège was early, and stood very straight, waiting for them, near to but not leaning on a wall. The adults gathered themselves and became serious and sedate, while Clara finished her cone. Inside, they walked around in a polite sort of way, looking for something to like other than the pure, hewn lines of the building. Janet said to Gina, "You might like the gallery in Falmouth better. They have some gems among the rubbish," but then Gina found a strange, perspectiveless painting by a fisherman called Alfred Wallis, and as so often in art galleries, if there was just one thing to hold onto, it was enough.

After the first few exhibits they split off into ones and twos: the space was not very big, and it was strange to walk around in a clump. Finally Gina came out onto the gallery and saw that the most impressive exhibit was the sea, framed between pillars, reflected in some kind of sheet metal, hazy and unstable. Clara was next to emerge, and Gina said, trying to make suitable conversation, "So you're going to be a Girl?" She observed the face of a passer-by register this and conceal surprise. "Yes," said Clara, "In September."

"Are you looking forward to it?"

"I think so," she said, looking doubtful. "Do you think I'll like it?"

"Oh yes, I'm sure you will," said Gina, with automatic reassurance, feeling like KayKaren Marlow being questioned by the twins.

"Did you like it?"

"Yes," said Gina, "I did, really. I mean, I really did." There was no point telling Clara about how it had been, or how it had partly been – the relentless low-level harassment, mostly simply for being a girl, partly also for being Gordon's daughter, the determined philistinism in the face of so much "culture", the codes she hadn't cared about enough to master (in this she was to some extent like Robert. It was a question of degree). It had been an exercise in learning not to be yourself in public, ever. You learnt, and quickly, that your real self was unacceptable. Gina hated having to think about how to be, rather than just being (and in this, she was also somewhat like Janet).

But she did not say this to Clara. She said, "It wasn't like it is now when I was there. They'd only just started taking girls, and only in the sixth-form. It wasn't very organised. They didn't have girls' hockey teams or anything like that. They didn't even have proper girls' houses. They hadn't really got used to the idea of girls, then."

"Why doesn't Grandad want me to go?" said Clara, with the sudden subject-switching of youth.

"Oh," said Gina. "I don't think that's true. I think he wants you to have a good education. I'm sure he does, of course he does."

"He said it's disgraceful that only the rich can afford first-class schooling."

"Well, yes," said Gina. "It is, when you think about it. Although it's all much more complex and local than that. But if you've got the opportunity, you have to go for it."

"He said they've pulled the ladder up."

"Do you know what that means?" said Gina, the lecturer in her anxious to instruct.

"That the people who had free grammar schools took them away for the next generation."

So Gordon had done a good job, according to his lights.

"Well all that is probably true to a great extent," said Gina. "But you're thirteen. You have to think about yourself. Just go there and do your best and then when you get the vote—"

"Grandad says he only votes to exercise his democratic duty. He says there's little hope of change for the foreseeable."

This did indeed sound exactly like Gordon. "You know, Clara," said Gina on a different, worried note, "If they get on at you, about being a matron's daughter, don't try to defend yourself. Just smile and be nice."

"What do you mean?" said Clara, wide-eyed, and Gina remembered that Janet had mentioned that she already had friends among the younger pupils, since she had been allowed for the last two years or so to share some of their activities – sports, and, if there was a place left, trips to Stratford-upon-Avon or London, so perhaps it would be all right. Now, though, she would have to say what she had meant.

"Well, until pretty recently it was only masters' children who were allowed to have those scholarships."

"I'm a master's grandchild," interjected Clara, missing the point and making Gina wished she'd never started on it.

"And then there was a boy who was really clever, but he was the school handyman's son, and a group of the masters asked for him to be accepted, and after that they pretty much had to open it out to everyone else."

"Was that Stopford?"

"Oh, oh no," said Gina, surprised. "Stopford was quite a different story. It seems Stopford died young", she added reflectively. "He ended up an alcoholic." But that was another affair altogether, so she said quickly, "This boy went to medical school. To be a doctor."

"But couldn't he have done that if he'd gone to any school?"

"Well yes, in theory. It was just that schools like Coombe's give you an extra chance."

Clara was doing ballet steps, not paying too much attention.

"It might have changed," Gina went on. "I hope it has. But there used to be a lot of – class-conflict. With the day pupils."

"Like what?"

"Oh, you know…" But clearly Clara didn't. "Not having the right dress for the house balls. Not using the right words or having the right accent…"

Clara looked dubious, and Gina was glad that she assumed that she would be all right, acceptable. With relief she saw Robert emerge from the white space within. He said to Clara, "So, you're going to be a Girl in September?"

Gina looked at her niece and saw that she had inherited something of Robert's sweet nature. She betrayed no impatience, but simply said, "Yes," and smiled again, and when he said "And are you looking forward to it?" she did the same. Gina wanted to leave them together but remembered what she had agreed, and stayed, and they all stood for a few moments, in what seemed to be a theatre within a gallery with the ocean as eternal and ever-changing backdrop. Nobody seemed quite sure what came next, and there was no prompter. Then Nadège came out to stand with them and the scene was over.

"Don't you think it looks like a stage, here?" said Gina to Janet, as she joined them, for something to say, and Janet said, "Oh, that reminds me. I've got three tickets for tomorrow evening, for the Minack. *An Inspector Calls*." They all looked at her expectantly – why three? "Clara will be doing it at school," Janet went on. Summer reading-lists before the third form now, thought Gina? Only now you had to say year nine, or, at Coombe's, the F-block. "I thought you may as well go," nodding at Robert and Nadège, both of whose faces registered surprise and dismay, Robert as almost a grimace, Nadège as a quickly-hidden but perceptible flicker.

"So, it's just the three of them?" said Gina, unable to ignore Robert's dog-like gaze on her face, but wishing she could find a more polite way to put it. He was clearly raking it over in his head, how to get out of it. It wouldn't be the Minack that bothered him, or Clara, since that was going better now, but the prospect of an evening with the woman who was still somehow his wife. Nadège was not willing to divorce and the whole thing had been left in abeyance. She set great store by being a married woman, even with her husband living the best part of two hundred miles away and in a monastery.

"Yes, just the three of them," said Janet uncompromisingly.

"What's the Minack?" said Clara, and Gina, who had looked it up when she had heard about the Cornwall jaunt, said, "It's an outdoor theatre right by the sea, and you all sit in a garden and you can see the cliffs and you'll get the sunset. It looks absolutely incredible," which of course made it sound as if she wanted to go, so she added, "Although I'm not mad on Priestley." This made it sound as if the play was not worth going to, which was no improvement.

"I had to work very hard to get those tickets," said Janet, her voice rising rather. "I could only get three and two of those were cancellations. I had to phone any number of times."

"Can't Gina—" began Clara, to her aunt's gratification and to everyone's mortification, but Janet said firmly, "It wouldn't be sophisticated enough for Gina. It's not even part of the season proper. Just some amateur group from some small town in the Midwest." Gina avoided Robert's eye.

"I'm sure it will be interesting," said Gina weakly, defeated by the conflicting needs to fend off Janet, stick up for Robert and betray no knowledge of the Midwest. "I'm sure it will be very good. There are lots of brilliant small theatre groups..." She trailed off. A tune was going through her head, something sentimental, sung around a piano— "When we are married". Wrong play: she remembered some appallingly misogynistic northern patriarch, stifling petit-bourgeois morality and "lah-di-da", but in spite of this unpromising backdrop, there it was, Eduardo's face before her eyes, and herself thinking, one day we will, we will be married. One day, quite soon.

"But why," Gina said as they walked back through the packed and narrow streets, and she got Janet on her own, "Why do you want Robert to go with Nadège?"

"Oh, it will give them a bit of time to talk things over," said Janet.

"What things?"

"They've got to make a decision. Is Robert coming back or isn't he?"

"I shouldn't think so," said Gina, rather brisk and distant. "Did anyone ever think he might?"

"Well, he's not going to stay a monk forever," said Janet. There was a lot Gina could have said to that, but since she and Robert were guardians of each other's secrets she only said, "Even if he doesn't, he won't want to go back to Nadège, will he? They just didn't get on, in any way. They barely knew each other when they got married."

"Look, Gina," said Janet, in her laying-down-the-law voice, which always seemed to sit so strangely with her profession. "I know you don't like Nadège—" The others were some way ahead, since Gina kept stopping to look at amethyst earrings or blocks of fudge and coconut ice in shop windows (Janet making an effort to be patient since she hadn't seen Gina for some time) so this was safe.

"Well, do you?" said Gina.

"That's not the point," said Janet, still very firmly. "As it stands Robert is still her husband and he will always be Clara's father. It's worth giving it another chance. Robert can't just run away from his responsibilities."

"Well, she does get tax credits, or whatever it is." They had had this conversation before on a number of occasions. It was not that Gina condoned her brother's behaviour, and she did think that if he had to leave he could at least have got a paying job; it was simply that there was no point endlessly flogging the dead horse of his purported inadequacy and irresponsibility.

"He should go back to Nadège and get himself a job and *sort himself out*" — this last with threatening emphasis. Gina said nothing. Robert was no more going back to Nadège than she herself was going back to her old life or, a cold and sudden thought from nowhere, Susie was coming back to them. She shook off the memory of Susie's hair – always her hair, always her face half-hidden – and stopped in front of a shop selling huge glass bowls with inset copper fish which were somehow mesmerising even though Janet was standing there, not quite with her arms folded, but as if she might fold them at any moment.

Impossible to take such a large and fragile object back, of course, Gina thought determinedly over her mother, focusing on an oval platter, but she wandered inside and found something called a rainbow wish-stick, about the size of a bookmark, made of bands of coloured glass, and bought that for Eduardo, asking for it to be well-wrapped, and wondering what he would wish for.

There seemed little point going back on the train now that things between Robert and Clara were going so much better, and the tensions of the morning seemed largely forgotten. Gina and Robert sat in the back seat of their parents' car (momentary ghost of a young Susie, wriggling between them). Clara had wanted to come with them, but Janet had said no, she was to go back with her mother, but she could stay the night at the house in Falmouth, on the bed-settee. It was only on the way back, as the two siblings sat silent, that Gina wondered how on earth Robert and Nadège were supposed to talk their marriage over with their daughter in the back of Nadège's car, the next evening. And then at the play, were they supposed to hammer out the bad sex and the broken promises in the queue for entry or the interval? Then it occurred to her that Janet was counting on the romance factor. It wasn't talking it over she had in mind, it was the view and the sunset and the catch in the throat and the sudden realisation that they loved each other more than anyone else in the world. For a psychotherapist, Janet could be astonishingly dense.

XI

They stopped at a pretty pub with a nondescript menu to have dinner, so Gina was able to have her salad. Everyone else had seafood tagliatelle, except Clara, who had missed out the previous evening, and ordered fish and chips. After this, Nadège drove straight back to her B&B. Back at the house in Falmouth, Gina had a bath, singing that silly song from the Priestley play, or the two lines she could remember, and went back to her room in her kimono, intending to go down and drink camomile tea in the garden – but there was Clara, sitting on her bed. Being out all day and with people she could just about cope with, finding her room inhabited after her bath was more delicate. But she could hardly ask her to go away.

"Oh, hi again," she heard herself say (shades of "good old Clara"). But it didn't really matter what she said, because it was clear that Clara had an agenda – she wanted to show her something, or tell her something, or both. She had a notebook on her lap, hardbacked, in a serviceable shade of green. Gina found moisturiser and perfume and waited for her niece to state her business, but, "Do you always put perfume on when you come out of the bath?" said Clara. Gina said yes, for a quiet life, wondering if Clara saw her as some sort of instructor in the ways of the world, and then thinking that might be rather nice.

"Did Susie do that as well?" said Clara, and now we're coming to it, thought Gina. She sat on the pillow at the head of the bed.

"I don't really remember," she said, and, then struck with inspiration, "Do you think she would have done?" She had no idea what Clara knew about Susie, although she could see it was inevitable that she would be interested in her.

"I don't know," said Clara, having her own good-old-Clara moment and hugging her notebook.

"I expect it must be strange for you," said Gina, helping her out. "Having an aunt you don't know at all."

"I feel like I remember her, though," said Clara. "I mean, I feel like there's a sort of gap, where she should be. And if *I* feel like that," went on Clara, who, at thirteen, was a new but keen student of the art of introspection, "Isn't it even stranger for all of you, when you're all together and Susie isn't here?"

Gina considered the question, and said, "Well, sort of. I mean, everyone wishes she could be here. Obviously. But it's not that often we're all together."

It was never. She could barely remember the previous time. "It's like a metro system where you have to go into the centre to get out on another line. Say there are three lines, and they all go into a hub...". And then a fourth, she had been going to say, which had fallen into disuse but could theoretically be renovated and reopened at some point, but it was all getting too complicated. As a simile it didn't entirely make sense, but it was a good reason to get out her pocket plan of the Paris metro and show it to Clara. Then pressing on, muddling even herself, Gina said Gordon and Janet were the centre, so maybe République, and she, Robert and Susie, and now of course Clara and her mother, were all on different lines. They didn't travel together. ("Is this where you live now?" said Clara indicating what had indeed been Gina's stop on line 6 – who had told her? – and Gina said, with an insistence on truth which seemed weaselly even to herself, "That's where my flat is, yes.")

"So... is that what it's like, with families, once you're grown-up?" said Clara. "You don't really see each other, not all together?"

"There are lots that do," said Gina. "Even in England". Her mind had been running ahead of her answer to Clara, on extended families in India or Morocco or wherever and how it probably was very odd, on a worldwide scale, the way the Ellises lived, and how there were other ways of managing and imagining family life. She said, *a propos* of fragmentation and estrangement in families, "Is it nice to see your dad?"

"Ye-es," said Clara, after a moment, in a dubious tone. Gina looked quizzical but said nothing. "It is nice to see him," went on Clara, still sounding doubtful, but more cheerful. "I didn't think it would be, but it is."

"You didn't think it would be?"

"Well, I don't really know him any more. And it was better, when he left. All those horrible arguments."

Gina had heard about these from Robert, and also from Janet, and their accounts converged. It took a lot to push Robert to shouting, but it seemed Nadège had managed it, by the simple expedient of refusing to answer him when he spoke or acknowledge him when he came into a room. It seemed she could keep this up for days. Robert bumbled most of the time, yes, but when necessary, he could be very direct: he could look inside himself, identify what he felt and somehow bring it to expression, even if clumsily. And then he would expect something back. If Nadège had blocked off his natural channel of communication, Gina could quite see that he would be driven to shouting. But there were other things too: according to Janet, Robert would come in from work, go to kiss Nadège, and she would turn her face away, and once he had bought her flowers and she had simply left them on the kitchen table, without putting them in water, and on enquiry said she didn't care for tulips. She threatened to leave a lot, but never carried through. It was amazing, to Gina, that they had got as far as having Clara: the conception had taken place well into the failure of their relationship.

"I don't like it when Grandma says I have to be nice to him," Clara said, her train of thought drawing to a halt.

"Nice? To your dad?"

"Mm." Unhappiness and embarrassment flickered on her face.

"When...?"

"When we got here. The other day. Before I went to the beach with my mum."

"I suppose she just wants everyone to be happy," said Gina, treading very carefully. This was not Janet at all, it was not in her world view, but Gina was trying to avoid words like "upset". She could see it must be destabilising, worse than that, somehow humiliating, to have a father who must not be upset. "But actually," she went on, more firmly, "I think you can just be yourself. You *are* nice!" She hoped Clara understood something of what she was trying to get across without saying it, which was that she didn't need to feel sorry for her father, but Clara was now off on a different tack.

"Did Grandma and Granddad argue?"

"You mean when we were growing up?"

"Yes."

"They did, I suppose. About making decisions. Your grandma would get pretty aerated. But your granddad's pretty good at diffusing things. Changing the subject. Pretending not to care about stuff, for a quiet life. Like your dad is, at heart."

"But they argue a lot about Susie."

She said this as if she knew it to be true. Gina realised she had no idea, but she said, "Well, you can see that they would."

"Because they don't agree?"

"I don't know if there's anything to agree on, really. If she doesn't want to be in touch, there's not much anyone can do."

Clara said nothing for a moment, and Gina wondered what she could add that would be acceptable to the ears of her thirteen-year-old niece. Human beings of that age did not need to hear that the people you thought were immutably part of your world could just withdraw from it, just stop supporting their particular pillar, make everything much heavier for the others and not care.

"Why are you learning Portuguese?" said Clara. The change of subject came as a relief, although Gina's immediate reaction was to slap her hand over the front of her volume of *Pratiquez le Portugais* with her MP3 lying on top of it. She had been going to do "No banco" before she went to bed. In the course of the day there had only been snatched texts with Eduardo, and somehow repeating "May I open a deposit account and request a cheque book?" in his native tongue made her feel closer to him. It was not really the right kind of Portuguese, since Eduardo was from Brazil and the book was European, but the world the two of them had created did not operate according to strict geo-linguistic zones. After all, where they lived was La Nouvelle France, an invented country, a piece of psycho-geography, a sort of Shangri-la where they existed among and between various languages. So questions of *estando* or *estou* or *tren* as opposed to *comboio* were nothing.

She said to Clara, "Oh, I like a bit of Portuguese. I've been to Portugal on holiday, a couple of times." She was gratified by a look which said, How wonderful, to be grown-up and to like a bit of Portuguese, and thought of the tiny pinpricks of possible future lives, like distant stars in a black night, of which childhood had been made. Then she saw that Clara was fiddling with the luggage label on her case, which stood between the head of the bed and the chest of drawers, and that the label said United. Next morning, when Clara's notebook came out again and she slid into detective mode, it occurred to her to worry about this.

But now Robert appeared in the doorway, hovering, looking as if he might like to talk, whether to Gina or Clara was not clear, so Gina said she would go down and make up the bed-settee for Clara, providing Robert with a pretext to follow her downstairs if he wanted and herself with the chance to score a rare good-daughter point with Janet.

"Are there some spare sheets somewhere?" she enquired. Janet was sitting at the kitchen table, reading a Good Food magazine.

"Those old flowery ones," she said. "The ones you used to have on your beds when you were little." Loopy seventies orange and yellow, unevenly faded: Gina remembered.

"You brought those on holiday?"

"They're just the right size for that bed settee", called out Janet from the stairs, with an edge of defensiveness. "I thought Clara might be round." Gina pulled out the bed, wondering whether Clara was pursuing the Susie conversation with Robert, who had stayed upstairs, or whether they were talking about something else, like why Clara, who was apparently quite gratified to see her father, never answered any of his e mails.

"There," said Janet, coming in. "Here's a single quilt." It was a new one, still packed into its zipped plastic case.

"It's pretty well equipped, this house," said Gina, and Janet nodded, apparently pleased.

Susie

XII

There had been a song Susie played so constantly that even Gina absorbed it on her visits home from university, trailing and yearning, with the words, "If we only had time, only had time, for you…". That long-ago summer, Gina had not had time for Susie. It had been like when they were much younger, doing acrobatic positions which needed two to make them, Susie balanced in an arc on Gina's hands and feet – and Gina suddenly letting the structure collapse and rolling away, saying she had to revise, or go and do some other important big-sister thing.

And while it had been clear for a long time that it had been a mistake not to make time, it was also equally clear, at least to Gina, that Gordon and Janet – particularly, she felt, Janet – should not have been outsourcing their problems with Susie to her, passing on their failure to deal with her, to get her, in Janet's much-used phrase, *sorted out*. But they had all pushed Susie away, without meaning to and without realising it would be forever. They had all assumed they could make up for it later on.

It had been the summer that began with Robert's appearance in Strasbourg and ended, for him at least, with his marriage to Nadège. For Gina the summer ended on the fifteenth day of September, with the submission of her doctoral thesis, after which, empty and unsettled, she might well have been glad of Susie's company. But Janet, when she phoned about Susie, had caught her at a bad time, a few weeks before the deadline. Gina was sitting at her desk, scrolling anxiously through a troublesome part of a chapter about the deployment of Ezekiel in Rapture literature, and at the same time checking the references against her card index and intermittently eating a baked potato. Having to pick up the phone put these arrangements out. Janet had jumped straight in with no preliminaries other than hello *("hell"*, answered Gina sotto voce as she got a crumb of buttery baked potato on an index card on Swedenborg).

"Look," Janet said, and it was almost "Now look here": "Susie's finished her exams and we don't know what to do with her." Susie at this time had just come through the lower sixth at Ashwick High, since she had refused point-blank to go to Coombe's, and the exams were internal school exams (as things turned out, she was never to go back for her A-levels). "She's got nothing to do and I don't want her here." Even by Janet's standards, this was harsh.

"Can't she get herself a job?" said Gina, who had spent her inter-sixth form summer working her way through reading lists, both standard and provided at her own request, but also on the till at the new Sainsbury's in Ashwick's just-opened "precinct". Now she saw that she had written Ezekiel where she meant Daniel and cast around for a biro, dislodging the handset from under her chin. Janet did not notice the series of small bounces and clatterings and Gina got the gist of her message in spite of them:

"... so inconsiderate... nobody but yourself... might be able to pull your wool out over your father's eyes..."

At this time Janet seemed to have taken up being extremely rude to people like a new hobby, but Gina had not yet thought of adopting extreme politeness as a strategy to fend her off. Still, she purposely set out to annoy Janet, who was clearly spoiling for a row, by refusing to answer her point by point. She merely said, "So what do you want me to do about it? She's your daughter."

"I want her to come out to you," went on Janet. "I'll get her a train ticket and give her some pocket money and she can go and do brass rubbings in the cathedral or something."

"Brass rubbings!" said Gina incredulously, thinking, No, *The summer is over and we are not yet saved* goes somewhere else completely (this was before everything was on the internet; she combed through the tops of her index cards). "What do you think this is, Barbara Pym? Anyway, Robert's sleeping on the settee – where am I supposed to put her?"

"Can't you ask one of your friends?"

"I can't just ask someone to have Susie to stay." Janet had no idea of the world of tiny, inadequately furnished flats and one-room 'studios' in which Gina and her friends existed.

"It's about time..." Janet was off again on her shortcomings: selfish; do what you want to do and everyone else can go hang. At this point Gina lost patience completely, screamed, "I've got my thesis to finish, it's bad enough with Robert here, *will* you just leave me alone!" She swore under her breath, crashed the receiver back into its cradle, felt rather than saw Robert loom behind her, said "*Go away*," and went on with her work. She heard him – in a flat that size it was impossible not to hear him – murmuring in the bedroom: "I know," "I heard," "Oh yes, she's pretty stressed", "Well why doesn't Susie—" and later "Why don't you—", so he was talking to Susie herself. Where was Gordon in all this, Gina wondered briefly, but she switched off that thought decisively and went back to trying to decide whether a reference to trash-Rapture literature deserved to be kept in or whether she should convey her contempt by deleting it. She went on with her work until one in the morning, when she had a bath, during which she heard Robert creep from her bedroom to his bed in her study, and then went to bed, without saying goodnight.

It was not until some time afterwards that she heard about what had been going on that summer with Gordon and Janet, and had to somehow square it with seeing them at Robert's wedding, where they had seemed perfectly normal, to make the stories match.

*

While Gina was finishing her thesis and Robert was working in the doll factory, Susie was finding out not exactly that there were limits on the duration of parental affection, but that family life did not necessarily go on until the last child had left home. She had almost forgotten what it was like to have Gina and Robert at home, yet a sense of emptiness and incompleteness still hung over Oak Lodge. This was unfortunate, because Susie was by nature a home bird. She liked to spend an afternoon turning out an ottoman or a chest of drawers, rearranging her bedroom, washing and rehanging curtains, or stitching a cushion cover. She would go into town, talk to her friends on the phone or go to their houses, but she preferred to spend long periods in her own company and at home. That was one reason why she hadn't wanted to go to Coombe's: the out-all-day structure of being a day girl, in for chapel, not home until after prep, doing everything like the boarders except sleeping at the school, did not appeal to her.

Janet had been annoyed about this: she was getting to the end of raising her family and she wanted to be free of the constraints of having her youngest child around. Perhaps they should have made her board, Janet said to Gordon, but there seemed no point going against her nature when Susie just was not attracted by any of it, the way Gina had been. She might have got herself deliberately expelled by going to a pub of something (much had changed since Stopford' time, but such expulsions were still possible). Besides, as it had turned out, Susie's exam results in the fifth form had been thin. Gina, hearing about this, had realised that while she herself had always been regarded as the clever one, and Robert as the one with problems, nobody had really ever categorised Susie, nobody knew whether she was clever or not, or what problems she had. She did all right. That seemed to be enough. The family had run out of energy to deal with its youngest member.

Susie herself had the impression of family life packing up around her. She no longer had a place: somehow it all seemed to be over before she had finished her childhood. She would trail over to the Allinghams when she was at a loose end, but Dr Allingham, while always polite and indeed sincerely glad to have a visitor, didn't feel for Susie as she had for Gina, and mostly what she wanted was to hear news of how Gina was getting on ("I think she's still writing her thesis," Susie would say, without much idea of or interest in what a thesis was). Gerry, when he was in, liked to look at Susie, and once sketched her beautiful cloud of pale hair, cinched in at the nape and escaping from a barrette, but he too could see that she wasn't what he was looking for (although he did manage to stroke her hair and neck, on the pretext of adjusting her pose). So Susie drifted to Crick House, sitting in the kitchen and talking to such of the boys who hung around there ("I don't want those boys dragging her down," said Janet, but Gordon shrugged it off).

It was not much of a kitchen as far as cosiness went: the longest side of the L-shaped room was entirely taken up with ugly industrial equipment and stainless steel surfaces. There was an institutionally-tiled floor, and an electric fly catcher; fire extinguishers and laminated safety-notices stood in for spice racks, wall calendars and the paraphernalia of home. There was also always a vague smell of bleach and catering-pack dinners (Mary did not do much actual cooking, except when it came to the eggs and vegetables, and the chickens brought in by the boys from the smallholding. These last she plucked, cleaned, and cooked without complaint). But in the shorter part of the room, perpendicular to the ugliness, so that from some angles it felt like a different room, stood a wooden table of a more homely vintage, with two hard chairs on either side, and at one end a more comfortable chair with a high back and a grubby paisley cushion, in which Mary took her breaks. At the end of the table was a small, dusty window surrounded by ivy, which could be propped open by means of a metal hook. On the sill Mary had placed a single geranium with variegated pink petals, in a cracked earthenware pot. It had, Susie considered, an improbable charm.

The kitchen boys were the quieter types, home-loving like Susie. There was pale, lanky, tow-haired Andy, whose habitual car-theft had landed him at Crick House. The expression "joy-riding" was not yet widely used for this offence, and Andy was in any case less joyful than doleful. There could be an emptiness in his expression, and he liked to sit and not say much. He had, Gordon said, a classic background for a Crick House boy: broken home, alcoholic mother. Crick House existed, as Gordon saw it, to help boys like him override these circumstances, and Andy was good enough at the various activities, if not at schoolwork. In any case, he was co-operative, he gave no trouble. Then there was Innocent, a recent arrival. *("Innocent?"* Damon had said scornfully, but Gordon had repressed this, saying "It's a good name, a good Christian name." "Pity he didn't live up to it," said Janet, when she heard).

Innocent was from a West Indian family in Hackney, and had been caught dealing drugs: a place had been found for this boy even though he was not from the county, because, his notes said, he would not thrive in a harsh regime, and his extremely beautiful face seemed to testify to this. Innocent's mother, who phoned Gordon often, seemed to feel both profound gratitude and profound shame. She didn't want him to spend more time than necessary with the other boys, she had said, several times. Gordon had tried in vain to explain that the whole Crick House project was about spending time together, helping and educating each other, but the upshot was that Innocent sat in the kitchen when he could, with "the quiet boys and the Master's daughter", as he told his mother. Only Innocent and his mother called Gordon "the Master", and continued to do so even when he pointed out that Masters were in charge of university colleges, not Community Homes with Education. But Susie's presence reassured Innocent's mother: if Gordon exposed his own child to this place, it could not be so bad.

And there was Luke, with his olive skin and shiny black hair, which could have indicated any origin from South America to much of Asia, but who himself had no idea "where he was from" (Susie had been naïve enough to ask). Luke's story, Gordon had said, was a sad one. He had been adopted by Christian fundamentalists with a number of children of their own, and they had been unable to cope with him once he hit adolescence and developed a propensity for petty crime. When he was fifteen they had disowned him. Gordon had explained to Susie that this meant reversing the adoption, signing papers to say that Luke was no longer their son. Luke had been brought up in Ashwick, and his family lived barely a mile away from Crick House. Gordon had worried about accepting the placement for this reason, but there was no acceptable alternative – not every town, or even every county, had a Crick House. It was an institutional anomaly.

"Would Luke's parents have done that," asked Susie, who was much struck by the idea that a child could be disowned, "if they hadn't had children of their own?" Gordon said he had no idea, but that one of their own sons had died of a childhood cancer, so maybe you had to cut them some slack, but he said it in a voice that lacked conviction.

Susie liked Luke in particular, for all he was a year and a half younger than she was. She began to look forward to bumping into him at Arthur's paddock (Susie visited Arthur, the donkey, several times most days, and Luke was often there mucking out the Crick House goats, a job to which he did not object). As her summer holidays went on, she would go over to Crick House to visit him specifically at the end of afternoon lessons. The Crick House boys did not have summer holidays, or indeed any holidays as such. Home leave could be arranged but was not encouraged: it was felt that it was better for them to complete their rehabilitation before they went back to their families, who had in one way or another, most of the time, contributed to their problems. Learning how to deal with family influence was one of the things Gordon talked about a lot on his camping trips and film evenings. But Luke now had no family to go back to. "Isn't that like..." Susie had said, struggling for words, "Isn't that like losing everyone in an earthquake?" Gordon had ruffled her hair and said that very probably it was. He approved of Susie's solicitude.

Luke would often be in the kitchen at the end of the school day, drinking tea with Andy, Innocent and Mary, while the other boys had theirs in the dining room. Susie didn't seem to mind Mary, perhaps because there seemed to be some connection between her and Luke. One day Mary had said, breaking one of her habitual long silences, "Came over here. They came over, when I start here." They had looked at her expectantly. "Who did?" said Luke.

"From that church," said Mary.

Mary's way of speaking was staccato at the best of times, but usually she went on if you said nothing. In this she was not unlike Robert.

"Made me go to meeting." Pause. "Bible meeting."

They nodded.

"Mrs Tredwell, Mrs Shaw. Pick me up in car. Give me books. God God God, blah blah blah. And then, when I go cloakroom, get my coat, I hear them. 'Guttersnipe,' those ladies say. 'That guttersnipe.'" Mary's eyes returned to her magazine – Gordon had started to pass on Janet's old copies of Good Housekeeping – and the account seemed to be over.

"That's horrible, Mary," said Susie, shocked. By virtue of not going to Coombe's, she had been less exposed than Gina and Robert to the darker reaches of human nature. Andy and Innocent said nothing. Luke squeezed Susie's hand under the table, because recently there had been kisses and he wanted her to know he was still on. A minute or two went by while they all sipped tea, and then Mary went on.

"Few days later, they bring clothing." It was one of her

peculiarities, to say clothing instead of clothes. "Old baglady bags."

"Clothing?" prompted Susie, feeling that somebody should.

"Old clothing in bags, all brown, green, grey," said Mary in disgust, although her own clothes were nothing if not drab. That day she was wearing a beige A-line skirt in some kind of polyester – it hung oddly on one side because the zip was not completely done up, which made a bulge – and a longline navy cardigan, grown skewed and baggy at the seams and buttoned all the way down. As far as could be ascertained Mary was not fat, but she had a shapeless, graceless, bundled-up look. She also wore a pair of old, flat moccasins that gaped at the sides ("like boats," Janet had said).

"But I take it back," Mary went on now. "I walk all the way to their church and I leave it on the step. I got my wages. I want clothing, I go to Marks and Spencer" – this last with intense pride.

"They sound like awful people," said Susie. She squeezed Luke's hand back under the table, and they all sat in silence for a while, thinking their thoughts and drinking their tea. It felt, Susie thought, more homely than home did. More like being with a family.

XIII

During this period, Crick House was in trouble, and had been for a few months. There had been letters from the Local Education Authority which had sent Gordon into foul moods that seemed to hang over the house like fetid odours, and then meetings. But Gordon complained that these were not honest meetings. They did not involve sitting around a table and thrashing it out: rather, a slick, self-satisfied little man, a Mr Jackson ("Call me Clive", but Gordon called him Jackson, without the Mr) drove down from his office at the Ministry of Education and told Gordon what to think.

Clive Jackson had himself been a teacher at a comprehensive for some years before being, as he irritatingly put it, "called to the Ministry", and he seemed to be constantly spoiling for a fight, at least verbally: he was puny and unattractive, and probably, thought Gordon, who was himself a tall man, and strong with it, scared witless of the boys. Jackson would arrive in his nasty car – too new, too shiny, too low on the road – and tell Gordon what was going to happen. Then Gordon would say why it shouldn't and couldn't, and there would be another exchange of letters. Jackson's complaints included "too much unstructured time," and "too little uniformity of provision". He had told

Gordon he was running the place too much like Coombe's, because of course he knew Gordon's background, although he had no idea of his ambivalence. Gordon needed to realise, he said, that he was not dealing with the same material. Gordon's letters back bemoaned Jackson's "fundamental lack of vision" and "a betrayal of the values of the foundation". He was tempted to add "ignorance" and "blind conformism to pointless diktats", but sighed and refrained. Then the whole thing would begin again: more visits, more letters, more strained conversations on the phone.

It was a time of change, not just for Crick House but for the whole education system in England. The national curriculum was coming, old freedoms had been called into question and were about to be withdrawn. New exams were on the way – Mrs Johnson came back to Oak Lodge to talk over "this *nonsense*," as she put it, not with Janet's querulous emphasis, but with a sort of wonderment.

"Of course, it doesn't affect us, not directly," she said, in her precise, emphatic way, looking from Janet to Gordon. "But as a country," she stabbed at the table, to highlight her words, "What are we doing to our young people? Battery hens, that's what it will be. There'll be no heart in teaching and no joy in learning."

Gordon had no doubt that she was right, and he worried that institutions like Coombe's might be exempt, creating further layers of unfairness. There was already talk of private schools creating their own qualifications. Gordon was appalled at how easy it was for the moneyed private sector to resist, how unthinkable for the great majority with no option but to remain under state control.

It was true that Crick House was also exempt from the reforms in many ways: it had always had a special curriculum and could never have anything else. But CSE exams, with their practical bias which Gordon regarded as sensible for his charges, were now on the way out, and neither Mrs Johnson nor Gordon had much heart for the new GCSEs. The newspapers were full of it – exams that were impossible to fail, Queen instead of Mozart in music, points for writing your name. Mrs Johnson worried that the boys would end up with meaningless qualifications which would not help them into jobs. What bothered Gordon was the threat of government control for teachers. It would become impossible for them to do their jobs as professionals; they would be relegated to the level of subordinates of some central bureaucracy. But these fears remained abstract. The problems that were beginning to loom locally were very much more immediate.

The point at issue was that an institution – a "structure", Jackson called it – with less than two dozen boys was a waste of money, and while the private funding for Crick House was not inconsiderable, the place could not exist without the local education authority. Centralisation of services, Jackson said, would ensure greater efficiency. Besides, the boys, as things stood, had too much space, too much time, too much freedom. They were, said, Jackson, "left to their own devices": pursuing worthwhile hobbies, said Gordon, and that under supervision. Gordon pointed out that the boys did surprisingly well in their exams, as things stood – Innocent, for example, was tipped for six top grades – and said that if they could in addition to that leave Crick House proficient in carpentry and able to grow their own vegetables and look after hens, he would consider his job well done. But, "We need to look forward," said Jackson. This was not the sort of education boys like that needed for the modern world. The idea of husbanding hens and digging up vegetables seemed to make him squeamish.

"These boys will be setting up home like everybody else", said Gordon, at which Jackson looked sceptical. "It they can build a set of bookshelves from a few bits of scrap wood and feed their families then they're half-way towards normal life."

This was perhaps slightly optimistic, and after the first of Jackson's visits, Gordon brought in car and moped maintenance and basic cookery. He himself provided the car and the moped ("You must want your head looking at," said Janet, "They'll sabotage the brakes or go off with the carburettor or something"). Cookery lessons were provided by Mary. Janet had much to say about this too, some of it connected with Mary's personal and kitchen hygiene. Gordon, who snapped a lot at this period for a generally even-tempered man, told Janet that if she had nothing constructive to say he would be grateful if she would say nothing. "And if you want to come and help the boys do cookery, you're very welcome," he added. There was a budget for paying so-called occasional speakers, as Janet knew, but she said she didn't want to be presented as some sort of drudge. "In that case, you might be kind enough" (he put an emphasis on "kind" which suggested that Janet was lacking in this department) to give Mary a bit of advice."

Janet had written a note to Mary and sent her an old Family Cookery book she hadn't used for years. The worst of this was that Mary had been pleased. It had moved Gordon, to see her sit and look through this book, nodding to herself, and he had thought how many opportunities had been missed, to do something for Mary instead of something about her, which was what had happened for most of her life.

So he invited Mary to dinner. Janet had been furious, because he had done it without consulting her, and Gordon had been in turn riled by this unnecessary fury. He had done what no parent should ever do, and gone to Susie to complain about her mother, thinking he might get a sympathetic hearing since Susie had been badly hurt by Janet more than once recently: Janet had first seemed to sour, then to withdraw, and Susie had been a convenient target for the performance of both these states. Susie would wander into wherever Janet was and start chatting and find herself so clearly surplus to requirements that she gave up. Moreover, since Gordon was so busy trying to save Crick House, and – part and parcel of the same thing – was also quite active in local politics, he was often absent in the evenings, and Janet had made it clear that the preparation and serving of dinner need no longer take place, or at least not on a regular basis. Susie often ate alone, and Gordon made himself eggs on toast when he got in, or ate what Susie had made, when she felt like cooking. So when Gordon came to Susie and said that he wanted to invite Mary to dinner, and said, growing bluff and hearty, "You're a good little cook – can you knock something up?", Susie decided that she could, and quite understood why he had not asked Janet.

The dining room, in which Janet had taken such delight when they had first moved in, now had a dusty and disused look. There were miscellaneous deposited objects, a pile of books, perhaps waiting to be returned somewhere, a bag of things to be taken to Oxfam, a box of used light-bulbs. Susie, daunted by the task of producing dinner for a visitor, worked around the dust and mess rather than dealing with it, and she also laid the table with an unironed cloth. Janet wandered in towards the end of the preparations. There was something odd about Janet these days; she had a rebellious, dare-you-to-bother-me air, almost like a teenager herself. She tutted at the dust and the tablecloth, but then said, "It's not as if Mary's going to notice." Gordon threw her an irritated look.

Mary's arrival brought confusion: she had a package in a plastic carrier bag under her arm, which Janet tried to take off her, assuming it was a hospitality gift of some kind, although it wasn't the right shape for wine and obviously wasn't flowers, while Mary hung onto it with some determination. In fact it contained Mary's indoor shoes, so that the evening began with an inelegant physical tussle, and Janet said "Oh, no need to change," in an over-gracious way tone which made it sound as if Mary had neglected to come in evening dress. But Mary was in fact wearing a black silk devoré tunic, very elegantly cut, over a pair of dark-green velvet trousers. The trousers could have been from Marks and Spencer – they were tapered in that sort of way – but the tunic, which might well have begun life as a dress for a shorter woman, must surely have come from the baglady bags, thought Susie. Good for Mary if she had cherry-picked before making her grand gesture.

Then Mary came in and sat straight down at the table, whereas Gordon had been intending to begin with drinks on the terrace overlooking the garden, which was slightly damp but pretty serviceable. But he brought the tray over to the dining table and carried on as if there was nothing strange in sitting down to gin and tonics at their places.

They seemed to have come to an arrangement that Janet would deal with bringing the food in, so that Susie could take a full part in the dinner, although Gordon took care to extravagantly praise each dish, thus seeming to Janet to be making a joke at her expense by letting it be assumed that she was responsible for the cooking, when three of the four diners knew she wasn't. This resulted in glares and sharply set down dishes.

The food was good: Susie had made mini-quiches and crudités with a garlic dip for a starter, and had baked a whole salmon, which she accompanied with buttered macaroni, to Janet's obvious surprise when she lifted the lid. There was also a green salad, and a mixed-fruit crumble for pudding. Conversation, however, was hard work. Mary did not seem to realise that it was a required component of a dinner party. She ate stolidly, drank a fair bit of wine, watched each face as its owner spoke but said nothing unless in answer to a direct question ("Have you been following the football?" tried Gordon. "No.") There were longish silences. Janet said, "I believe there was an American President's wife who used to write down topics for conversation on slips of paper. Or was it the Queen?" which didn't help. Susie felt increasingly anxious, but she saw that her father was not anxious at all: he was perfectly relaxed. Later he said to Susie, praising her once again for the food, "I think Mary had a splendid time." Gordon liked these old-fashioned, Enid-Blyton expressions, it was something he had learnt at Coombe's and carried over. "Did you see her face? She was thrilled. I bet she's never been invited out to dinner before."

"Never?" said Susie, pondering the possibility of this.

"People like Mary don't get invited out for dinner," said Janet, coming into the kitchen with the tablecloth and napkins in a bundle, to go in the machine. She said it expressly to annoy Gordon, but it was clumsy and fell short of its target

*

Mary took Janet's remark about writing down conversational topics on slips of paper quite literally. A few days after the dinner, she came to Gordon in his break and gave him a list of subjects, written in blue biro on a piece of lined A4 paper.

"Why the Queen is important," he read. "Harm caused by religion. Common varieties of garden bird."

"Thank you, Mary," said Gordon. The obvious thing would be to say, "You must come for dinner again," but he couldn't say that and then just leave her hanging. Next day, he asked her "for a drink" at six, making it clear than no dressing up was required, and hinting that Janet would not be in. In the event, nor was Susie: she was off with Luke, in a field behind Arthur's paddock, although Gordon was not to know this.

Mary, when she arrived, was tremendously changed. It was not so much her clothes – something best described as slacks, and a sort of ethnic blouse – but the smell she gave off, which consisted of various slightly clashing scents, bath oil, soap, shampoo, some sort of perfume. She had applied eye make-up, rather heavily, and although the effect was somewhat ghoulish, it did make her look more... feminine, said Gordon, searching for a compliment. He sat her in an armchair in the sitting room, and courteously read through her list. How this led to the two of them making love on the sofa was anybody's guess.

It didn't come to light straight away, and besides, Janet's business took place in parallel. All this had its own logic, it was not a simple case of tit for tat. As Janet saw it, Gordon was completely bound up with what would turn out to be the long, slow and agonising demise of Crick House, and she herself had simply had enough. She had had enough of being a wife, a being with a secondary existence only, entirely contingent upon Gordon.

"But you've got a job," said Gordon, and Janet told him that was absolutely not the point. She had followed him and fitted round him. Every major decision they had taken had been based on his needs, his wants, his convictions. What she did not explain to Gordon was that she also had a restless, desperate sense of time passing, of something running through her fingers like sand, something she could never get back. In the mirror the skin under her eyes had a new quality, like the topskin of a cake seen through the glass door of an oven just as it begins to rise. Some permanent, irreversible mutation was about to take place, and in a few months or a few years the change would be baked in, irrevocable. In her early forties, Janet had felt she could still run back and touch the young woman she used to be if only she could get more sleep, more sunshine, or more something. As her forties wore on, as she herself wore on, she was forced to acknowledge that that young woman was gone forever, and the most obvious manifestation of this was anger. She was angry with Gordon, angry also with Susie, for being there when Janet felt that if she could only get them all out of the way she could be herself again, or at least she might stand a better chance of remembering what that self had once been.

Gina was not there, but Janet was angry with her too, because she had so decisively disconnected herself from anything Janet understood as normal life. "I don't want children," Gina would say, as if a close study of her mother's failures had brought her to this conclusion. It sent Janet mad, and this was also why she felt that if Susie needed sorting out, then Gina should be the one to do it, and why she had the idea that Susie should be packed off to Strasbourg. Janet did not stop to think that Gina was already sorting out Robert.

So Janet phoned Gina in France and said, "I don't want Susie here," but Gina was no help, Gina, who was more interested in dwelling on the end of the human race than perpetuating it. And as for helping out her family... The very thought of Gina irritated Janet now. She was all set for an easy life, once she'd finished writing whatever it was.

And somewhere in this period Janet began, as far as Gina could reconstruct events afterwards, to drive off quite late in the evenings. She would stay out all night, and come home without saying where she had been. She had always been combative, but now she developed something brazen, not so much in how she looked – she had always been nicely, if conservatively, turned out, and continued to be so – but in her attitude, her expression. It must have been, to her husband and younger daughter, disconcerting. In fact, Gina thought, as she mulled it over, it must have been terribly hard for Susie, already living at the end of family history, with things breaking up around her, to find her mother suddenly no longer her mother, as if she had been replaced by someone else (at this point, Gina's thoughts would always wander off into how this was apparently a syndrome, believing your family and friends had been replaced by people pretending to be them... Then getting back on track, she would think – it was all so inevitable, so rehearsed – about how many, many young people of Susie's age, and far younger, had to deal with their parents' marital difficulties, and didn't use it as a reason for disappearing and never being heard from again).

Although there had been more to it than that. There always was. It was all knotted up, Gordon, Janet, Mary, Luke, Crick House, like some sort of complicated monster that had swallowed Susie whole.

XIV

When Janet phoned to ask Gina to have Susie for the summer holidays, Gina had not spoken to Susie for some time. Phoning abroad in those days was still an expensive business, e-mail had not yet come in, and letters were the preferred form of communication. Gina and Susie corresponded regularly, as they always had since Gina had left for university. Susie liked stationery of all sorts, and for birthdays and Christmas Gina would give her writing paper with envelopes in different colours, a fountain pen with bottles of green and purple ink, and stickers you bought off big rolls in Paperchase. Susie was still using all these in the lower sixth, which was one reason why she would never have done as a Coombe's girl and hadn't wanted to try.

"I am really missing you," Susie wrote to Gina, in Gina's first few weeks at Durham. "Robert never talks about anything interesting." Gina had smiled over breakfast in the college dining room, well able to believe it. "What's it like to live in France?" a later letter had enquired. Susie's envelopes arrived like little scraps of the fabric of home life, when Gina's existence was a practically solitary round of library, gym, and flat, and Friday evenings, after her classes, brought an ache for human company. She sent back postcards of storks and

Alsatian houses, and tried to sound cheerful, although she had, for that first year, never felt so alienated, and had been unprepared for the sublime indifference which seemed to be her lot. She told Susie about her bike rides at the weekends, taking the train out to the villages, cycling around places that were quite pretty but, she didn't say, meant nothing to her at all; then pedalling furiously back to beat the infrequent train to the station, and how the driver once had seen her coming and waited, and how nice she had thought that had been. Gina at this time was well into the zone of the comfort of strangers. A kind word from a shopkeeper could make her day. "Are you making friends at the university?" wrote Susie, but that wasn't how it was, it was each to her own in the university library. By the following year it would all be much better, but Susie's letters, at that time, had cheered Gina up more than their writer knew.

Afterwards, when there were no more letters from Susie, Gina was immensely glad she had kept this little series, some of which were decorated with doodles in coloured pencil – hearts, flowers, whorls. In various house moves she had succumbed to the Zeitgeist and "decluttered", thrown away letters and photographs, and later she regretted this bitterly, not just because of Susie, but because previously people would have kept these things all their lives, and there would have been not just room for them but an appointed place, and what sort of life was she living, forever in small, squared-off flats with no room for anything extraneous? Was it not the general clutter of life, the unstructured accumulation of years, that made you human? In Eduardo's house in Waldo, she would find again that missing protective layer.

Susie's letters the summer Gina had not allowed her to visit had been about how horrible home had become, about how sad Gordon was and how sharp Janet's tongue, about how Arthur seemed suddenly much older and slower and how she was worried about him and thought his joints might be hurting – and about Luke. "I really, really like him. He's had a really terrible life. He was in St Vincent's before he came to Crick House". St Vincent's was the county hospital. "He tried to kill himself." This in itself was not that unusual for Crick House boys, but it must have been the first time Susie had come into direct contact with the phenomenon. "He got home from school one day and his key didn't work, so he rang the doorbell and his dad came to the door and he said, 'You are no longer our son and you don't live here any more,' and then he said, 'Your mother has packed your things,' and handed him a suitcase, just one suitcase. His mum didn't even come to the door. Luke said, 'Where am I supposed to go?' and his dad gave him an envelope with a piece of paper in it, and said, 'That's no longer our concern'. Can you imagine? He just said that because he wanted to say something horrible. He could have said 'Here, look in the envelope and you'll see where you have to go.' But he wanted to say something really pompous and stupid. So Luke got a bus and found the house and rang the doorbell there and there was a nice woman who came to the door" —as opposed to his mother, thought Gina, who enjoyed Susie's way of writing— "and she showed him his room and made him a cup of tea, and told him he could stay there until they got him sorted out."

Gina, like all the Ellises, was used to the boys' depressing life stories, but there was something particularly distressing about this one. Perhaps it was the deliberate, conscious parental failure, which was not quite on the same level as alcoholic mothers or fathers who let violence get the better of them or any of the other situations which developed and festered and grew too big. There was something excessively self-righteous and unattractive about the father on the doorstep with his prepared lines.

"They're all really weird at that church," wrote Susie. "They're not allowed to watch TV or do homework on Sundays. And they're supposed to get saved, and Luke couldn't do it, so he was going to hell. So he couldn't get baptised. They have this sort of pool and you have to testify about all the terrible things you did before you got converted, and his mum said he was still walking in darkness and he would probably *never* be allowed to be baptised. I asked Dad if that was why his parents didn't want him any more, and he said those people have some very strange ideas."

Gordon's idea of Christianity was pragmatic: in his view it provided a framework of basic moral values, however open to interpretation in the modern world, while churchgoing, at best, refreshed and focused the soul. Attendance at the Sunday morning service had been expected at Coombe's – it had its own chapel, and a rather nice choir, even if the chaplain's sermons tended towards the pedestrian – and Gordon took such Crick House boys as wanted to go to St Peter's, Ashwick's parish church, on a Sunday morning. Take-up was quite high: the boys didn't see much of the outside world, and the vicar always welcomed them especially. Perhaps they enjoyed the ritual, which harked back to simpler times. Besides, the alternative was woodwork, and they got enough of that in the week.

"On the first Sunday evening, his girlfriend went round because she was really upset," Susie's letter went on. I bet she was, thought Gina. "His parents wouldn't tell her where he was after the morning service (they had to go to church three times a day, once in the morning, once in the afternoon, once in the evening, and then there was the Young People), but she cried so much that her parents made his parents say what had happened and then they told her so she went round when she was supposed to be at church. And she said they had prayed for him to be rescued from the devil and it was in the sermon. But she was only fourteen." Gina presumed that this meant, only fourteen and so couldn't do much about it, or only fourteen and so withdrew for her own protection.

"Vicky was really nice (she was the house mother), and it was like a family, because there were only four other boys, but Luke got really depressed and he went down to the old railway and a master from Coombe's found him with his wrists slit, and he said, 'Thank God it's not one of ours'. Then he (I mean Luke) went to St Vincent's, then he came to Crick House. He's really nice, Gina, really good-looking and funny, and all he did was swear at his parents and some shop-lifting and things like that." Gina smiled, wondering which things. "Dad says it's only the sort of behaviour which is to be expected." Gina could hear Gordon say it. "Dad says Luke's mum and dad weren't capable of dealing with the issues, because they know who his real mum is but they wouldn't tell him, and children need to know where they come from because it's just human nature. And anyway they had too many children, so they couldn't concentrate on him like he needed."

"I see him every day," Susie went on. "He comes up to my bedroom (Mum's never here so she doesn't know) and sometimes we go to the field". Gina knew which one, behind the paddock. Susie had added a note in the margin, written sideways: "Guess what – once we were there and we looked up and there was Gerry Allingham, watching! Can you imagine?!!" Gina could. Susie went on, "We haven't got any money so we can't go to the cinema or anything."

Going to the cinema from Crick House involved a bus to the station and a train to Birmingham as well as the tickets, so Gina saw the problem. The boys at Crick House did not have pocket money, it was part of the regime, designed really to keep them away from cigarettes and alcohol. If they needed money, they had to make a request for it. Gordon was good at granting these, if they wanted some domestic item like new coffee cups for the house, or even a new pair of jeans, although strictly speaking new clothing went through different channels, and he encouraged the boys to ask for books, to not much effect. Gordon felt outings into the town to buy things were good for them, were normalising, and it was enlightening for the people in the town to get visits from pupils from Crick House as well as Coombe's, and to see them behaving well in public. (It was true that it was an entertainment for the Crick House boys to wait until one of the Coombe's Boys – or Girls – paid with a "note", and then shout "Eton rifles." There had once been a bit of shoving. But boys would be boys, in Gordon's view. He felt they could take it, at Coombe's. Janet told him this was irresponsible.)

Gordon, as Gina knew him, would certainly have given Susie money to go the cinema with Luke on a Saturday afternoon if she had asked. The boys were allowed out, although there was much signing of ledgers and many warnings about the penalties of being late back – in this it was not much different from Coombe's. But it was equally certain that Gordon had no idea what was going on between his daughter and his ward. What would he have done, had he known? He had brought up his family to mix with the Crick House boys and to understand them, but it had probably never occurred to him that one of his daughters could fall for one of them. However equal Gordon wanted them to be, he started out from the view that they were essentially different.

"So finally... we did it!!!!!!," continued Susie's letter. "I was scared but it was really nice. It did hurt a bit but in a nice way. Luke said, 'I love you, Susie,' and I wanted to cry, but I didn't." Oh Susie, Gina must have thought, even reading this for the first time: I hope you're being careful. Thinking about it later, she sometimes saw Susie in her mind's eye, aged about eight, stepping onto a helter-skelter. At the bottom she had cried and said she didn't think it would be like that. "Like what?" they had said, and Susie had replied, "Just, *horrible.*"

XV

On the second night in Falmouth, Gina, who should have been tired from the sea air and the many conversational demands of the day, found herself unable to sleep. She had phoned Eduardo, and they had talked in a pleasantly inconsequential way, and he had mentioned various agreeable things he would like to do to her when she got back, but just as she should have been falling into a deep sleep, she found herself wide awake. Maybe it was because it had seemed so real, Eduardo's voice in her ear as if her was there with her, and now he wasn't. She found herself thinking once more about Melanie, wondering if she had shared her bed with anyone, and if it had been strange to find herself alone, in prison. From what Robert had said, she thought probably not. He had given her to understand that Melanie was quite a solitary person, unconventional, and that this had counted against her at her trial. She kept herself to herself. Maybe this included her bodily self. Whether there was bed-sharing at St Agnes Mount Gina had no idea, and hadn't felt able to ask.

She sighed, pulled on her kimono, and made her way down the two flights of stairs where moonlight filtered palely onto the sage-green carpet through narrow stained glass. She had an idea that red wine was what was needed. Failing that, she would make camomile tea.

Going into the kitchen, she nearly jumped out of her skin: but then the white face, uplit in swimming phantom light, resolved itself into Clara, sitting at the kitchen table with a tablet. She was, she announced to Gina in an anxious voice, reading *An Inspector Calls*, and had had to move into the kitchen because the wifi in the sitting-room kept cutting out.

"But you'll be seeing the play tomorrow", said Gina.

"Someone might ask me something about it", said Clara. Since it was unlikely Robert or Nadège would think to do so, Gina presumed she meant Gordon. Gina gave up a brief and fruitless snoop for red wine and put the kettle on.

"Well, the main thing about it is that a young woman dies – she commits suicide, I think – and it turns out that everyone in the family, it's about a family, had a hand in it." It was a long time since she had read it. "The daughter gets her fired, the son gets her pregnant – no, I think it's the daughter's fiancé who gets the girl pregnant, not the son. And the mother refuses to give her charity... I don't remember what the father does."

"But what about the inspector?"

"The thing is that he isn't really an inspector at all, I mean, not a police inspector. He's supposed to be the voice of conscience, or something. It's a sort of morality play." Nothing from Clara. "You know – they all think well of themselves but it turns out they were all responsible in some way for the death of the girl, and they have to face up to it. I mean they have to face up to themselves. I think that's the thing. Schools love it because it's about integrity. Self-censorship. That sort of thing."

Clara, in her large-framed glasses, looked attentive but still worried.

"I can write that down properly and email it to you if you like," said Gina. "But honestly, you shouldn't worry about it. You'll get it as soon as you see the play."

Clara nodded, yawned and put down her tablet. Gina, sipping her tea, braced herself for a reprise of the conversation about Susie, or Robert, but Clara said, looking more cheerful, "What's it like to live in Paris?"

"Oh, well," said Gina, considering what she could say. "It's got a certain charm. If you like that sort of thing. I mean, it's a very beautiful city." It was, you had to give it that, whatever her own recent problems with it. And the rats. And the dirt. "But where I lived was really small. And you can get sick of that. But surely," remembering her niece was after all half-French, "surely you must have been to Paris?"

"Only through it," said Clara. "When we get the Eurostar. We only go to France to see Mamie".

"And how's that?" said Gina, interested. "Does she still live in the Vosges?"

"Yes. St Pierre-le-Vieux."

"And is it fun, going out to see her?"

Clara looked judicious rather than dubious, as if she was straining to be fair, although Gina could not imagine it was fun from what she had seen of the place some two decades previously. Clara said, "Well, Mamie gets me lots of cakes and things. And they've got a massive garden, and there are these goats at the bottom of it. But apart from looking at the goats, there's not that much to do."

"So what *do* you do?" Gina was curious.

"We go to Cora." That was a hypermarket. "And sometimes we go the market. Sometimes we go swimming. And Mamie makes me watch a lot of TV for my French. And sometimes," she yawned again, putting her hand over her mouth, "I have to watch Mamie cook things, so I learn how to do it. Coq au vin and things like that." Ah, lessons had been learned, thought Gina, remembering Nadège's culinary shortcomings and at the same time imagining the torpor and the boredom and the seemingly endless wait, for Clara, for real life to resume. "But it's much better here," Clara went on. "There are loads of things to look at in the shops. And places to go."

"Yeah, it's not bad," said Gina. "So far."

"And also," Clara went on, looking down at the table, just as Gina had been about to indicate that perhaps she should go to bed, "It's not just that it's boring and there's nothing to do, at Mamie's. It's just that – I don't really *like* her. I mean, I can never get through to her. She's like something made out of plastic. She's not like a grandma." Gina filtered out a query about Janet on that last score, and focused instead on the extraordinary closeness of Clara's feelings about her grandmother to Gina's own about Nadège. (But actually, if she thought about it, Janet seemed to do pretty well with Clara. She seemed pretty grandma-like to Gina).

"Do you think it's awful, not to like her?"

"No, of course not," said Gina, shepherding her niece into the sitting-room, where she got into bed and sat with her arms around her humped knees under the quilt. Gina smiled at the clash of Clara's fuchsia daisy-print pyjamas against the hectic tangerine swirls of the sheets. "It's not awful," she said. "But she's quite old now, and she must like having you around. I mean, you're part of her life. And she's part of yours. It's irrevocable. Even it it's all a bit... unsatisfactory." She heard herself sounding like Gordon. "The thing is," Gina went on, gathering her thoughts, "I do think, I *really* do think, that family has to be the bedrock, whatever happens." This was pretty much what she had formulated recently. "I just think whatever it's like, we're stuck with it. So we might as well make the best of it. And besides," fiddling with a corner of the quilt cover where the pattern was much darker as it had been less exposed, "she's not that bad is, she, this Mamie? I know she's a bit – austere." Gina was against dumbing down for the younger generation.

"How do you mean, you know?"

"Well, she didn't seem fun, exactly."

Clara's was all wide-eyed astonishment. "You know Mamie?"

"I only met her briefly. At the engagement party, and the wedding."

"You mean my parents' wedding?"

"Yes, of course."

"Oh," said Clara, dumbfounded. It has apparently never occurred to her that these two family satellites which she had always regarded as entirely separate should have intercepted one another's orbits. Gina could see her niece's worldview slide a little more clearly into place, like hitting on the right correction in an eye test.

"Can I see that?" she said, indicating Clara's novel, *The Attic Term*, which lay on the coffee table by the head of the settee.

"I got it from a bric a brac," said Clara, moving on, trying out a new word.

Gina flipped over the cover, was glad to feel herself yawn, because now sleep might come. "I used to love these books. I think they're quite valuable now."

"It was 50p."

"There you go then. The gods were smiling on you. 'Night." She rose, took up her teacup, and left Clara to the nascent amours of Ginty and Patrick and the wrath of the icy Miss Keith. There had been a rather stern French grandmother in that, if memory served her well, but one time she came up trumps by inviting Ginty to Paris and buying her racy lingerie...

As Gina made her way upstairs, still sipping her tea, she heard Robert cry out. Thinking she must have disturbed him, she made her footsteps as silent as possible, lifting her feet up like a pony. Then from her room on the second floor, she heard something else beginning, a rumble of short exchanges between Gordon and Janet, a door opening, something called out impatiently, quite loud. The house seemed unquiet. Or perhaps it had nothing to do with the house. Perhaps it was just them, held in this strange matrix of intimacy and secrets, words spoken and unspoken, hearts guessed at and hidden. She pulled up the blind and looked out at the stars.

XVI

Barely two months previously, at the beginning of May, Gina had been back in Eduardo's house for ten days. Waldo, in a very short time, had become the centre of her operations. Helga, one of Eduardo's colleagues in the philosophy department, bumping into Gina on campus at the end of April, had said, "I haven't seen you for a while – been busy?" So being away for ten or eleven weeks was insignificant, it seemed, and now it was Waldo she went away from and came back to.

The intervening semester in Paris had been strange – living in an *appart-hôtel* on the outer reaches of the metro, teaching an unreasonable number of hours to build up her savings, eating cheap Japanese takeouts with her friend Maud, comforting herself by thinking of Simone de Beauvoir's library women with their everlasting *jambon-beurre* and their almost penitential accommodation, to make it seem not so bad. But the semester had also been, as Eduardo said, "victorious": the Fulbright application she had written while still in Waldo at the beginning of February had been successful. Jean-Louis had written her a reference he had not allowed her to read but which apparently had done the trick, or part of it, and now she was back in America with a research contract and a year-long visa, working on apocalypse in 21st century literature as a precondition for creativity. It wasn't about catastrophe scenarios, or not only, she had explained at the interview (taking line 6 out to Passy, glimpsing her flat, another life). It was to do with how human beings, lost in the unimaginable continuum of time, needed mythologies to impose beginnings and endings, timespans to which they could relate. This constituted a suitably upbeat version of death and destruction for such a project, Eduardo had said, and so it had proved.

Gina had spent her first week or so working hard on an article, and felt like a day off. Eduardo was at the university: this time of year meant endless meetings. Jupiter was sitting on the dining table, very upright, planted directly opposite her laptop and looking at her through narrowed eyes. "Did you have sisters?" Gina said to him. "Or were they brothers?" He closed his eyes slowly, which could have meant yes. Or no. Perhaps he looked on them with resentment. According to Kelly, he had got left behind when his mother was transferring her litter from one place to another – she must have been a feral cat – hence his sudden appearance under a bush in her garden, aged about four weeks and still requiring feeding with a dropper. A squirrel had been investigating him, Kelly said: they had been pretty much the same size.

Gina was scrolling through a website called Part Of Me. She had decided to fill in a questionnaire. This venture had grown out of a conversation with Kelly some months before, towards the end of her first visit to Eduardo – although Gina no longer thought in terms of visiting. Kelly had been sitting in the kitchen, as she liked to do, talking. She was a good talker, with a rich, resonant voice, and a certain dryness, and she liked to drop in, since her husband was away for long periods, working on-site in Canada (he was some kind of engineer). On that occasion Kelly had started talking about her sister, whom she hadn't seen for many years: she had apparently produced and abandoned two children.

"She just took off," said Kelly. "Didn't want to know. One good reason not to have children. Who knew you could just change your mind? All your life you hear 'There's nothing like mother love', 'You never regret having a child'. Turns out it's just not true. Go on the internet, there are a million stories like it."

Gina had looked up expectantly, unsure whether they were now supposed to talk about not having children. With time it became a question you learnt not to ask. She didn't like being asked herself.

"Never wanted them," said Kelly, guessing what she was thinking. "And if I had, there were two second-hand ones waiting for me."

"Hand-me-downs," suggested Gina.

"Yeah, take these, your sister's grown out of them," said Kelly.

"There's still a lot of wear in them?"

"Yeah, exactly. The good news is, it's a permanent alibi. No pressure to have any of my own."

"From your parents?"

"From my mum. Dad's been gone a while."

Gina was silent, thinking that her own parents had not pressured her either, although for different reasons: because she so obviously hadn't planned her life that way, and because the grandchild they did have, or at least the way they had her, posed enough problems, and because possibly Janet herself hadn't been keen on the realities of family life. Pressure to have children had come mainly from Jean-Louis. Thank goodness she hadn't; it would have complicated things unspeakably, now. Unable to go into all this – there was too much to explain – she told Kelly about her own missing sister. It was the first time she had thought of Susie as missing, exactly.

"There are a few sites you could try," Kelly said.

"Have you tried?"

"I don't even know if I want to, half the time," said Kelly. "But you get on there and it's sort of addictive. All those stories. Then there's the guilt."

"Guilt?"

"Yeah, Lisa was the bad one, I was the good one." Kelly was now a family lawyer, working part-time, choosing her own hours. "And you know, looking back I think my parents were happy with that. They wouldn't have been so pleased to have little Miss Successful," she fluttered her hands in ironic self-congratulation, "if they hadn't had the one who screwed up all along the line. Isn't that bizarre?"

"Families are bizarre," said Gina. "So – what about your sister's children?"

"Two boys, sixteen and fourteen now. Live with their father. They do ok. He takes them to Florida twice a year to see their grandma."

"But do you know where your sister is?"

"No idea," said Kelly. "Sometimes I don't even know if I want to. Sometimes I get sick of all the misery, you know? It gets under your skin, you can't get rid of it." Darkness flickered for a moment across her big, open face.

Gina knew what Kelly meant, about not knowing if you wanted to know, although the misery about Susie was of a different order. She did not know what kind of life Susie was leading but she couldn't imagine her being a bad person, the sort of person it made you miserable to think about. It was her absence that made for unhappiness, an ongoing pain. But the problem was that Susie would know this, she could not fail to know it, and she kept right on doing it, as if it didn't matter, which arguably did make her a bad person. But perversely, there was guilt too, for Gina: if she had only agreed to let her stay that summer... As it turned out, Robert had left for the Vosges a few days after that terrible phone conversation with Janet, so Susie could have had the bed-settee. And then, if Gina had tried harder to get in touch with her during her year in Italy... Now, three months after that conversation with Kelly, Gina began to fill in an online form.

Name of missing person (when you last knew them):

It was strange to see Susie make the leap from something undefined to "missing person", but Gina could quite see that the missing person diagnosis shaped the mess and clutter into a story everybody knew and could understand, including, perhaps, Gina herself. The two words conferred the purity of the urban myth, readily accessible: a man goes out to buy a pack of cigarettes and never goes home... Of course, this was not exactly what had happened, in the case of Susie. There had been no disappearance, as such. She had an email address, and Gina had heard from her, albeit at very long intervals – emails which said nothing, answered no queries. Now she typed,

Suzanne Isobel Ellis.

They had matching middle names, Georgina Imogen, Robert Ian, Suzanne Isobel, a perhaps surprising touch for Gordon and Janet, who didn't go in for cuteness, but Janet's

middle name was Irene and Gordon's was Ian, so it seemed
they had gone with the theme. They hadn't wanted Ivan or
Ivor or Isambard for Robert, so he got Ian too.

Relationship of missing person to you:

Younger sister.

When did you last see the missing person?

Seventeen years ago.

**Do you believe the missing person to be
deceased?**

No.

No, definitely not.

Are there any adoption issues?

Only very indirectly. She wrote,

No.

So far so good, but then:

Are you actively seeking the missing person?

What do you want from this site?

These were more difficult.
And lastly:

**Briefly describe the circumstances which led to the
person going missing. Include dates and place
names. Describe any contact you have had since
that time.**

Which should have been straightforward, but there was

the effort of going back over it, expressing it clearly. Gina sighed and got down to it, as she had sighed and got down to so many things, writing proposals, projects, papers, abstracts, course descriptions. For a moment, any of those seemed preferable.

Yes

she wrote. She was actively seeking the missing person. Otherwise she would not, presumably, be doing what she was doing. For the moment she seemed to have outsourced her volition – it was as if she was observing herself from the outside.

Under "What do you want from this site?" she typed, "To have a chance of finding Susie", then deleted that and wrote instead, "To find out if anyone else knows what it's like". Jupiter favoured her with a slow and severe blink of his emerald eyes.

And now the last question, about the circumstances which led to the person going missing. How strange, Gina thought, that she had never tried to do this before. Susie's absence had become absorbed into things in a messy, day-to-day way. She hadn't tried to untangle it. She tried now.

Susie got pregnant at the age of seventeen. By a pupil at the reform school run by my father.

(This sounded too dramatic, so she deleted it and tried again).

Susie got pregnant at the age of seventeen. Because this fell at a bad time in the school year (she conceived in August), she ended up not going back to school for her final year.

172

She went international, didn't mention A-levels. She wanted to be understood, for the people out there, whoever they were, not to stop reading.

> She was supposed to be having a year out and then going back to take her exams.

Gina considered this now: it sounded strange, that a pregnancy stopped almost before it had started had prevented Susie from going to school for a whole year. It had been the upset, she supposed, the upheaval, and not wanting to have to explain to her friends at school and have teachers talking about her. But still it seemed odd, she thought now. A year out seemed overly dramatic.

All this had happened not long before Robert and Nadège arrived at Oak Lodge, after their wedding. Had Susie felt the need to avoid them so drastically that she had allowed herself to be be bundled off to another country? But Susie got on well with Robert: they all, more or less, and in spite of everything, got on well.

> She went to Italy to be an au pair.

Gina stopped typing. There had always been something odd about that plan, and even odder about all the business that came after it. Even at the time, Gina had had her doubts about the Italian adventure. Susie had been doing art history, ancient history and Italian at A-level, so going to Italy had seemed a logical idea, some small town not too far from Milan, but an au pair's lot was so hit and miss, so contingent on the whims and idiosyncracies of strangers. On her year abroad from Durham, Gina had met a gap-year au pair whose host family went away for the weekend more than once with friends of theirs, leaving this bright and pleasant but wholly out-of-her-depth eighteen-year-old au pair with their five assorted children to look after single-handed. (She had shut one of them in a cupboard, and asked Gina if she should feel bad about it. Gina had hedged). Of course there were thousands of good experiences every year, young women, and young men now, who were taken to the bosom of their host families, there was the blossoming of everlasting international friendship – but should Susie really have been exposed to this sort of arrangement, at that time?

Susie had gone very silent; there was no postcard or letter on colourful stationery to say she had arrived, and there were no phone calls. Gina got sporadic news through Janet. It was clear that Janet suspected that Susie would have passed on a lot about the events of the summer, which was indeed the case. In fact, Susie was Gina's sole informant on this score: "Can you imagine Dad sleeping with Mary? I can't really imagine anyone sleeping with Mary!" Susie had written, with rather sweet restraint. "And they were screaming in the kitchen (I mean Mum and Dad, not Dad and Mary), which was good because Luke was in my bedroom and he needed to get downstairs without being noticed. Mum was saying, "How could you, with that slattern?" And then Dad said, "Gerry! Utterly pointless, spineless" (sorry, cos I know you used to like him)". Susie, at seven years younger than Gina, had been far too young for confidences about exactly what went on between Gina and Gerry, but Gina had told her a few things, thrown her a few scraps she had thought, in a lordly older-sister way, suitable at the time.

So Gina had not been surprised to find Janet brusque and brittle on the phone. She would emit bulletins, rather than converse: Crick House was in much worse trouble than they'd thought, there was talk of tearing it down and building a

Young Offenders' Institution in its place for two hundred inmates – talk that would eventually solidify into Fairfields; Gordon was barely at home and when he was he hardly spoke; Robert and Nadège were settling into their flat at Coombe's, Janet had finished sewing a set of curtains and cushion-covers for them. On the topic of the newlyweds she would sometimes unbend a little: Nadège had no idea how to do the simplest household things, hang curtains, clean windows. She couldn't imagine what that mother of hers (Janet had not taken to the distant, unbending Frenchwoman) had been thinking of.

"I sometimes wonder what Robert sees in that girl," Janet would say, dismissively. Her tone grew bleaker as the first months of the marriage wore on. And it would have been fun, Gina thought, for Janet to have had the sort of daughter-in-law she could go for coffee with, or clothes-shopping in Birmingham. Nadège was a dead weight (not that there was much weight on her).

"And how's Susie, has she phoned?" Gina assumed that Susie was experiencing restrictions on phoning from where she was and that that was why she hadn't phoned Gina herself.

"Susie's all right," said Janet, perhaps a little cautiously. "She'll need a bit of time to settle in."

A bare three days later Janet phoned Gina again, her voice tense even by her standards.

"You won't believe what's been going on here," she said, very grim. Gina's mind flicked through various scenarios: Susie suddenly back, Mary blackmailing Gordon, Robert and Nadège divorced (too early – it wasn't yet possible). Gordon and Janet divorced?

"You'd better tell me," said Gina.

175

"That boy," spat Janet. "That boy who got Susie into trouble."

"Do you mean Luke? He's all right, isn't he?"

"I don't know what you mean by *all right*."

Gina meant he shouldn't necessarily incur Janet's automatic disapproval, because if there was any fault it was Susie's fault as well, but Janet was already steaming on, "I don't know what you mean by *all right*, because just at this moment he's in police custody and I really don't care whether he's *all right* or not."

"Why?" said Gina, confused. "Do you mean because of Susie?"

"*Because,*" said Janet, with heavy and ominous emphasis, "Because last night when the boys were supposed to be asleep he set fire to Crick House."

"He set fire to Crick House?" Gina was having trouble believing her ears. "Why?" she said again.

"Gina, I do not care a jot *why*. What I care about is that Susie has been involved with this psychopath." Being a psychotherapist did not stop Janet from bandying such terms willy-nilly. "And that my husband" —this was typical of Janet at times of stress, Gordon became hers alone and nothing to do with her children— "could have been killed by that juvenile delinquent."

"Was Dad there?" said Gina. "At the time? When did this happen?"

"No he was *not* there," thundered Janet. "It was two o'clock in the morning."

"So—"

"That violent, criminal thug! Gordon did everything for him, he trusted him with *his own daughter*—"

It hadn't been exactly like that, thought Gina, and, pursuing various trains of thought she managed to come out with "Is Mary ok?" Mary, of course, lived in.

"Mary! Mary!" shouted Janet. "Why this sudden concern with Mary?"

"I mean, is everyone ok, was anyone injured, what about the supervisors?"

"Harry Binley and three of the boys," said Janet. "Smoke inhalation, and Harry's got minor burns. They're still in hospital."

"Oh no."

"And the downstairs windows smashed and as much damage as he could cause with his bare hands."

"Harry Binley?"

"No, Luke!"

"And this is because of – because of Susie?" *Because of the abortion* sounded so bare.

"Who knows what goes through that boy's twisted mind," said Janet, "But if he thinks he's fit to be a father—"

To cut this short Gina said, "So Luke's been arrested?"

"Luke is in police custody and it's the best place for him," said Janet. "He can rot there for all I care."

"Does Susie know?"

Janet sighed a terrible sigh. "I suppose she'll have to," she said, and after a minimum of pleasantries, hung up. Gina phoned Robert.

In spite of what Janet had said, of course there was no rotting in police custody, they would either have to charge him or let him go. But according to Robert, he would certainly be charged and would almost as certainly end up in an institution less enlightened than Crick House. "But why?" said Gina yet again. "Why would he do that? He didn't really expect Susie to keep it, did he?" Robert could not cast any light. But after some weeks Gina learnt that there had been a trial, and that Luke had been sentenced to a year in the youth detention centre in which he had already been held on remand since the fire.

"Terrible place they've put him in," said Gordon, when he spoke to Gina about it. Most of the time Gordon said that whatever was wrong was "nothing I'd bother you with". Confidences were rare, but on this occasion he said, "What they put those boys through. You can't imagine."

Gina, thinking imagining might be worse than knowing, had said, "What, what do you mean?" and Gordon had talked about beatings behind locked doors, and putting boys in stress positions. In a more innocent world, so long before Guantanamo, Gina did not know what this meant, had to ask and then wished she hadn't.

"A short sharp shock, they call it," said Gordon. "These places are run by fools who can't see that once you break a boy you can't easily put him together again."

"Have you... have you visited?" said Gina in a chastened voice. Gordon said he had seen all he ever wanted to see of Haverley Youth Detention Centre a few days after the fire, and that anyway Luke had refused to see him, and had not so far changed his mind.

XVII

Gina, realising she had been looking out into Eduardo's garden for some time – the last of the largest snowheap still had not melted – clicked her screen back into life and applied herself once more to the Part of Me site.

She began once more to type:

> She went to Italy for the academic year, and I met up
> with her on her way home.

They had had lunch on the on the terrace of the rather nice, old-fashioned station bistro in Basel. Susie hadn't eaten much, hadn't even said much, really. Gina still remembered now an odd, luminous quality about her too-pale face, although her hair had still been as wild. At the same time she had seemed somehow grounded, less elfin than she used to be – altogether older.

> But she never arrived home.

This made it sound like a completely different kind of story, like the poor young language assistant who had disappeared during a train journey not long before.

> My train left Basel first. Susie said she didn't mind.

Had she even insisted on it? Gina couldn't remember, but she did remember that she had waved from the pull-down window and had not been sure whether Susie had seen or not, something that had nagged at her over the years.

> And then my mother phoned the next day to say she hadn't been at the station where they were supposed to be meeting her, in London. She just

– not disappeared, that gave the wrong impression –

> went off on her own. It seems she stayed in London with people we didn't know, then she went to Australia on a working holiday visa, then she travelled around the world.

> For the first few years, Susie sent postcards to all of us, intermittently.

There had been a long period in which Susie only seemed to be practising cutting them off, as someone might attempt suicide several times before succeeding, thought Gina. But maybe Susie didn't see it as like suicide, maybe she saw it as saving herself.

> She never gave an address or phone number. After a while the postcards stopped.

When had this been? Gina could not remember. The last one had been, she thought, from the Philippines.

> A bit later, everyone started using e mail and we did have an e mail address for her. We would all write her messages and sometimes she would write back.

Ah yes, the hopeless messages, thought Gina:

Hi Susie, I hope you're ok. I haven't heard from you for ages. It would be great to know where you are and what you're up to. Lots of love.

These were messages you might send to someone you'd known at school, decades since, who had suddenly popped into your head but was really of no importance. The answers that came back were no doubt what the messages deserved. A few days would go by, or a few weeks, then:

I'm ok, hope you are too, xx.

And that would be it, which had had its annoying side: Gina had wondered if Susie got some sort of kick out of all that withholding. When the messages had ceased completely, perhaps seven years previously, it has not been, at first, worse. It has been less irritating. But as time went on, and irritation curdled into a helpless, retroactive grief, Gina had looked for her on social media, and drawn a blank. If Susie was out there, it was clearly under a different name.

*

Now Gina uploaded her form and clicked on the confirmation e mail. Then she went back into the Part of Me site, feeling suddenly tired, and began to scroll through the other stories. Jupiter had moved over to her side of the table and was curled up with one paw dropped down towards her lap, and she stroked his head absently.

The website looked oddly like a dating site: you clicked on the profiles you found interesting. It was organised into "Adoption issues", "Drugs and alcohol", "Debt", and "Other" ("Some stories are published in more than one category"). There was a warning in a fluorescent box that anyone whose sibling had disappeared in suspicious circumstance should go to the police. Gina went into

"Other", and found "Sara, 48, Mass; brother; twenty-three years," "Martina, 22, Texas; sister, five years." The second figure indicated not the ages of the siblings but the time they had been absent. There were avatars, android figures or flowers or ducks. Gina clicked on "Zoe, 44, NY; sister, fifteen years", because her circumstances were the most similar to her own. Zoe's avatar was a teddy bear, but her words were harsh. "I'm pretty sure my sister gets off on this," she wrote. "Breaking my mum and dad's heart, creating a void at the centre of every family occasion: it's a twisted way of finally getting the attention she craves. It makes me so angry that my sister is so determined to ruin our lives." There was a comments section at the bottom of the page, which consisted mostly of "I hear ya" or "Right on the button" on the one hand, and, on the other "Take a good look at yourself and you'll understand why she never wants to see you again". But there was also "Family is an open wound that never heals," which seemed harder to classify as encouragement or censure. Gina clicked off the site, decided to go and do something homely and wholesome, make a chicken pot pie, stew some fruit.

Later that evening, when the chicken pie had been eaten, she told Eduardo how she had spent her afternoon. There had been a lot of evenings, by this time, to talk about their families, to make them strut across the stage like marionettes and say their lines. By now, his background was familiar to her: the bush upbringing in the state of Sao Paulo in the early years – no shoes, and eating iguana meat because you didn't have to pay for it – then the coming of roads and electricity and running water, and the move to the city for the children's education and to prepare their flight out, away. It had been a source of great delight to his father, said Eduardo, that his granddaughter, Eduardo's daughter, had chosen to go back to Brazil to study, that success now meant being selected to go to Brazil, not leave it.

Eduardo liked to draw broad historical sweeps, while Gina took a more psychological approach: of course she had explained it all, Coombe's and Crick House, and the events, public and private, which had brought all that to a close and had somehow, inexplicably, led to the mislaying of Susie. Whereas Eduardo's cast of characters gave out information about an unimaginable elsewhere, her own family puppets tended to make speeches about their inner motivations and duplicities, which Gina sifted through and analysed from one telling to another. But now he told her something he had never told her before, which was that he had a brother who had been shot, and died. "Families shape themselves around these things," he said. "It never heals. But new things come."

Gina nodded, against his shoulder, and he rubbed his cheek against the top of her head, Jupiter-like. She thought of the various people she had known, at school and university, who did have a dead brother or sister, more than you would imagine: a bike accident, a speeding car, meningitis, a mishap while scuba diving, and there, you were *that* student, that family. At least Susie wasn't dead.

Later still they sat half-watching a silly series on his big screen TV. Gina's mind wandered back to Susie: it was perfectly possible that she had her own Eduardo now, maybe children also. There was the thing with Robert: he had said, during their email exchanges when he had first gone to St Agnes Mount, how he sometimes expected to see Susie checking in as a new arrival. He had seen her, or thought he had seen her, on Victoria Station, about three years before, with a child of about four. Gina had jumped on this and phoned him straight away.

"But didn't you speak to her?"

"No, she was too far ahead."

"But do you really think it was her?"

"I don't know, I only saw her from behind, but yes, I think so, it was the way she walked, and her hair."

And it was no good, as it was so often no good with Robert, getting aerated and shouting, the way Janet would have.

Gina sometimes thought she felt Susie coming through *The Guardian*. She was aware there was a word for this, that it was a type of insanity, thinking special messages were being addressed to you in the newspapers. Janet, whose skill as a psychotherapist was largely confined to her knowledge of such classifications, would know. But in these days of reader comments it was perhaps not quite so fanciful. Laying into the family problem page was a weekend entertainment for thousands: the themes recurred, and so did the comments. "My mother behaves badly towards my partner," "My parents will not accept my stepchild", "My sister refuses to invite my fiancé to her wedding": all were followed with variations on "Cut all ties with your family", "They will only make you miserable, life's too short, blood relatives are nothing special, they're just people like anyone else, you're better off without them". Sometimes Gina wondered if Susie herself might be behind some of these comments – could she be A Horse Called Alex (not that far from a Donkey Called Arthur), Zan2000 or ID283153?

But it seemed unlikely; and there was a very uncomfortable element of childish vindictiveness about it all, Gina thought, as well as a rather stupid denial of the basic laws of humanity. In the end she had deleted her account.

*

In bed, Eduardo told Gina that it had been two years after his brother had died that he and his then-wife had adopted their daughter, Julia, and that this had been his new thing. She had been in an orphanage in the north-east of Brazil. His voice grew tender when he talked about his daughter, who was on an honours programme in Ann Arbor and had gone back to Brazil the previous year, not as an orphan but as a privileged American, to spend her junior year abroad at the university in Sao Paulo.

"Did she like it?" said Gina, feeling unqualified to discuss Eduardo's daughter. There were various photos of her around the house, olive-skinned, silken-haired, solid and smiling – probably she had mixed south-American blood, Eduardo said, since she was paler than many in the North-East. She was tremendously clever, it seemed, and would be going after some high-powered job in Washington or New York.

"She loved it," he said. "Absolutely loved it. But she came back saying she was glad to be American." And he laughed privately, thinking about something Gina could not see.

Gina had not yet met Julia. Eduardo had gone to Grand Rapids to have lunch with her and "her mother" (he always said "Julia's mother", never "my ex-wife") between Christmas and New Year, but Gina had not been invited and would not have wished to be. It was far too soon. Nonetheless,in recent Skype calls to her father, Julia had taken to saying "Say hi to Gina", to Gina's tremendous gratification, and Gina would say hi back.

Day two

XVIII

On the morning of the second day in Falmouth, Gina, wandering down to the kitchen in her kimono at past nine o'clock, intending to get some coffee and biscuits and head out into the garden, was intercepted by a forbidding look from Janet, who was busy at the kitchen worktop, filling rolls for later on. Gina understood that she was not to speak or go outside and also that Janet was trying to listen to what was going on without making her presence known. Since both the door and window were open, it was difficult not to hear. "He's just found out she gave him the wrong address for Clara," Janet hissed out of the side of her mouth. "Sshhh." Gina, who hadn't said anything, heard Robert's voice saying, "...just can't understand it. Why would you do that?" Gina could see the top of Nadège's mousey hair from the window – she must be sitting on the wooden bench which stood against the wall of the house.

"I already told you. It was for the best," she said.

"But how could it be for the best? You let Clara think I didn't want to keep in touch at all."

"It would only have confused her," came Nadège's flat little voice, now with a defensive edge.

"But, but—" Robert was not the type to go off on a

furious riff in the garden – he was simply trying to get the words together to express an argument that seemed to him reasonable. "But it must have confused her much more when she never heard anything from me."

"You could have phoned."

"I find it much easier to write," said poor Robert. And since he obviously wasn't going to get angry, at least not verbally, Janet broke her cover and asked Gina how strong she wanted her coffee. Nadège, realising the conversation had become public, got up and walked through the kitchen without saying a word and let herself out of the front door. After a minute or two, Robert came in and sat down.

"All those emails I sent Clara," he said to Gina, picking up their conversation from the train down from Paddington. "It wasn't the right address. Nadège set up a false one. I mean, an address Clara didn't even know about."

Janet harrumphed and left the room.

"And the other way round too?" asked Gina.

"Eh?" Robert looked confused, and Gina felt sorry for him, so she said, rather than barked, "Did Nadège give Clara a false address for you as well?"

"I don't know," said Robert. "I didn't think to ask. But all those times I wrote and Clara didn't write back. She must have been wondering why I never got in touch. I don't think I even kept copies."

"Of yours, to Clara?"

"No. I mean yes."

"But that's got to be easy enough," said Gina. "You just need the log-in for the account Clara didn't know about, and they should all be there, in the in-box. Nadège can give you the password."

Robert regarded his sister bleakly, and Gina remembered

that Nadège had, according to what Robert had said in the past, a stubbornly secretive streak, was, in fact, so reticent as to be devious. Gina thought of her sister-in-law as a smooth, silvery fish, forever on the verge of darting into some back-channel where she could not be pursued. It was not until after the wedding that Robert had found that she steadfastly refused to reveal the identity and circumstances of her father. Robert had presumed this person long-gone in one way or another, dead, divorced, disappeared, and had not been greatly interested, but he had been dismayed by his new wife's refusal to discuss the subject.

"You must have seen his name on her papers, when you got married," said Gina then, but Robert said no, it just said unknown, and that Nadège kept her papers first inside a locked box in a suitcase, and later in a locked box in a locked drawer. "I don't know how you put up with it," Gina had said, and had not been very surprised when he had decided he no longer could.

"But it doesn't really matter what you said in the emails," said Gina now, 'Or not exactly what you said. What matters is that Clara knows you sent them." She had been about to wonder aloud how best this could be arranged, but at that moment Clara appeared in the doorway, yawning in her pink pyjamas, and saying "What emails? What emails did you send me?" From somewhere Gina summoned the presence of mind to say, "It seems your mum made a mistake when she gave your dad your email address, and you didn't get his messages. But your dad can tell you what he wrote. More or less." She felt quite proud of herself about this for the rest of the day.

"Did you really write to me?" said Clara, turning a hopeful, still-sleepy face towards Robert. At that point, Gina took her coffee and yogurt out into the garden, because, unexpectedly, tears threatened. Still, she looked forward to a conversation with Robert at some point about whether Nadège's own strange relationship with her father, or her father's memory, had led her to intervene in this way between her own daughter and her daughter's father, or whether it was just vindictiveness.

Coffee finished, she went to make up the sofa-bed and straighten the front room, so Janet didn't have to. Robert and Clara were still sitting in the kitchen, Clara eating toast, Robert drinking tea. They were not, apparently, conversing, but Gina thought that another thing she could say to Robert at some point, later on, was how amazingly well he had done.

*

The plan for this second day, Janet had announced the previous evening over dinner, was for all of them to drive down to Land's End, taking both cars. They would have a picnic, go for a walk by the sea, go to the gift shop (Clara had brightened at this), and then drive over and have a look at Porthcurno, leaving Robert, Nadège and Clara at the Minack, with another picnic (there would be soup in a thermos and pasta in a food flask, said practical Janet, because no-one wanted cold food twice in one day). Now Gina could hear her mother's voice upstairs – not the words, just the tone of anxiety and complaint. After a few moments Janet appeared on the stairs, calling over her shoulder, "I know they're around somewhere," and then Gordon's voice came: "I wasn't reckoning on going into the loft this morning."

"Why d'you want to go into the loft?" said Gina, who wasn't sure what time they were leaving and still wasn't dressed.

"Oh, good morning, Gina," said her father, who liked

things formal. "Yes, your mother thinks the theatre-goers should take some waterproofs. And there might, er, be some in the loft."

"Oh," said Gina. "It will ruin it if it rains. What's the forecast?" But it was probably easier to find out on her mobile, so she made to go up to her room.

"Those waterproof trousers you used to have, and the cycling cape," Janet was calling now. "Those would do for Robert. And I think my old red cagoule must be up there, Clara can have that, and just grab whatever you can find for Nadège."

Gordon sighed and asked Gina to help him with the slide mechanism for the fold-down ladder, which was stiff. "Have to get onto someone about this," he said.

"But why did you put things in the loft?" said Gina. "The house is big enough. You could have put them in the front room or the kitchen."

"You know how your mother is," muttered Gordon and went up the ladder, which he did not like to do as it hurt his arthritic knee: "It's not the going up, it's the coming down," he would say.

In her room, Gina saw that a bright afternoon was forecast over Land's End but possible showers in the evening. She had some idea from a guide book she had flicked through that you weren't allowed umbrellas at the Minack. Ah well, she thought: at least Clara would have seen the play, when she came to do it at school.

Clara appeared as Gina was applying make-up – eyes and lips only, for the summer – and trying to find a different pair of earrings, because she had been wearing the same ones since she set out. Clara still carried the green notebook. Coming into the room she said, "You've taken the label off."

"What?"

"The label on your suitcase."

This was perfectly true: Gina had removed the incriminating United label after Clara's visit the previous evening. She looked guiltily towards the bin and thought, I don't have to account for my actions to my thirteen-year-old niece, but found herself thinking simultaneously, How bizarre for me to be here, with Robert the only one who knows I've moved to America. Is that normal family behaviour? She collected herself, and said, "So is it ok, about your dad's emails?"

"It wasn't his fault," said Clara, fiddling with Gina's roll-up travel jewellery case and apparently in no need of a heart-to-heart on this issue. "Do you want to see," she said, with a doubtful, trailing emphasis on the "see", "Do you want to see a photo of Susie?"

"Susie?" said Gina sharply. "What photo?"

Clara brought up a photo on her phone, opened her notebook and said, "It was six years ago. The seventh of July, in Amsterdam."

Gina peered at it. The photo was blurred and the figure was turned away from the camera. There was a plume of pale hair caught up in a high pony-tail; the neck was long, the shoulders slim. It could have been Susie, but with so little of the face, only a part of a cheek and forehead—

"Where did you get this?" she said.

"A friend sent it to me," said Clara. "It's tagged. Susanne Ellis. Look."

"It's Suzanne with a z," said Gina. "And she's always been Susie, really. No-one's ever called her Suzanne." Although these things could change, as she herself, reincarnated as Georgina, had discovered. "So – you're looking for Susie? And your friends know?"

"My best friends do," said Clara modestly. "Maya and Alicia."

"What do they say?"

"They try to help. Maya was the one who sent it."

"Oh. Let me see again." Yes, it could be Susie. But equally it might not be. And even if this was Susie, years ago at some sort of event in Amsterdam, what did that prove or disprove, what did it help?

"So," she said, more gently, to Clara, "You're trying to track her down as well."

"I just want to know she's all right," said Clara, and Gina thought how extraordinarily and unexpectedly adorable thirteen-year-old girls could be. Clara sat on the bed and opened her notebook. There was a page headed "Auntie Susie" – the letters had been coloured in in turquoise, and a cloud drawn around them in dark blue – and quite a lot of writing followed, which Gina felt she couldn't ask to read. Clara, it seemed, just wanted her to know that it existed.

"You do know she's got a child?" said Clara.

"I don't *know*," said Gina. "I don't know at all. I know there's been... *talk* of it—"

"My dad saw her with a little boy," said Clara. "In London."

"Did he tell you that?" said Gina, surprised.

"No, I heard mum talking about it to Grandpa once," said Clara. "So if Susie has got a child, don't you think you ought to do something about it?"

"Well," said Gina. "Just because you're with a child doesn't mean it's yours. And even if it was, nobody can do anything about it if we don't know where she is. And she doesn't want us to know." Besides, what exactly were they supposed to do?

"But don't you mind?" went on Clara.

"Yes. Of course I mind." She didn't say that she also minded Robert's slowness, his failure to act that day at Victoria – why on earth hadn't he run after her? Had he had nothing on his Oyster card, had he tripped over his habit? "We all mind, very much, but we can't do anything about it," she said, and thought what a dusty answer this sounded, and how incomprehensible adult reasoning must seem to the young. "Come on," she said. "Let's get going. Hay while the sun shines and all that." Good old Clara.

*

Nadège drove down on her own, which was perhaps for the best given the revelations of the morning. Janet drove the rest of them. Robert had his eyes closed, probably going over the enormity of Nadège's behaviour, or possibly, Gina thought, praying – she supposed monks did pray. Gina looked out at buttercups against very green grass, at purple foxgloves, at the odd rabbit, at the astonishing gentle repeated rise and fall of the landscape which seemed to mark out this part of England, while Clara, in the middle seat, commented on various places she would like to go:

"Oh look, there's a sign to a seal sanctuary."

"Now that I think of it, we could have gone on a seal-spotting tour at St Ives," said Gordon.

"Look at that, it looks exactly like Mont St-Michel, only smaller." Clara had been there on a school trip the previous year.

"Quite a lot smaller," said Robert, opening his eyes.

"Is it an island?" went on Clara.

"Only at high tide," said Gordon. "The rest of the time you can walk over."

As they skirted Penzance she exclaimed, "It says there's a sea water pool!"

"The Jubilee Pool," said Gordon. "Nineteen-thirties. Quite impressive, by all accounts."

"They've put in heating. You'll all have to come back and we'll go there," said Janet, and Gina wondered whether trips to Cornwall were now going to be a feature of latter-day family life. Perhaps, she thought, since she was at the stage where any mention of the love object was gratifying, even to herself, perhaps she could come back with Eduardo.

Nadège was waiting for them at Land's End, in the carpark. They sat and ate their rolls and yogurts on benches overlooking the sea, zipping up their jackets against the wind, looking out at the greying horizon ("Of course it won't rain", said Janet), and watching two Chinese tourists in flimsy, strappy dresses and high heels take photos of each other striking poses against the sea. Once the picnic things were stowed back in the car, they wandered down to the shops: "Tourist trash," said Janet, but Clara's eyes lit up, and they hung back so she could have a look at the scarves and the belts and the postcards and the calendars, while Gordon headed for the end-of-the-land walk beyond. Gina, straggling behind so she could get Robert on his own, said, "It's going pretty well, then, with Clara?" It was not quite what she had intended to say, but probably he got the message, which was that she was trying to be supportive, although you never knew with Robert.

"Yeah, not too bad," said Robert. "I think." There was a longish pause, as there so often was with Robert, and then he said, throwing an arm out to indicate the tussocky grass, the wild flowers, the deep blue of the sea beyond, "So what's it like then? America? Do they have things like this?"

"I haven't really seen that much yet," said Gina. "Only Michigan. Not even much of that." It had been strange to become suddenly aware of new seas, inland seas, the existence of which she had never really registered, just as she had never previously seen the mitten of Michigan on a map of America, whereas now it was the first thing she looked for, the lovely gestalt of it between the Great Lakes, with Waldo low down in the heel of the hand, and Port Huron, with its hypnotic procession of slow, purposeful steamers down the St Clair River, in the thumb.

"It's very beautiful, Michigan," she went on, "With the Lakes." She had learned to count them off, Michigan, Huron, Superior, Erie, Ontario, and to add that only Ontario did not border on Michigan. "You go to the shore"— how American that sounded— "and it's like the sea. Waves. Sand-dunes. And on the way you drive past vineyards." She realised she was not giving any sense of it, and that she herself was really no good at seeing landscapes and reporting on them, so she talked instead about the fruit pies with Bible verses in the lid that came from an Amish farm, the fruit wines ("cherry pie in a bottle"), the Cornish descendants selling pasties at the farmers' market, the artisan brie with apricots and almonds. "Oh, and the deer: once we drove up from the beach in St Joseph to this pub in the town, and there was a deer. Just standing there in the car park. It had these huge brown eyes and it just stood there. It didn't even run away."

"So you like it, then."

"Most things I like. There's so much space. And people are so polite, in Waldo. They give you a huge amount of room, to get past." She suddenly thought of Paris, the Métro, the appalling proximity, and surprised herself with a rush of nostalgia.

"But?"

"Oh... there's the way you have to drive everywhere. Pretty much. There used to be a direct train from Waldo to South Haven, on Lake Michigan. And there used to be all sorts of ferries to Milwaukee and Chicago. But not now."

"So not much of a complaint."

"No. No, not at all. I've just got this feeling—" Gina went on. "This feeling of being in a New World. Capital N, capital W." She could feel her own face full of wonderment: there were times these days when she was aware of this uncontrollable radiance. She said, out of politeness, to deflect attention from this, "And St Agnes? That must be really beautiful in the summer," and he said it was, and that she must remember, from Durham, which she did: the last spring she had spent a week cycling around the lanes after term had ended, just wandering, sleeping at bed and breakfasts, and had wondered why she had spent so much time in the city. But now she thought landscape was all very well, but what she really wanted was for Robert to talk about the Sisters and the Ladies, for him to count them off as she had counted off the lakes: Sister Agnes, Sister Philomène, Sister Angélique, Sister Bénédicte, Sister Maria; Lady Melanie, Lady Tilly, Lady Phyllis, Lady Jane, Lady Margaret, Lady Tanya.

"Any news, from all of them up there?" she said.

"A couple of texts," said Robert.

"From Melanie?"

"No. Sister Bénédicte. About the meeting I missed."

"Was it important?"

"Oh, they'll all repeat the same things a dozen times when I get back." He sighed. "It boils down to whether or not God can work through a holiday resort, really."

"Oh," said Gina, who had never considered the

possibility, and was more interested in the day-to-day, in the details of being a Sister or a Lady. She thought suddenly, horrified, that in this she echoed Gerry and his fascination with what girls did, although her own interest was much more pedestrian (who did the ironing? Was there any resentment between the Sisters and the Ladies?). She said, careful to betray only a neutral interest, "So how does it work? Do they all shout at each other? Or is it really decorous and holy?"

"A bit of both, really. Sister Bénédicte lays down the law, Sister Agnes gets the wrong end of the stick, Sister Angélique keeps the peace, Sister Philomène goes to sleep when she's been doing the gardening."

"And Sister Maria? What does she do?"

Robert gave her a sideways glance. "You can probably imagine," he said.

"What? Sits in total silence?"

"No, not total silence. You remember how she was. Mistress of the inappropriate remark. Or more the misplaced biblical quotation. Beware the lusts of other things, I think it was. Sat there and said it like some little old gnome."

Gina had stopped in her tracks, she was staring after Robert open-mouthed. Now she ran a few steps to catch up with him. "Robert," she said, pulling at his arm. "Robert, are you telling me that Sister Maria—"

"Yes?"

"That Sister Maria is *Mary*?"

"Ah, well," said slow, stupid Robert. "I thought you would have worked that one out a long time ago."

"I—", said Gina, "I—". And she was struck afresh by what always had struck her, from what Robert had said about St Agnes Mount – that it was just the sort of place Mary would end up in; she had even thought at one stage what a shame it was she hadn't committed a crime so she could be a Lady. And look at her now, gone one better: not a Lady but a Sister, with lifetime membership.

"*But,*" said Gina, knowing there had been something, "Mary got married! I know she did, I remember Mum saying!"

"She did," conceded Robert. "She did. Didn't last long." It had been some spare bachelor from the fundamentalist church which had got its tentacles back into Mary after the fire, vindicated when Luke had been publicly proved to be the devil incarnate. Now Robert said, "He hit her, apparently."

"But if she was married, how did she…"

"They're Sisters," said Robert mildly. "They don't have to be brides of Christ".

"No," said Gina, "I didn't mean that. What I mean really is, how did Mary end up precisely where you were? Did Dad tell her about it?"

"It was the other way round," said Robert. "But nothing to do with Dad. I used to bump into her, at Coombe's." Gina remembered now that Mary had got a job there, when Crick House folded, working in the kitchen of Dickens. Accommodation was not provided for cooks and cleaners. Maybe, Gina thought, horrified, that was why she had agreed to marry again – to have a roof over her head. She had been conditioned to look for safe havens. But surely Crick House, after all under the aegis of the state, should have looked after her better than that? But she didn't want to interrupt Robert, in case he never got back to the point.

"One day," he went on, "she told me she was leaving her husband and going to live as St Agnes Mount. I don't know how she knew about it." Gina would have wanted to know, would have wanted detail on the genesis of the whole thing.

"But it happened that I remembered the name."

"Well," said Gina. "I'm amazed." She was, on many levels, not least that anyone could want to spend the rest of their life with Mary. But she could quite see that once the name was known, once the seed had been sown, it had been a matter of time. Robert had never belonged with Nadège. "Do Mum and Dad know?"

"Not as far as I'm aware," said Robert, so Gina said kindly, as if they were still twelve and ten, "Don't worry, I won't tell them," and thought what a strange secret it was to keep. "How does she get on up there?" she said. "What – what's she like?" For Gina knew Mary mostly through hearsay and family lore. She had been gone before Mary became a part of the fabric of family life.

"She's pretty good on the domestic front," said Robert. "Very dedicated. She does ok." Which confirmed Gina's suspicion that Sisters and Ladies were mostly about mopping floors and other domestic inconveniences.

She dropped behind Robert a little, because the path narrowed but also because she wanted to stop talking, to take it in. Ahead, Janet led the procession with Clara just behind her, while Gordon was walking with Nadège, no doubt keeping up a stream of commentary on local history, flora or fauna: emitting information was his usual method for dealing with his daughter-in-law. It struck Gina that since she had arrived she had not had a heart-to-heart with Janet, nor had Janet shown any desire for one. She was then compelled to ask herself whether she felt any desire for such a conversation with Janet, and was forced to conclude that with so much that could not be said, or at any rate could not be said yet, it was probably best avoided. It was not as if they were in the habit of intimate chats anyway... Was Janet happy, she wondered?

She seemed to be, she looked contented enough, indeed more so than usual, although perhaps a little tired. Maybe later on, thought Gina, when the others went to the Minack, and she would be alone with her parents.

But by the time they had looped back to the signposts where you could be photographed with your names slotted in under Land's End (Clara did this with her grandparents) she found that Gordon and Janet had picked up a couple of a similar age to themselves, whom Gina recognised after a moment as Stella and Peter Carr, from Coombe's, looking like their own parents, since it must easily have been twenty-five years since she had last seen them – Peter, now baggy-faced but still affable, Stella as ever a little severe with her neat long bob, now iron-grey. There had been a lot of "Gina! Robert! What are you up to now?", and Janet talking over everyone and louder so it didn't come out that Robert was a monk, and how was Andrew, the Carrs' son (working in the City), and what a coincidence to see them down here, and they really must have dinner. Nadège, who of course saw the Carrs quite regularly, at least from a distance, stood a little apart, but Stella said to Clara, "So you're going to be a Girl in September!" and Gina was once more amused to notice a couple look mildly surprised as they walked past.

It emerged that the Carrs were staying in Penryn, which was no distance at all from Falmouth, and Janet said how about tonight, since Robert and "his lot" would be at the theatre.

"You won't mind, will you," said Gina, who had got better with time at imposing her own will, "But I was thinking of popping over to Truro later on, to see the cathedral. It will give you a chance to catch up."

"No, no, you go," said Janet, expansively. "Do whatever

you like." She seemed extraordinarily pleased to see the Carrs, who had been living no more than four miles away from Oak Lodge for the past two decades. Did they meet, in Ashwick? Gina had no idea, but Janet certainly seemed thrilled to chance upon them now. It must be the sea air. Anyway, a little trip on her own would be just the thing, Gina thought. She could find somewhere quiet and phone Eduardo, sit outside a pub with a book. Recharge. There was only so much socialising she could stand, family or no. She might go and see Robert's painting for him, as it looked as if he probably wasn't going to get to see it himself. At least not this time.

XIX

It felt strange and uncomfortably over-intimate to drive back with Gordon and Janet to Falmouth, as if she had regressed thirty years while Robert was still grown-up. Robert and Clara had driven off to Porthcurno with Nadège, for the theatre, and Janet had decided she wasn't that bothered about seeing the Minack, if nobody minded, and that it would be better to let them go off by themselves.

"We can have a bit of a sit in the garden before dinner," said Gordon. Gina simply nodded, then wondered what it was like when your children slipped into middle age and stopped howling in derision at remarks of this ilk. The Carrs were driving over because it had been decided that they would try a seafood bar in Falmouth.

"Still," said Gordon to Gina, not turning round – he was driving back – "I can run you over to Truro if you like. Or pick you up later. Can't be more than a dozen miles."

"Thanks," Gina, "But I'll go on the train. I've checked the times." She had liked the idea of the little shuttle, chugging along with its windows open, parochial and pleasant, and she left the holiday home with a sense of freedom and adventure. Early at Falmouth Town – Gina was always early for trains – she got on the train as it went past in the wrong direction, rode up to Falmouth Docks, where she admired the mosaic of a train which made her think of Lisbon Oriente with Karin – how long ago it seemed hen rode back along the whole line. Trains were useful, she found, to think, and trains were also universal, they brought all the poles of her life, her lives, together, and to this extent there was something soothing about them. Eduardo had asked once if it wasn't worrying, symbolically speaking, that she preferred to travel on rails, from predetermined point to predetermined point. He planned for them to go to the Upper Peninsula later in the summer, where she could drive and get her confidence back: there was hardly anybody on the roads, he said.

Back soon, she thought. She no longer used the word "home" to herself, it had grown too confusing. But she had left Waldo on the previous Sunday, arrived in Cornwall on the Tuesday, and now it was Thursday. She would be back in Waldo on Monday, back at the frame house that certainly looked like home, with its gables and its midnight blue-painted wooden slats and its porch and garden. This was a good thought, but it did not prevent her from being vaguely annoyed with Janet for arranging this evening's separation from her brother and niece when time was already so short. Gina had hardly seen Clara at Land's End; Janet had hogged her. Gina smiled as she thought of the one representative of the new generation (the hope, the new ships) as a resource that should be fairly shared out.

And something else was niggling Gina. She couldn't put her finger on it. Mentally she rifled through possible sources of unease – Susie, money, flying? – but could not think what it could be. Outside, all the light had veered to the west, while the east was grey with a clay-like greyness which did not bode well for a dry evening.

Gina arrived at the cathedral in Truro to find a queue outside, apparently for a concert by the cathedral choirs: some Bach cantatas, Pergolesi's Stabat Mater and various other choral works she hadn't heard of. The queue was moving quite fast, and looking round Truro in the rain seemed unappealing, so she joined the tail-end, intending to ask if there were any returns, but she found one thrust upon her without having to request it. There was something domestic about the Victorian cathedral Gina rather liked, and the music washed over her pleasantly, while she thought of nothing in particular, but saw Eduardo's face very near to her mind's eye. But by the time the first Bach cantata was over – *Ich hatte viel Bekümmernis* – the thing that had been niggling at her in the train had wriggled its way out. The facts of the matter, as she saw them, were these:

1. Janet had been bizarrely thrilled to see the Carrs earlier on, oddly anxious to pin them down to dinner, immediately, that very day;

2. In the car, Janet had said to Clara, "You'll have to come back." She had not said "We'll have to come back";

3. (A). Gordon and Janet had brought with them, for a week's holiday, a set of old flowery sheets which dated from the nineteen-seventies, on the pretext that they might be useful for the bed-settee. And yet the house was a fully-equipped Airbnb rental;

   (B). In addition to the sheets, they had brought a box of old waterproofs, and had placed this box in the loft.

The only conclusion to be drawn from all this, thought Gina, as the introduction of the Pergolesi broke over her, presenting her mind, for some reason, with a clear vision of liquid honey and golden dessert wine, was this:

Gordon and Janet were not on a week's holiday. But, for some bizarre reason of their own, they were pretending to be.

She longed to discuss this with Robert, but clearly neither of them was in a position to talk on the phone. She wondered what it was like, watching a play in an outdoor theatre in Cornwall in the rain.

*

Robert could have told her that it was not very different from sitting under a cold shower fully-dressed; that rain had begun to seep through the seams of his jacket and had been creeping down his neck for so long that one of his shoulders had gone numb, while the one that was trying not to get too close to Nadège, and had a touch of arthritis, was aching horribly; that the seats were unbearably uncomfortable notwithstanding the cushions they had hired; that in spite of the fact that it was the middle of the year when the nights were at their shortest there was no view at all over the sea, only mist; that a precious two minutes in the shelter of the toilet block during the interval was the part he was looking forward to most; that if it hadn't been for Clara, whose waterproofs seemed actually to be waterproof and who seemed happy enough from what he could see - her eyes and the end of her nose - he would have been long gone.

*

Gina was not the only one who was wondering about Robert. At St Agnes Mount, Sister Agnes was sitting at a corner of the refectory table with Melanie and Mary. Sister Maria, while she did not let on about knowing Brother Robert from a former life, seemed to take a vaguely benevolent interest in him, and once she had said to Melanie, a propos of nothing, that St Agnes was the one you prayed to to get a husband, and laughed.

The women were streaming a webcam on a tablet (Sister Agnes was surprisingly good with technology). "Might get a glimpse of him," she said, nodding at Melanie. But the webcam proved disappointing: all you could see was a view over the amphitheatre and down to the sea, according to the caption, although what you really saw was nebulous, formless grey.

*

In the interval of the Truro concert, Gina managed to force her way against the flow of the crowd towards the refreshments table where busy-looking well-dressed ladies served ice-creams and bottles of mineral water, to the Chapel of St Margaret, to see the painting for Robert. It was actually a set of four panels, the mountains purple, the sky vermillion, showing Christ on the cross from different angles. In the last, the cross stood empty. She quite saw its stunning simplicity, the gloriousness of the Mediterranean colours, the puzzle of the crow and the dog; she felt the shock as her gaze travelled to the fourth panel. But what, she wondered, was Robert's take on all this? He had never been, as far as she knew, particularly religious, yet now he was a monk. Had he been converted, suddenly seen the light? Or had it simply been a rational decision, a good match for his talents and failings?

But here she was herself, Gina reflected: she had spent more than twenty years of her life interpreting and reinterpreting rewritings of Apocalypse, poring over Revelation and Daniel and Ezekiel. So perhaps people wondered the same about her. "You shouldn't wear long skirts," Jean-Louis had said once: "It makes you look like a Protestant." Looking like a Protestant, to Jean-Louis in the entirely secular circles in which he moved, apparently meant looking something like a puritan or a Handmaid. Gina had pointed out that she often wore her skirts with scoop necks or vest-tops, but the problematic combination, for Jean-Louis, was long skirt plus biblical intertextuality. Low necklines and bare arms had nothing to do with it. How strange it all had been, thought Gina. Like a foreign country. Like a long time ago. It had, of course, been both these things, in a way.

What if she had said, "I *am* a Protestant"? she wondered now, listening to the warm rise of a setting of part of the Song of Solomon thrown in as an extra, in this great edifice to faith (the piece was by someone called Arthur Frackenpohl, and it ended with "our wedding day" sung very quietly on one note. Her cheeks were wet. There were these flashes; they were, quite simply, the pangs of love; Eduardo got them too). She was, of, course, nominally a Protestant, an Anglican, it was how she had been brought up, and sometimes she had missed it as a benign, well-meaning background. Some of the university people in Waldo were Unitarians, and Gina had been to one or two services with Eduardo. She liked the idea of a divine being known by many names, and the many names not mattering very much.

She had worked out, recently, that what she probably was was a post-Christian, or a meta-Christian. Human beings, as she understood it, had always needed these myths, these stories, these historical and divine figures, and probably always would, so it was better to celebrate this than fight it, but at the same time to stand outside it (not, please not, like those awful people who had got their claws into Mary). The point was, surely, to come to terms with it in one's own way. If the Rapture came now, thought Gina idly, would people like her be taken up? People who carped and qualified, who said yes if, and yes but, and wasn't the whole thing best understood within an intellectual framework? Trumpets and horsemen and the moon turning to blood while she argued the toss about post- and meta-...

The orchestra was tuning up again, and she had to nip very fast up to the pulpit, to see the Truro Noah carrying his ark, like a toy boat. Noah-myths were apocalypse-myths, Noah and Revelation all part of the same thing. She caressed his stone robe fleetingly, glanced at the dove and the rainbow for long enough to say she'd seen them, then went back to her place and spent the rest of the programme chewing over her extraordinary surmise about her parents.

XX

After Jackson's first visit to Gordon, Crick House had limped on for a few years. Luke's fire had, of course, been a boon to the opposition: the boys were out of control, they had problems Gordon was not equipped or qualified to deal with. When it was finally decided that its doors would close and that the nine remaining boys would be dispatched to other institutions or, in one case, home, it was almost a relief; better to know the worst than to live with that level of threat, rumbling on and on, with deceptive patches of normality between meetings. Gordon, who had been saying for years, "I just need to know where we stand," now said to Janet, with a wry smile, "At least we do know now. Where we stand." He moved to embrace her – they had been having breakfast at Oak Lodge when the final letter arrived. But Janet was not good at comfort, and turned away, saying in a bitter tone, "Well, where *do* we stand? You'd better let me know. When you've decided." Gordon shook his head. He was all too aware that these past few years had taken a toll on both of them – he himself had aged, and there had been a dramatic increase in the ratio of ice-chips to human warmth in Janet's soul.

When it came down to it, the options were few. The

original idea of expanding Crick House to accommodate four or five times as many boys had been abandoned, which was why Gordon had been left pretty much alone for all this time, and Jackson's asinine comments on his methods had been what would later be called kicked into the long grass. The new plan was bigger and bolder: in fact, it was hideous, figuratively and literally. Crick House was to be demolished altogether. Its grounds, Arthur's paddock, and what was known as "the wasteland" beyond, although it was pretty tame and families walked there on Sunday afternoons (it was here that Susie had lain in the actual long grass with Luke) was to be subsumed by a Young Offenders Institution, the name of which would be Fairfields. Nothing of Crick House was to go into it; nothing of Crick House would remain. Fairfields would be a prison for minors, not, or at least not primarily, a place of education and enlightenment. Gordon had wept tears over this, over the wrongness of it, his big face balanced on the fingers of one hand, and he had begun to keep a bottle of whisky in his study, which, through all these years of all those boys, he had never needed before.

The building itself was to be unsightly, a geometrical, hangar-like structure in red-brown brick. Supermarkets looked like that now, and so, ironically, did the brand-new Arts Centre at Coombe's. At a little distance from the central structure, on what was currently the paddock shared by Arthur, the goats, and, behind a fence, the boys' kitchen garden (divided into allotments in recent years, to encourage a spirit of healthy competition), would be staff housing, mean-looking squared-off little flats. Oak Lodge was scheduled for demolition, and it was in one of these "units" that Jackson, who somehow seemed to have wormed his way up to overseeing the changeover, expected Gordon and Janet to live once Gordon took up his post at the new institution.

"You can't say *expect*," said Gordon to Janet. "They don't expect anything. They don't care."

"That's not true," said Janet, who was trying to be, at last, supportive. "They know a good thing when they see it." They had indeed offered Gordon quite a senior post, to end his career on a high note, as they saw it.

"It's more a case of keep your friends close and your enemies closer," said Gordon, and of course they didn't want him on the side of the opposition, which was growing more vocal: who wanted a Young Offenders Institution on their doorstep? Not the Allinghams – old Dr Allingham, who had rheumatoid arthritis, was in a home now, but she was still outraged – and not Coombe's, which feared that the town would become better known for its junior prison than its minor public school. There was also anxiety from the general public. Job creation was promised – Harry Binley and the other supervisors from Crick House had been invited to a presentation of what was on offer – but people were worried about what these jobs would entail, worried about the general tenor of Fairfields. Harry Binley's wife felt that if a boy in a place like Crick House was capable of setting fire to the place, more desperate boys in Fairfields would do much worse. And when it came down to it, the public preferred the whole idea of Crick House. There had always been complaints ("delinquents wandering around the lanes"). There had also been occasional trouble, as how could there not be, mostly centring on attempts at underage drinking, successful or otherwise; there had been the odd run-in in the town. But the mood now was nostalgic: the Crick House boys were part of the community, Gordon's work was heroic, wayward teenage boys should be helped back onto the straight and narrow, not locked up.

So yes, of course, Fairfields wanted Gordon "on board". He would be a "valued member of the team"; they considered him "very able," they admired his "inter-personal skills". All this left Gordon in despair. "It's the hollowness of it," he tried to explain. "The insincerity." In later times, he would say "manipulation". When Gordon stalled instead of accepting the offer and the flat that went with it (and after Janet grabbed the phone from him and shouted at Jackson or his minion or whoever it was that if they thought she, Janet, was going to live in one of those pokey, disagreeable little boxes with everyone else's children running around the corridors they had another thing coming), he was offered more money for the same job, and given a guarantee that Oak Lodge would not be touched "for the foreseeable future".

"That's all right then," said Janet, "We'll just have a bloody great prison practically in the garden". But it was the lesser of two evils.

Fairfields made no particular offer to Janet. If Janet wanted in, it would be as an employee of HM Prisons. There were no more unofficial nooks and crannies, as there has been at Crick House or Coombe's. There were only pawns, centrally deployed.

Once Gordon had it in writing about Oak Lodge – it was made clear that it was a favour, and no time span was specified, but it seemed unlikely that the plans would change in the immediate future – he simply ignored the letters about joining the management team at Fairfields, and looked for another job. Coombe's, of course, knew all about what was going on – everyone knew everything in Ashwick, it was that sort of town, with overlapping circuits of information and gossip – and offered him a post teaching history part-time and experimenting with a new politics AS-level, but going back to

Coombe's seemed almost as much a capitulation as moving to Fairfields. In the end, he was saved by the very prosaic circumstance of a history master at Ashwick Boys' Grammar taking early retirement, which was possible now, with all the reforms. Before that, he had been off for nearly a year with "stress". The dissenters were being paid off.

"Pity you can't take early retirement," said Janet. Gordon mumbled something about giving of oneself, and service, which Janet had anyway never understood. But he had already decided to keep his own views on what was going on to himself and just get on with the task in hand at Ashwick Boys', which really amounted to getting the boys through the exams as best he could.

Janet did understand that something big was ending, that the longest and probably the most defining chapter of their lives was drawing to a close. Since Susie had left for Italy, Janet had taken to visiting Arthur in her daughter's place. She did not put her arms around Arthur's head and murmur in his ear as Susie had – sudden, acute memory of Susie's long back, her hair, her yellow wellies – but stroked his nose and fed him carrots. Since he had lost his youthful habit of running over to greet people, Janet was less alarmed by him. Now he walked slowly, and, according to the vet, didn't see very well. In fact he was dead before Fairfields took his paddock away, which was probably for the best.

"Have you told Susie?" said Gina, when she heard. Janet did write and tell Susie. She went to some trouble to find a rather lovely card with a donkey in a meadow. But she didn't hear back.

XXI

Gina got back from Truro to find Janet and Gordon in the kitchen, picking over their evening with Stella, Peter, and the monsters of the deep. The Cornish lobster had met with approval, while the Indonesian curried oysters had not gone down so well. Peter had had heart trouble, but was being well looked after; Stella had taken up long-distance cycling.

"But don't you see them in Ashwick?" Gina said, as if innocently.

"Oh yes, we went to Andrew's wedding," said Janet. "An awfully nice young woman. Awfully pretty."

"Rather a *large* young lady," said Gordon, explaining Janet's uncharacteristic gush of approval.

"How young?" said Gina, interested. Andrew was the same age as Robert.

"No idea," said Gordon. "Poetic license."

Gina smiled at the wall, thinking vaguely about how it must be to be a bride, caught Gordon eyeing her, and took control of her expression. Would her parents come out, she wondered? Or would she bring Eduardo back to England on a wedding journey?

In the train on the way back from Truro she had entertained the idea of confronting her parents about her new

217

knowledge, but as a family they didn't go in for confrontation. There was no real sense, as there seemed to be in both higher and lower social classes, that what one person did was any concern of the others. Janet had always been almost pathologically individualistic – "I shall do what I want, what does it matter to anyone else?" – and Gordon had a natural discretion which made it difficult to provoke scenes of any kind. Besides, saying nothing about their secret helped her to feel less bad, less mean, less undaughterly, for so closely guarding her own. She would tell them when she was ready. And she would invite them out, not necessarily for the wedding, but just for a holiday, to spend time with them. She had already identified various resorts where this could take place: on the shores of Lake Michigan: New Buffalo, South Haven, Traverse City (just thinking the names was magical). And she would book tickets for the Chicago Symphony, show them the city. So she stopped poking sticks into her parents to make them give themselves away, and said what a shame it was about the rain and the Minack.

"But it's going to be beautiful, tomorrow," said Janet. "Just a bit of rain in the morning, then sunny for the rest of the day."

"What are we doing tomorrow?" said Gina.

"Your mother's putting on a buffet," said Gordon.

"In the garden," said Janet. "To celebrate."

"To celebrate—?" said Gina, in spite of her previous resolution.

"To celebrate being together," said Janet firmly. "We'll start with drinks around one".

Gina saw the next morning disappearing into the preparation of savoury tarts and gateaux. "I'll help you with the food," she said nobly.

"No need," came the airy reply. "We're having it catered."

At that moment, Nadège's car was heard to draw up on the drive. Janet went out into the hall, while Gina put the kettle on and found a packet of biscuits. She heard a general scrum as outer garments were wriggled out of in a small space, and a chorus of weary and wet voices. Nadège was saying, "No thank you; I'd rather go back to the hotel." Robert and Clara came in, both looking frozen and subdued, and Gina got into older-sister mode, chivvying Clara into the shower in the first-floor bathroom, and Robert up into "her" bathroom. It didn't appear to be the time to ask him, with sisterly sarcasm, whether he and Nadège had managed to talk over their marriage as Janet had seemed to expect, but if she had, she might have learnt that Nadège had informed him, quietly and without preamble, in the minute or two in which they waited for Clara to come out the toilets at the end of the play, that she would agree to the divorce: that, as she put it, she wanted no more to do with his family. He hadn't asked her, as most men probably would have done, what she meant by that, and there hadn't been time to discuss the fact that Clara was, ineluctably, an Ellis.

When he had had his bath and the appalling evening had begun to fade into something which might one day begin to be funny, Robert came out in Gordon's borrowed bathrobe, sat on Gina's bed and told her what had happened.

"That's brilliant," said Gina, then backtracked and added humbly: "I mean, I suppose it's for the best. I've never been married. I wouldn't know." Her brother humphed, then said, "I should never have married her."

"But you've got Clara," said Gina. "She wouldn't be here, if you hadn't."

Robert nodded. Once more his broad square face looked

as if it might break into tears.

"Will you tell Melanie?" said Gina, tactlessly, clumsily, just trying to cheer him up. But Robert's expression brightened at this and he said, "I'll go and get my phone." Gina called after him, "I'll make you a cup of tea." She went down to the kitchen and sat eating shortbread biscuits shaped like dogs (the evening in Truro had not involved dinner) and speculating on what had made Nadège suddenly give in. Clara came in in her pyjamas to say goodnight, hair fuzzily blow-dried and up in a high pony-tail, yawning, already half-asleep. There would be no more from the green notebook tonight.

*

At St Agnes, Melanie was lying on her bed when Robert's text message came, reading an old Virago book of case-studies about women prisoners. There was a relatively extensive library on prison issues, most of it much more weighty than this. The case studies had nothing and everything to do with Melanie's own life. She had never been a single mother, an abused wife, never taken drugs, never slept on night buses for want of anywhere else to go, but she had done the thing that had to be done, the thing there was no way out of, and she knew the inside of a cell, the night screaming, the retreat into the darker reaches of the self and the inability to get back at will. It was like being swept out to sea, in Melanie's view, and having to use all your energy to tread water just to stay alive. Impossible to get back in: the currents were too strong.

She was reading with a purpose, looking for inspiration, for how these things might be expressed. It was the first time in a long time that she had managed to do anything with a purpose. She felt like a very old woman heaving herself onto a bicycle, back bent, knees stiff, preparing to cycle uphill. Part of the project, at St Agnes Mount, "the project" being synonymous with Anthony's personal vision (people who minded that didn't really get on there) was for everyone, Brothers, Sisters and Ladies, and perhaps in the future retreaters and visitors, to write their testimony for the library.

"Not 'testimony' in the evangelical sense," Brother Michael had interrupted, when Anthony had mooted this. "No need for any road to Damascus moments."

"And not too much emphasis on sin," suggested Sister Angélique.

"Yeah, forget all that," said Anthony, who did not care to be interrupted in his moments of vision – blue eyes shining, chin balanced on his fingertips: "Let's go for uplifting."

Sister Maria nodded, several times. She had had a basinful of sin and damnation at the church down by the gasworks in Ashwick.

Anthony himself was currently dealing with copy-editing and formatting the testimonies which had been come in so far. He had gone off on a little riff at one meeting to explain that he meant formatting in the editorial sense only. There was no right or wrong way to do it. He had plans to put them online, "at first"; perhaps later there would be a book, drawing on them. And this was how Melanie came to be thinking about her testimony now, although she felt she had little to say. She had not, she felt, had much of a life. Contrary to what people tended to think, contrary to what her lawyer had argued, she had not sacrificed her own life to look after her mother. There hadn't been much to sacrifice. People assumed that because she had a degree in geography from Manchester she would have made something of herself without her mother, as indeed all her busy friends had done, but the truth was she hadn't really wanted to do anything in particular, had had no burning ambitions or desires. She had been, for the first few years after university, happy enough, living in her mother's house, temping in offices locally, pottering at home, dabbling in romance for a little diversion. Then her mother's illness had come. Dealing with it had taken all Melanie's time and energy, and she had watched herself getting older, and wondered why she had never seemed to have more of a hold on life, more of a grip. Recently Robert had been her mirror: he was here because he was good for nothing in the outside world, said Sister Agnes (who herself could not go outside the precincts of St Agnes at all). Melanie wasn't good for anything either, so she saw herself reflected in him. She might centre her testimony on that, but she would have to find a more tactful way to put it, not to hurt Robert's feelings.

Anthony, in his introductory interview, had said, when Melanie had had nothing to say about her mother, that perhaps she had not yet been in the right space to mourn her, that it could be not just a question of time, but also of being in a place which made it possible. He didn't say that just because in the eyes of the law you had murdered your own mother didn't mean you weren't destroyed by her death: he took this as read. Melanie had still been finding it difficult to do much besides nod, but she had been pleased that he had made his remark about mourning in the right place gently, as a hypothesis, a mere suggestion, that he didn't tell her what to feel or what she ought to experience.

What she had felt for a long time was that because time had stopped, it didn't really matter where she was. Now, though, following Robert's text about his divorce, a euphoric sense of a possible future suddenly stretched like a rainbow across the permanent moment in which she seemed to be suspended. It might be all right, with Robert; they might be able to make themselves some sort of life: a possible life. She might one day be able escape from those few seconds in which she had eased her hands out of the plastic bag, made safe the rubber band, when it had just been a question of the final vanquishing of the stubborn mechanism that inflated the lungs, drove on the heart. (Her own hands, cupped around her mother's face inside the plastic. The warm dry skin, where soon there would be rivulets of condensation. There had been enough Temazepam – bought in a pub, which hadn't helped her case – to make it less terrible, for both of them. But nothing could dim the memory of the final sliding out, the letting go.)

Then Aileen, her mother's sister, claiming Melanie's mother had never wanted to go like that, had always been opposed, that Melanie had fed off her like a parasite, was too lazy to get a proper job and make a home of her own. Auntie Aileen who only phoned at Christmas, who had not visited in years. Thinking of her made Melanie feel so bitter she could taste it on her tongue. So perhaps she hadn't let go yet, all this long time later. But perhaps she might begin to, now. Rereading Robert's message for the third time, and taking in the reality of his impending divorce, she was aware that at one time she would have smiled. She didn't smile now, but she saw quite distinctly in her mind's eye, a large, circular station clock, black hands shaped like arrows, a wrought-iron frame, and she heard in her mind's ear the click as the hands sprang on.

*

In Anthony's study, Sister Bénédicte was going through the documents which would allow St Agnes to be turned into a "retreat". There would be jobs for all who wanted to stay, said Anthony: not just jobs, but real *roles*. It would be a new dawn, a new chapter, but imbued with the spirit of what they had all worked so hard to create. Sister Bénédicte looked as if might prefer him to save his inspired voice and his face bathed in evening sunlight for a plenary meeting where they would be appreciated, but she nodded and said it all seemed to be turning out as well as could be expected.

Day three: morning

XXII

On the morning of the third day in Cornwall, Gina woke from some ungraspable dream about being at an airport and crying out, "I need more time!" She lay in bed for a while, feeling upset about the next day's trip back. Chicago suddenly seemed a frightening place to be going, and so terribly far away. Coming back to England had upset her equilibrium; she had lost her nerve. How had it come to this, she wondered – split between France and America? Neither had anything to do with her: England was her home.

At the same time, she ached for Eduardo, with a physical longing in her solar plexus. "You'll be back before you know it," Eduardo had said, his nose against her hair. "Don't worry. I'll be with you, right – here." And he had kissed her forehead again, between the words, which was something he did not do often. They had, for those last few nights, gone to sleep facing each other, tightly bound together, brooking no separation.

Perhaps, she thought wildly, they could come back here, the two of them, make a life here. Eduardo had French nationality, it would be feasible even now, just a question of getting some kind of residence permit. Then she thought about English universities, and how they had been turned into businesses, and how bringing in funds had never been part of her job and she wouldn't know where to start, wouldn't even want to start. In America there were people employed to do that, but in England it seemed to be a job for academics. She was much given to these circular arguments with herself, even though recently she had worked out what she wanted, what she needed, which was not to be fixed anywhere, not in any particular system, but to live in the State of Betwixt and Between: to live in Waldo, teach in Paris, at least for a while, return as tourist and visitor to the country of her birth. She needed this plurality, could not function without it. Eduardo had said he felt to some extent the same, about America, France, Brazil.

She couldn't hear anybody around the house. She remembered Janet had mentioned going to the supermarket, and thought she probably should have got up early enough to go with her and help stow the bags. But too late now, and if there was nobody around, she thought she would go out, have coffee and a Danish pastry, look round the shops, chase the darkness away by purchasing notebooks or scarves or souvenirs; find an owl for Eduardo, who collected them. In the hall, she saw two envelopes on the mat, one brown, one white, both quaintly addressed to Mr and Mrs Gordon I. Ellis. She picked them up and put them on the hall table, then put them back on the mat. She didn't want her parents to know she had blown their cover, even if they had no talent for crime.

Turning into the main road along the harbour at the bottom of the hill, she bumped into Gordon and Robert, and asked if they wanted to come for coffee, "Or have you just been?" Gordon said he would pop back to the house as he had one or two things to do, but Robert, who looked rather subdued, said he would come. Gina thought she detected relief as they walked away from Gordon.

"Where's Clara?" she said.

"With Mum," said Robert. "She wanted to go to the supermarket."

"Nadège?"

Robert shrugged. "Not around yet."

"Is there something the matter?" Gina asked, as they sat down at a table outside a bakery near the harbour.

"You could say that," said Robert, sighing.

"So?"

"Dad's been having a go at me." There was a long, Robert-ish pause. "About Clara."

"Why, what's happened?"

"Nothing. I mean, nothing new. It's just that they've been on at me for ages to *sort it out*". The tone was Janet's, in hectoring mode.

"But what exactly...?". Gina was not being entirely disingenuous. She knew that Gordon and Janet frowned on Robert's skills as a father – Janet in fact frowned on all his skills, and latterly Gordon had not shown much encouragement – but things between Robert and Clara in the last few days seemed to have been going better than anyone could have expected.

"'Now that contact is re-established' – I'm supposed to make arrangements. Make sure I see her regularly. Not drop in and out of her life. Think about her needs, not mine."

"And will that be ok with Nadège?"

"She can't refuse. Not without a reason."

"But surely if you're getting a divorce, the judge will sort all this?"

"Doesn't stop Dad form putting his oar in. About my

duty. Which I seem to have neglected. All along the line."

"Do they think that?"

"Don't they tell you?"

"Well. You know how it is. They do go on. I mean, they used to go on. But not recently, not at all. And anyway, I haven't really spoken to either of them on their own this week." She wondered suddenly whether they had been doing it on purpose, pushing her away for reasons of their own, and felt resentful. Nobody ever worried about her, about how she was. Gina felt the burden of Susie's desertion, felt that she had to be a markedly good daughter, to make up for it, and also that she constantly failed in this. But her parents, she thought, did not seem to see things the same way: we've lost one, better be careful with the other... Certainly, it had never been easy to be close to Janet: she did not seem either to require it or to be capable of it. But for Gina there remained a sense that if she had been a different kind of person, a better daughter, Janet would have relented, let down her guard. Then she remembered she was excluding both her parents from her American secret, and wondered if they somehow knew about that, and were paying her out for it, saying nothing to punish her. But it seemed unlike them.

"Anyway," she went on, as she ate her pastry after a pause of Robert-like proportions, had she but known it: "At least I haven't had to hear about my shortcomings."

"Yeah, right," said her brother. "*Your* shortcomings. What might they be? Doing too well?"

"I haven't really done well. Not the way you're supposed to. Doing well in academia means going after power. And caring whether you get a prestigious publisher or just a publisher."

"And you don't?"

"No, not really. Power isn't my thing. Leading or following, I don't want to do either." Gina had recently developed an interest in Myers-Briggs. "And I want to get my stuff published so it gets into libraries so people can read it. Other researchers. Students. That's all." This was not strictly true: she also took some satisfaction in updating her CV, but she could not say this to Robert.

"But you still write books and do conferences. And you were always so into it."

"Yes. I still am into it. I mean, you get dips, big dips, but I still am. Or I am again now. And now I've got a Fulbright, so I've got a visa for another ten months in America." She nudged her brother towards understanding.

"Isn't that pretty good? A Fulbright?"

"Yes. I mean, I'd think it was if it happened to anybody else".

"There you are then. Nobody else I know does anything like that." She considered saying, "But there's actually something really wrong with me. You all think I'm go-getting, that I take it all in my stride, but Jean-Louis had it right, I'm deeply flawed. And you had it right as well, Robert: you showed me the broken dolls, which were always somebody else – Susie, Nadège, the St Agnes Ladies – but recently I see that I am there also, peering through the slats of a crate, waiting to be mended..." . But she couldn't really go into all this now, with Robert needing her support about Clara and what Gordon had said, and besides, while it was true that she had at one point lost her way, she was settling now, finding her place anew in the order of things. So instead she chose a different tack, and said, "But I could never do what you do. Live in a group. Follow a leader. Be a good person."

"It's not exactly like that."

Gina shrugged. In fact, she thought of Robert as some kind of scapegoat, the *souffre-douleur* of St Agnes Mount, but she went back to her own preoccupations. "Actually, what I meant, about my shortcomings, was not having children."

"There's still time."

"There really isn't. You have to really want it, to be an older mother. And I don't."

"But they've never held it against you. The parentals." He had heard stories, at St Agnes, of pressure brought to bear to have children, or not have children. Lady Jane had said once she quite simply hadn't wanted a child, that in retrospect she felt pregnancy had been a way for her husband to control her, get her where he wanted her. And Lady Kate, who had left now but was the one who had rented the house in the village, had wept bitter tears, more than once, about her elderly parents' will to keep her at home, to prevent her from having a husband and a family of her own.

"No," agreed Gina. "They've never put any pressure on. I suppose I'm lucky. And I don't really think about it much. Not like my friend Ella. She has this big theory about how not having children is a process in itself. It's not just something you don't do, it's something you do do, a negative process. A decision that you have to see through, or something." And then there was Karin, who said she wouldn't really be alive until she had one, which she somehow squared with her attempts to suppress her own life.

"But the strange thing about Mum and Dad," Gina went on, as Robert said nothing, "Is that they seem to let me off because I went into academia. As if most female academics don't have children!"

"You mean they do?"

"Of course they do. I mean, maybe not most, but a lot.

232

There's probably at least an even split. In some ways it's the perfect job for it, at least in the humanities. Lots of autonomy, lots of working from home."

She hadn't meant to talk about herself: she had meant to sympathise with Robert about Gordon. She wondered if she should tell him what Clara had said, about not minding when Robert left, but decided against it: it was open to misinterpretation. The two of them had found each other again, it wasn't for her to shoot holes in their boat. To lighten the mood, she told Robert about what she thought she had discovered, about Gordon and Janet's holiday rental. She told him about her charge list, the various moments when Janet had given herself away, and the conclusive evidence of the post that morning.

"But they said it's an Airbnb," said Robert. "How can they live in an Airbnb?"

"It might have been once," said Gina. "Maybe until quite recently. But I reckon they've bought it."

Robert, sipping his coffee, said, "It is a bit bare. Not much furniture."

"And what there is is very new. The beds, the sofa. And the kitchen units."

"So what, you think it was sold all-in?"

"Could be. And they've got their own furniture coming, once we're off the scene."

"But why would they move down here? They're not even retired. And why would they not say anything?" asked Robert.

"Probably they're just not ready. Or else they're going to make a big announcement. Maybe even later on today. This lunch in the garden – Mum said it was to celebrate."

"You don't have to tell me not to say anything."

"I know."

XXIII

The previous September, Gordon had received a second, and portentous, letter from the Ministry. Janet had been extremely annoyed that it had been addressed to Gordon alone. The knife-edge they had been teetering on since Crick House had "ceased trading" – this was Gordon's new expression, better to make a joke of it – had become blunt with time: several years had passed and Oak Lodge was still standing, even if "the essence of the place", as Janet said, had changed forever, with Fairfields squatting in front of it like a great unwelcome toad.

According to this letter, a person called A. E. Boyle, with whom they had never had any contact, was "inviting" them to move into a flat in the staff "complex" on the Fairfields site ("Why 'complex'? It's simple, brutal," said Janet, and she had a point). For this they would be expected to pay the same nominal rent they had been paying for Oak Lodge in recent years (while Crick House was in operation, it has been free). The reason for A.E. Boyle's invitation was quite simple: Oak Lodge stood on a site which would be needed for the expansion of the hideosity in front of them. No details were given.

"What do they mean, expansion?" said Janet. "A leisure centre? A hairdressing salon?"

Gordon had given up lecturing Janet on the realities of the Fairfields regime. Ironically but inevitably, she now looked back with nostalgia on Gordon's reign over Crick House, harping with approval on the gardening, the livestock management, the camping trips, the emphasis on healthy hard work. She seemed to have some idea that the boys in Fairfields had it easy in comparison. Gordon was not sure about this. Conscience had driven him to join a committee which oversaw the regime, and as far as he knew there had been little outright abuse so far. But the policy of treating young people like prisoners felt wrong.

Now, with the letter in his hand, Gordon did not answer Janet. The thing was to decide what to do. They had of course talked about it before. The hope had always been that they would be able to stay at Oak Lodge until Gordon officially retired, which was still a mere few months off, although he had always intended to go on working to some extent. Janet, who was still practising part-time, sometimes said she would never retire completely, because she was simply too interested in other people's lives.

"One thing's for sure," said Janet, who did not care not to be ignored. "We won't be moving into any of their flats."

"Obviously not," said Gordon. There had been no real need to talk about that, they were both agreed.

Two days later, over breakfast, Janet suddenly said, as if they had been half-way through a conversation, "Of course, if you're going to just teach, we could live anywhere."

Gordon sighed, but did not challenge "just teach". He said, "How d'you mean?"

"We could do a Lilian Johnson," said Janet.

The demise of Crick House had coincided with the death of Mrs Johnson's husband. Gordon and Janet had gone to the funeral, where they had found her looking better than she had for weeks. "It's terrible, but it's over," she had said. A few days after that she had dropped in to say goodbye – she had always been a dropper-in, never a phoner. She had said she was going to live in Scotland, that she had always wanted to, that it had been her husband's dream of retirement too, but now she would go alone. She had an old friend there, from Oxford. Janet had felt at a disadvantage, as if they should have had something to offer, something for Mrs. Johnson to take away. Although they had never spent much time together, her departure seemed another blow, another part of their life dismantled.

"You mean move to the Borders?" said Gordon now.

"Not necessarily there," said Janet, in a careful voice. "But there's no reason to stay here."

Gordon could have said, My job: he had not been able to help throwing himself into it, had quickly become head of department, and had a made a bit of a speciality of organising extra-curricular activities that involved boys from both Ashwick Grammar and Coombe's. He was seen as able, and valuable, but at the same time he disliked having to function within a large structure, missing the days of Crick House as his own world over which he had ruled supreme. Besides, there was so little time left before he was due to retire anyway. It was no good wanting to stay rooted. What he did say was, "What exactly did you have in mind?", and he too said it rather carefully.

Janet took a steadying breath. "I went to see Gerry."

"Oh yes?" said Gordon, after a moment, very dry. A year or two previously Janet had said it had been the simultaneous nature of their extra-marital affairs that had saved them from the danger zone. Gordon had asked her what rubbish she had been reading. That was the last time Gerry's name had been mentioned between them.

"When it all folded" —Janet always said folded, as if Crick House were somewhere between a business that had gone bust and an old newspaper— "I went to ask his advice." She had been convinced they must be due some redress, some compensation. Gerry, looking older, a little bowed, still living in his mother's house, had received her in the rarely-used drawing-room, listened to what she had to say, and a week later phoned to tell her that because of the way the endowments had been set up, if they were evicted, and if Oak Lodge were demolished, it might indeed be possible to argue that compensation was due. At the time eviction had not been on the cards and Janet had let the whole thing slide, but now that the situation had changed, she had consulted him again (looking not just older but old, four years on, sallow and skeletal. It was clear that he was quite ill in some way, but Janet felt she couldn't ask).

"To cut a long story short," Janet went on, watching Gordon spread butter and marmalade with an expression of absolute neutrality, "There'll be a cheque at some point." She named the amount.

"Hmm," said Gordon, considering. It would be a very considerable boost to their investment account, which had taken a battering in the various recent crises.

"You could go on teaching to supplement your pension," said Janet. "Even supply. Or you could do tutoring. That's the big thing now." It was, and Gordon disapproved of the new educational system which made it necessary. But for a second he considered being the sort of man who saw only his own advantage, who didn't consider it his duty to see the bigger picture.

"And I could go on with my clients," Janet continued. Recently she had made a speciality of couples' counselling after, or sometimes during, middle-aged adultery.

"It sounds rather, rather – *random*," Gordon said now, using his pupils' word. He was a planner, like Gina. He liked to see the sense in things, the patterns. Although pursuing that train of thought was depressing: neither he nor Janet had many relatives, so no real reason to be anywhere. Gordon had a brother in South Africa, Janet a sister in Croydon, and cousins who had emigrated to Australia, thirty years previously, with whom she exchanged Christmas cards.

"It was random when we came to Ashwick," said Janet. "We came here for your job. There was no other reason to come here and we've spent decades of our lives here. Now we can leave because the job's gone."

"My real job went years ago."

"All the more reason."

He knew she was serious because she was speaking in sentences, paragraphs, rather than her usual little bursts of impulse or anger. Janet knew he was listening because he said nothing. And so the seeds of the plan were planted.

Some days later, Gordon said they could go and live in France, to be near Gina. "Don't be ridiculous," said Janet, aware that she no longer needed to push her advantage: really the deal was already done. "Gina wouldn't want us in France. She's got her own life." Gordon would have not put it quite so bluntly, but he could see she was not that kind of daughter, not the kind to buy a house in the country and do it up and have her parents round to sit in the garden. ("All those years of encouraging her, and this is what we get," Janet had said, some time before. "Gina encouraged herself," Gordon had replied. "She didn't need us." This was perhaps worse.)

Later still, Janet said, "What if it all goes wrong, Gordon?" He hadn't heard her so gentle and supplicative for years. They were sitting in the kitchen, leafing through a pile of brochures. "Holiday places," Gordon had said. If they were going to do it, they may as well do it properly. No point living in the middle of nowhere, or just moving to some other, neutral town (he didn't say their marriage wouldn't stand it but they both knew this was true).

Gordon sipped tea, thought about it, and said: "We don't actually have to tell anyone. Not at first. We can try it out. No need to rush into buying. We can rent a place, dear." He hadn't called Janet dear for decades. And in the euphoria of it all being all right, the invitation to the children to spend three days by the sea was born. Next day, Janet went into town to buy the cards with the sails and the sunbeams.

Gina and Robert were more or less right about the furniture. "Let's just get rid of it," said Janet, her brusquerie returning. "I've seen enough of all this junk to last a lifetime. We'll take the decent stuff, such as it is. Get rid of the rest."

Gordon thought at first that he would not allow Janet to get rid of Susie's things, her bed, her desk, her old cheval mirror with a felt Woodstock hanging off one corner. The general clutter of her clothes and belongings had long since been tidied away. Much of it Janet had thrown out or given away, over time. She had said if Susie were still around, an expression Gordon did not care for since it could imply that she was dead, she would not be storing her things in the parental home, not at her age. Gordon acknowledged there was truth in this, and could see that it would be grotesque to keep her room as some kind of shrine. One might do that if one's daughter was dead, he reasoned, but for a daughter who simply did not want to come home—. He had, years before, gathered together a few of her things: a threadbare teddy, a woolly toy rabbit, her jewellery, a pencil pot made and decorated by Robert with paisley stencils, that she had had on her desk. He had put these things in a wooden box one of the arty boys at Crick House had painted for him, with flourishes and flower motifs, in the style of canal art – his family had lived on a barge. So these things were safe, they had gone into the ark. Now that the waters were finally rising, Janet could get rid of what she liked.

Gordon replied to the Ministry with a very short, very bland letter: in connection with the forthcoming demolition of Oak Lodge, he and his wife would not require accommodation on the Fairfields site. The flat put aside for them could thus be freed up for employees who needed it. Gordon wished the department all the best in its future endeavours. He said nothing about the settlement or about their plans, to these people who had been waiting for years now for them to leave. He had a sudden, sad sense that the world was waiting for them to die.

Still, organising the move had, in its way, been fun. They had gone down for a few days to see the house in Falmouth, and sign the papers for the rental, the plan being, if that one did not suit, to get the agency they were using to show them others. It had been, as Gina and Robert had worked out, a holiday rental. The owners, who themselves had moved to Falmouth for their retirement had made a lot of money on it over the years but grown fed up of the constant upkeep and administration. They were now looking to sell, but were happy with a longer-term rental over the autumn and winter, and in no hurry for Gordon and Janet to make up their minds. Gordon had been worried that they might be resented by the locals, that incomers might be frowned upon. "Not in

Falmouth," said the agent, a no-nonsense woman who was herself from London. "Maybe further out, but not here." He had let himself be persuaded. There was no viable plan B.

Gordon and Janet had stayed overnight in Exeter on the way, in Bath on the way back, and in Falmouth had "splashed out", said Janet, since they couldn't yet stay in the house, and booked a hotel with a spa which billed itself as "luxurious", and was rather, with everything very clean and sleek and modern. "I shan't miss Oak Lodge," Janet had said, looking around and deciding that partly it was the emptiness that made this place luxurious, the lack of clutter. And then when they got back to Ashwick, against all expectation there had been an almost festive air in the preparations for the actual move. As Janet said, it made it so much easier, not having to worry about cleaning or touching up the paintwork for incoming tenants: "I'm not going to go to too much trouble for a wrecking ball." It had seemed almost hilarious, at the time, and there had been a certain glee in packing up and heading off. They had left without saying anything, not creeping away, Gordon said, just hedging their bets. No sense in having a goodbye party if they might be back in a few weeks looking for a place in Ashwick. Janet gave out a cover story: they had put their furniture in store and were taking a holiday. She said this to Nadège as well, but she wasn't really worried that Nadège would pass anything on to Robert or Gina, since she made such a speciality of never telling anyone anything.

The Ellises' friends in Ashwick presumed they must be extremely upset about Oak Lodge and quite saw the wisdom of the plan. Behind their backs they speculated as to the amount of the settlement.

XXIV

Gina and Robert finished their coffee and decided to stay out for a while, both so that Gina could complete her purchases and to allow Robert to give Gordon a wide berth. Once the shopping was done, they walked up the hill and then down past Castle Beach and over to Gyllyngvase, stopping in the Queen Mary gardens along the way. Gina wanted, she said, to take a photo of what appeared to be an artichoke tree. She was delighted with its bareness, its prickliness, the huge and bulbous flowers. "I didn't even know they grew on trees," she said. "Do you have these, in the north? Do you sell monkish artichokes on the market?"

Robert said they did not, that anyway he dealt with the mead stall, not the garden produce, but he posed obediently in front of the plant, then sat on a low wall looking at the sea while Gina, whom he had never known to be particularly interested in nature, went off round the garden taking photos of this and that.

"Look," she said, sitting down beside him, tilting the screen of her phone towards him. It showed a pale grey stone wall, a paler grey sky – although sunshine was indeed promised for later – and, between the two, growing behind the wall so that it seemed to be growing out of it, a single flower with narrow and spiky pinkish-lilac petals radiating from a dark centre.

Robert looked. "What does it mean?" he said, since it seemed to mean something.

"I'm not sure yet," said Gina. "But there's something about it. Flower from stone. Colour from no-colour. Things growing where you don't expect them. Maybe it's Mum. Or my relationship with Mum." Robert looked dubious but interested. "I'm doing metalwork," Gina announced.

"Really?" Robert sounded gratifyingly surprised.

"Sort of collages, with different shapes. I'm not very good yet. But I like the way you can see what you want to see, when you get rid of words." She saw it as a remedial exercise, and bent herself to it, humbly.

"Brother Gareth says something similar," said Robert. "At St Agnes. He paints – well, abstracts, I suppose you'd say."

Gina had been to a workshop in Waldo: it was part of working through her feeling, as Kelly would put it, that there were other things in life beside texts, or that there needed to be such things in her life. So far she had started on a panel showing aluminium fish jumping in the river in Port Huron. The tutor had said this was an excellent subject, that it was good to begin with things you saw as silver. Gina also had more ambitious plans: she wanted to do one of a group of black men she had seen in Waldo, standing not in a group, but singly, strung along the street, listening, faces lifted, to music from a festival they couldn't afford to pay to get into. Gina had been much struck by this – the unofficial listeners generally sat on the grass outside the gates, with blankets and beers. These men were a whole new layer, something secret, something she wanted to acknowledge.

243

She didn't go into all this with Robert. Much of her new world was still too complicated to explain. They walked along the path behind the beach, saying nothing. Gina gazed at the empty horizon, and had a sense of emptying her thoughts into it. It was restful. But once they had walked back along the beach itself, really it seemed to be time to go back to the house if they were to appear not only in time for lunch, but for some token offer of help.

"Oh good," said Janet, hearing them come in. She looked remarkably buoyant, more so than Gina remembered seeing her for a long time, and Gina went through to the kitchen and kissed her on the cheek, at which she looked surprised but pleased.

"It's all arrived," said Janet. "I'm just warming the oven, then we'll start putting it all out."

Duck pâté crostinis, read Gina from one box. Caramelised red onion and goat's cheese tart; smoked trout pinwheels; porcini and sea salt twists; parmesan crisps. Plates, medium; napkins; crystal-look glasses. Already unpacked were a large bowl of crudités and several lidded pots which must be dips. "Shall I take these out?"

"Give the table a wipe first, if you would. Then it's this cloth, with these clips. Evenly, all the way round, not just the corners."

Gina did as she was bidden, and by the time she had laid the table, been upstairs to tidy and perfume herself and collected Robert on the way down, everyone was gathered in the garden, and Janet's celebration was ready to begin.

"So," said Gina to Clara, as Janet passed plates ("Tuck in, help yourselves"), "What did you think of the play?"

"I really liked it," she said, in a tone which combined doubt with deference to her grandmother for the treat. "But there were things I didn't really get. I mean, how could someone get a shop assistant sacked, just because she smiled behind her back?"

Gina saw her father shaping up for a teachable moment. "Rights for the working classes don't go as far back as you think," he began. But at that moment, she also became aware of Nadège, who was sitting on the bench along the kitchen wall, neither eating nor drinking. Gina could not remember, afterwards, how it was that the attention of the group suddenly turned to her sister-in-law. Gordon said, to be agreeable, to include her, "And what did you think, Nadège? Deluge aside, of course."

Nadège made a small, throat-clearing noise, and said, "I have decided to grant Robert a divorce."

"Yes," said Gordon, since she seemed to be addressing him. "Yes, I believe, I believe he mentioned it. Bit of a chat this morning." He tried to smile at Robert, but there was something in the atmosphere that made it difficult. Was there any need to make quite such a public deal of it, wondered Gina?

"And I've got something to say," said Nadège.

They waited, still making their way through the various delicacies (and they really were very good) in a silence which suddenly seemed rather too animated by cutlery scraping on plates.

"Well, what is it?" said Janet, as nothing came. "Rather good, these goat's cheese tartlets."

"Very," agreed Gina.

"They can't be that difficult to make. I think there might be a bit of honey in there."

"Janet," said Gordon, warningly.

"Well?" said Janet, again.

Gordon nodded towards Nadège.

"I want to tell you that I'm leaving this family," she said, in a tone of enormous finality.

"How do you mean?" said Gordon.

"*Clara* is part of this family," Janet jumped in, with an emphasis which suggested that Nadège was not. Clara was staring at her mother wide-eyed. Whatever was coming had clearly not been discussed.

"After the divorce, I want nothing more to do with any of you," went on Nadège, in her flat, composed little voice. Gordon, seeing Janet about to start again about Clara, placed a warning hand on his wife's arm.

"Separation is never easy," Gordon began. "But such a radical stance—"

"I'm being as radical as you were," said Nadège. "Or perhaps not as radical. No-one could be as radical as that."

This fell once more on silence, and Gina said, with a little malice, "I think you'll have to give us a clue." If anyone was going to let on that they knew about the secret house move, she didn't see why it should be Nadège.

"You disgust me. All of you."

"Steady on," said Gordon.

"Don't you think," said Janet, in an indignant voice, "That this might be better discussed between you and Robert? There's no need to spoil our day. This is supposed to be a celebration."

"A celebration!" said Nadège. "How can you celebrate? Your daughter is not here." Oh, *Susie*, thought Gina, out of a moment's confusion. "All these years you haven't seen her, haven't taken any news of her" —the deterioration in Nadège's English was the only sign of her emotion— "just haven't bothered –"

"How dare you!" said Janet, banging her plate down.

"I think you'll find there's more to it than that," said Gordon, his face growing still.

"Oh yes, there's more to it than that. But it's not as if you two ever cared enough to find out," nodding across the table.

"Us?" said Robert, clumsily indicating himself and Gina.

"Yes, you," said Nadège. "You don't care what happened to your sister. You're so involved with your own stupid little lives—"

"Possibly less stupid than being an under-matron at Coombe's," said Gina, but Gordon said, quite loudly, across her, "If you've got something to say, Nadège, then please tell us what it is."

"And if you haven't, just go," said Janet. Gordon did not countermand this order.

"I talked to Susie."

"*What?*" It was almost a shout, and strangely enough, it came from Clara, whose face suddenly seemed to collapse in on itself.

"When?" said Gordon, quietly. "When was this?"

"It was many times," said Nadège, still composed.

"But how did you find her?" said Gina, who could feel a rush of anguished anger rising inside her and felt like first slapping her sister-in-law and then banging her head against the wall.

"On the internet."

"So have you actually spoken to her, or is this just someone in a chatroom who might or might not be Susie?"

"It is Susie. And she told me about her son."

"I told you!" cried Clara; turning to Gina. "I told you my dad saw her in London, with a child!"

"No," said Nadège. "I'm talking about the son you took

247

away from her." She looked steadily at Gordon.

There was silence for a moment.

"We did no such thing," said Janet. "*No such thing.*"

"Janet," said Gordon, and once more laid a hand on her arm. "We don't need to go into it now. Not like this."

"Go into what?" said Gina, looking at Robert, who shrugged and raised his palms upwards, mouth open in incomprehension. "What? What are you talking about? What do you mean?" She could hear her own voice rising.

"Clara should go inside," said Janet. "Go upstairs, Clara."

"Oh really, she's got this far," said Gina. Clara stayed where she was. Gina poured herself another glass of wine, then poured all round, except for Nadège, who could hardly expect it. She threw half a glass down her throat, and, in defiance, went back to eating what was on her plate. "And if you think we haven't looked for Susie on the internet, you have no idea," she went on, turning to Nadège.

"Yes, she knows where you looked," said Nadège, and Gina felt as if she was the one who had been hit, hard, in the stomach, and stopped eating. "But you looked in the wrong place."

"That's enough," said Gordon. "That's quite enough."

"Get out," said Janet to Nadège.

"You can't say that to her in front of Clara," said Gina, getting up, putting her arm round her niece, down whose cheek a tear was rolling. Although she could quite see why Janet would.

Gordon rose and followed Nadège round the side of the house to the driveway where her car was parked. A few moments later he reappeared and said to Clara, "Your mother's going to be on her way. She says we can keep you for a day or two, send you back on the train. Go and give her a kiss."

"Come here," said Robert, and dabbed gently at his daughter's cheeks with a paper napkin. The four adults sat and looked at each other and the world seemed to have grown very quiet. Nobody knew where to start.

"Susie didn't know what she wanted," said Gordon, after some moments, and Janet, "Somebody had to make a decision."

"To help her make a decision."

Of course, most of the detail didn't come out then. They were only heard the bare bones of the story. The rest, Gina, Robert and Clara, each of them had to reconstruct for themselves,.

Susie

XXV

"She wouldn't have it," said Janet. It was the summer of Robert's dolls and his engagement, the summer of Mary and Gerry, the summer that marked the beginning of the end of Crick House, when Gina was finishing her PhD and Robert was courting Nadège. Janet crashed into the kitchen, banged her handbag down on the table.

"You mean she's changed her mind?" said Gordon, who had been sitting reading *The Guardian.*

Janet tutted in exasperation, as if she didn't think Susie really had a mind.

"She went in, all ready, and half an hour later she was out again. Still pregnant!"

"Where is she?"

"Wandering around somewhere." Janet didn't care where she was (Susie's shamed face in the mirror on the way home, looking like a child who'd wet her knickers at a party). Janet was furious, and was to remain so for a long time.

In fact, Susie was in the kitchen at Crick House. Mary was on her own at this time of day, the boys, including Luke, busy with their afternoon lessons. Mary was sewing, mending a large, striped blue chemise that had torn at the shoulder. Susie had a lurching feeling inside her. Gina had explained once that it was her solar plexus and she needn't take much notice of it, but Susie had a feeling of nebulous terror and she couldn't ignore it. She had a sense that she could not be left alone, not for a moment, that she couldn't be trusted, or could not trust herself. But she didn't want to see her schoolfriends. Four of them were supposed to going on a week's holiday at the end of August to a caravan in Cromer owned by a relative of her best friend Rachel, but she wouldn't go, not now. She was much too near the beginning of the pregnancy for it to show, but she couldn't imagine getting through the week without the whole story coming out, and it was too secret, too private, to be told. Nobody could understand, about Luke, about what she felt for him, about his real mother, giving him away, and then those people, those awful people who made him do all those weird religious things and then thrown him out of their house.

Neither could she bear the idea of being a pregnant schoolgirl. There had been quite a few of these over the years at Ashwick Girls', frightening and hybrid and slightly obscene, child-women with uniform blouses straining over their bellies, ties foreshortened by the curve as their time grew near. Sometimes the pregnant ones lost their old friends and acquired a little troupe of the curious and well-meaning. Sometimes they suddenly seemed years older, and shook everyone off and walked alone. Susie could not, would not, be one of these creatures. And so these past weeks she had stopped going for coffee in town, stopped going to Alison's house – the closest, geographically. She had a horrible sense of having left them all behind, in spite of herself, without wanting to, without getting a chance to say goodbye. Panic rose inside her. She wasn't ready, she needed more time.

Mary had received Susie, who looked dishevelled and a

little pale, without surprise, and poured tea in silence. Susie had told her story with no effort to dress it up: "I'm pregnant. It's Luke's. I went for an abortion but I couldn't do it. This morning."

Mary said nothing.

"You know," said Susie, "You know when you, when you, with Dad?" She had a sense of womanly solidarity with Mary, comfortable, silent, strange Mary, which allowed her to ask this, but it would have been too much to attach a verb to it. "Did you use, you know. How they say you should. A condom." Susie's mind had been running on this – at what moment should the object be produced? Who was supposed to deal with the practicality of it? Just how idiotic was she, not to have made Luke do this?

"I had operation," said Mary.

Susie gazed at her. "You mean you had an abortion too?" She didn't know why she said "too". After all, she hadn't done it yet herself.

"No. Sterilise," said Mary. "Long time ago." Susie felt she should have something to say to this, some acceptable reaction, or that she should ask more about it, but she couldn't. She just sat at the table and cried, without energy or hope. Mary went on sewing. It was restful. More restful than being with Janet.

*

Susie "hadn't been prepared," Gordon said later, making Janet feel as if this was her fault. "She was frightened," he said. "The equipment frightened her."

"Oh for goodness sake," said Janet. "It's quick and painless. There's nothing to be frightened of."

Gordon had been outraged at this. He had told Janet that

if that was the best she could do as a mother she had better keep out of it, which was what she was doing, largely. Apart, she thought bitterly, from dealing with the hospital, driving Susie to and fro, rescheduling appointments with her clients to accommodate her. She had heard Gordon's tread on the stairs up to the top floor, presumed he must be going into Susie. Janet could imagine her daughter lying weeping on her bed but for the moment she was too angry to care. What an utterly stupid thing to do, to sleep with Luke of all people, to let herself be spoilt by him, and not use contraception – what girl of seventeen these days did not know about contraception? Janet knew there would come a time when the flames of her anger would die down, she would be able to see her daughter again, to comfort her, to prepare little feasts and treats for her, but she knew this only as a fact, without being able properly to imagine it. Just now it was better that it was Gordon listening to Susie's words of sorrow trying to force themselves through her torrents of tears.

*

Luke came up to Susie's room late in the afternoon of the next day, when normally he would have been among the Crick House kitchen boys. Susie wasn't even careful about it any more – what did it matter if they were seen? The thing was done, now. Although as far as she could tell, her mother was not around, and Gordon must be at Crick House, dealing with the after-class activities, optional at this particular time of day. The boys were allowed to go to their rooms and read, draw, or, as the official schedule quaintly put it, "listen to the radio".

Susie lounged on her pillows – pregnancy was making her langorous, she needed to hunker into herself – and told Luke about the hospital appointment, about what had happened. "I didn't plan it like that," she said. "I just couldn't do it." She paused, expecting a response. "I needed to be sure," she prompted. "That you didn't mind."

Luke, sitting perpendicular to her with his back against the wall and his legs across hers, said, "You shouldn't let this ruin your life, Susie. You've got everything ahead of you, you're going to do your A-levels, go to university... You don't need this, not yet. Maybe one day."

There was a wistfulness to "one day", as if he knew – which he did, really, and which she did also – that the Susie of a decade hence, who might be settling down and thinking about babies, in her home-loving and domestic way, would certainly not be doing it with him.

"You're too good for me," said Luke.

"That's not true," said Susie. "We're the same." They had talked about this before, about how there was not much difference in their backgrounds. Luke hadn't passed the exam for Ashwick boys' grammar but there had been talk of transferring him for the sixth form. He had lived in a pleasant house. He had never been poor, or what Gordon called "disadvantaged", although it must surely be a disadvantage, Susie thought, to end up with parents like that.

"You are," said Luke, moving now to lie beside her and take her in his arms. "You're much too good. You need to forget me, you do. You deserve much more."

"So you think I should go through with it?" said Susie. "With the termination?" The doctor at the hospital had offered this kinder word.

"You don't want to marry me, do you?" Luke had said.

"I don't want to get married yet," said Susie, helplessly. Sometimes she felt that Luke was saying the opposite of what he meant, that he wanted her to say that yes, she did want to get married and that she didn't deserve anything, not any more than him. Susie wasn't sure what she deserved, but she couldn't imagine being with Luke forever. She wanted to go to Italy, she wanted to go to Australia. She wanted a baby one day, but not now, not like this. She hadn't seen anything, hadn't been anywhere, and sometimes that made her panic, made her want to run away, never to see Luke again. She began to cry, which was another thing that pregnancy seemed to make her do. She loved him, but she could feel him infecting her with his sadness, his sadness that would never go away. Sometimes the thing in her belly seemed exactly that, an infection. But now Luke had rolled over her, and he was lying holding her so that she was between him and the wall, and he smelt of cigarettes and the special smell that was his skin and hair, and the aftershave she had given him, from Boots. She felt completely safe, completely secure. It was impossible to think, about what she wanted and what she didn't. Something else had taken over, some inevitability, some force she wasn't strong enough to resist.

Susie was hopelessly split, and it seemed that Luke must be too, because that was the night of the fire, and the night he was arrested and, after some time, sentenced to his year as a Young Offender.

XXVI

Susie's appointment at the hospital was rescheduled for a week later. "There's no *real* hurry," said the nurse carefully to Janet, on the phone. "We've still got a couple of weeks in hand." It was nice of her to say "we", Janet thought, sharing the weight of the problem. "Still, better to get it out of the way. Psychologically."

Janet was past caring about Susie's psychology. Her entire life had been derailed by Susie's problem, she had been plunged into it as into a cold sea and could feel the shock of it, couldn't get her breath. She was already badly shaken by the fire, even if Gordon hadn't been in the building at the time. Nothing like that had ever happened before during Gordon's tenure at Crick House, but it was the sort of thing Janet had always feared, and now it made her fear worse. What if the boys mutinied? What if they did something to Gordon, or to Janet herself?

And now Susie, imagining herself in love with this delinquent, and Gordon, telling her there was a conflict between Luke's intellectual and affective judgment ("Intellectual!" Janet had scathed). But she thanked the nurse, wrote down the new time, and thought that it would, soon, be over, and that life would go on as before, and that even if it hadn't been perfect, it at least hadn't felt like it did now, as if she had capsized in a small boat among huge waves and couldn't get righted.

*

"She kept changing her mind," said Janet, in the Falmouth garden; and Gordon, "She was so young. So easily influenced."

*

The second appointment at the hospital was worse. The outcome was the same, but the process was terrible. Janet was trembling with anger as she told the story to Gordon.

"Those – those church women. Getting at her. I don't know how they can show their faces." She meant after what they had done to Luke, although they weren't the ones who had done it, not directly.

"They were there, waiting. The cheek of it. It's got nothing to do with them." Mrs Shaw and Mrs Tredwell, bringers of second-hand clothes to Mary, had met them outside. (Had Mary, in return, brought them this nugget of information, about Susie? Her relationship with the church was ambivalent. You never knew. And if not Mary, then who?). "They said they wanted to have a word with Susie. They said it was about Luke." Although she disapproved of what had been done to the boy by his parents, Janet's tone made it clear that as far as she was concerned, Luke no longer figured in her world-view. She had regarded the ladies with scorn, their cake hats and their dusty tweed skirts and naked faces.

"Whatever it is you want, can you please be quick," she had said briskly. "My daughter has an appointment and we don't want to be late."

But Susie had stood there, a rabbit in the headlights, and

said, "Mummy, I do need to talk to them. Go inside and I'll be in in a minute."

Janet had still not grown used to seeing her youngest child as in some way grown-up, autonomous, now that she was pregnant, but Susie's tone was decided, and, said Janet now to Gordon, "I wasn't going to stand and have an argument in the hospital car-park."

"She came in and she didn't say a word to me," Janet went on. "Just went in to see the doctor. And when she came out again she said the doctor wanted to speak to me. And she said—"

"She?" said Gordon. "I thought it was Dr Greening."

"Well it wasn't, it was a Dr Elton, there's more than one of them. *She* said," said Janet, who had somehow felt worse, more judged, when she had discovered the doctor was a woman, "she said that even if Susie changes her mind again, they won't do it now. They can't in all conscience" —Janet's voice mimicked, sneered— "sign a form to say that continuing the pregnancy would have a detrimental effect on Susie's mental health. She said she clearly doesn't want to end the pregnancy and she asked" —unbridled indignation— "she asked whose idea it was to have a termination, hers or mine? Not *yours*," Janet raged at Gordon. "Oh no. Mine. I've got to be the one who's making her do it."

Gordon, face set, said, "So where does this leave us?"

It was a very good question, to which Janet had no immediate answer. She heard him go upstairs.

"I can't," wept Susie, as Gordon perched clumsily by the head of her bed on an easy chair strewn with his daughter's paraphernalia, "I can't do that to Luke. He says he doesn't want it to die. He told Mrs Tredwell. He says he wants it go out into the world and be the best part of both of us. He says he wants it to have a chance. He says…"

The rest was incoherent. Gordon patted her shoulder awkwardly, went downstairs, and phoned Mrs Tredwell. "She's coming over," he said, coming back into the kitchen. "Oh, that's all we need," said Janet, almost weeping with frustration. "Why did those bloody women have to involve Luke? It's nothing to do with him. That little thug. He's obviously going to go from bad to worse."

Gordon said, "I think it was probably Susie who told Luke. She must have written to him." Although he wondered why these women felt the need to involve themselves.

"Luke," said Janet, to Gordon and again to Mrs Tredwell, "has forfeited any right he ever had to make decisions about our daughter's life." Mrs Tredwell, still in her ugly felt hat, sat and said that abortion was an abomination in the sight of the Lord, quoting various Bible verses. Janet left the room. Gordon thanked her for her visit, and reclaimed his share of the moral high ground by asking her to send his regards to Luke, should she visit him again. He was deeply annoyed by her assumed monopoly on Christianity.

*

"You have to understand," said Gordon, in the Falmouth garden, "That we were under a lot of pressure from the church. They put forward two families to adopt the baby. They were having papers drawn up. We had to find another way."

"Susie wouldn't be swayed," said Janet. "Her mind was made up."

"But," said Gina, outraged, "Did she want the child adopted? Did she agree to it? Who made her agree?"

"She certainly didn't want a baby," said Janet.

"It was Susie's decision," said Gordon, in a voice which had become, over the years, inhabited by doubt.

"We kept telling her," said Janet ("You kept telling her," Gordon had learned not to say), "It's just a ball of cells, it's not a baby at all, you're not killing anything, and she kept saying she loved Luke and she couldn't do it to him because he wanted it to go out into the world. Whatever that meant."

"And did it?" said Gina. She was making a tremendous effort to remain outwardly calm, to let the story come out, because there was so little time, and so she was controlled when she said, "Did it go out into the world? And what was all that, that" —she stopped herself from saying "rubbish"— "about Italy?"

XXVII

Susie had gone to Italy, but not exactly to be an au pair. The Thomsons, from Coombe's, had by this time retired to the Tuscan countryside, where they were working, to the amused contempt of those they had left behind, on a series of Italian cookery books in English, with Felicity writing the recipes and Oliver doing the photos. What made it easier was that they had been so good, Janet said, with the Browne-Williams girl. This was the daughter of a housemaster at Coombe's who had got involved with drugs, as Janet put it, and earned herself a police caution. She had gone out to stay with the Thomsons for several weeks, in return for a modest contribution to board and lodging, and come back in a more constructive frame of mind. "Not that it's a punishment", Janet had said, warningly to Gordon, who said, "Of course not. Obviously not. It's just that if she doesn't want to stay here— . And at least she'll be going on with her education. To some extent. I hope she'll get a chance to speak some Italian."

*

In the garden in Falmouth, there was really there was only one question: "How could you lie about something so big for so long?" dressed up as, "Why didn't you tell us before?". But

Gina was aware that if she said anything of the kind they would never get to hear the story. She said now, "A pregnant teenager in Italy! How did that work?"

"They were very good to her, the Thomsons. Exceptionally good. They took her about, when she still felt like going. Showed her all the architecture she was interested in. All the art."

"But how did they... explain it?"

"There was nothing to explain, Gina. Italy is a perfectly modern country. At the hospital they knew she was having a baby for an infertile couple. It was a good deed. The staff told her that. Over and over."

"But who did that in the 1980s?" cried Gina. "Nobody did! Nobody!"

"What else could we have done?" said Janet, still combative but with an edge of wretchedness. "Just what were we supposed to do?"

*

When the social worker came, it had been enough to make you wish for the church ladies. It was Gordon who had called social services. It was the best way, he said to Janet, to get the church off their backs. Janet had been horrified.

"So now we're the sort of family that requires *social workers*?" she said, outraged. "I can't believe how far that boy has dragged Susie down. Dragged us all down. Why did you ever have to get us all mixed up with those criminal boys!"

"If there's going to be an adoption," Gordon said, ignoring this, because they had already been over and over it, "It should be done by professionals. I won't have some private business cooked up by that church."

They sat in the front room, Gordon, Janet and Susie. Janet

had made tea, properly, in a tea-pot on a tray. The social worker, a Mrs. Judd, arrived in a muddy estate car. To Janet's relief, she looked as if she could have been anyone, visiting the house for any reason. She looked like one of them. Mrs Judd, both motherly and business-like, smiled at Susie as they all sat at this very awkward tea-party, and said, "These days there are so few babies for adoption, and so many couples looking to adopt—"

"It's a sellers' market," said Janet.

There was an uncomfortable silence.

"You have no idea what the families go through to be approved," said Mrs Judd. "We leave no stone unturned—"

"Actually I do have a pretty good idea," said Janet repressively. "I *am* a qualified therapist."

Gordon and Janet had done nothing but quarrel over the last few days, with a bitterness which exhausted Gordon, although he suspected that something in Janet fed on it. Now he no longer had the energy to intervene. He sat and looked at the carpet between his feet, and thought, for the first time, that it was rather an unpleasant shade of maroon. Mrs Judd said, "Oh good, so you're well placed to, er…" and then got lost, and it was Susie who said, sitting forward in her armchair, with her hands joined on her lap, her hair a cloud of almost-silver in the light behind her, "So what's going to happen?"

Mrs Judd said, "It will only happen if you agree, Susie. We prefer to think of it as something that you're going to do rather than something that's going to happen."

Janet looked scornful, and Mrs Judd suggested going for a walk with Susie so they could have a little talk on their own.

*

"And don't think," Janet had shouted, not at Susie but at Gordon, "Don't think I'm going to be the one bringing it up. I've had enough of all that. I'm not starting again. Not at my age."

Janet was forty-eight. In another generation, it would not have been unusual even to be a first-time mother at forty-eight, but Janet considered that the time for having babies was well past. The trouble was that this thing of Susie's was stirring feelings up inside her, making her wonder if the time for having babies had ever really been. Had she wanted children? You took it as read, as axiomatic; or her generation had done that; or she had. Janet now was not sure she'd ever questioned it, and wondered if she should have done. You did well at school, got engaged, got married, had children: that was the way it was, that was what being a woman was, that was taking your place in society. Yes, education was important, and work, but they were secondary to that great design. The default position towards women who didn't do this had always been pity and contempt, and Janet had internalised this attitude. Mary was a good example of a woman who drifted around the universe, a person who did not really qualify for the epithet of "woman" at all. Mary's very existence had made Janet angry, even before the business (she always thought of it as "the business") with Gordon.

And at the opposite end of the spectrum there was Gina. Janet sat on the edge of the marital bed, a place she rarely lingered, and thought about her eldest child. Gina had always been so certain she wanted no truck with babies and families, so sure she had other, better things to do. She had never entertained the idea of imitating her mother, not for a moment. She had been sure that she was better than that, destined for higher things. Gina had given herself permission to live as she chose, to place herself, shamelessly, at the centre of her own world. There was a part of Janet that would have liked to see Miss Gina brought low by pregnancy and childbirth and the daily grind of bringing up children, forced to be, she thought venomously now, like everybody else. And there was also another aspect to all this. It had been common, at one time, for misbegotten children to be taken in by aunts or uncles. This could have been Gina's comeuppance. But she wouldn't have it, thought Janet. She would have no problem whatsoever saying no. And besides – as reality caught up – with no husband, no house, no garden, no time... Her animus towards her eldest daughter flared and died.

Later Janet said to Gordon, "And it's not as if it's going to be an easy child, with some sort of juvenile delinquent for a father."

Gordon tended more and more to ignore Janet when she went on like this. She had already blamed him, over and over, for bringing them to Crick House, for exposing Susie to those boys. Gordon thought back with bitterness to how much she had wanted to get out of Coombe's, how dearly she had wanted Oak Lodge. But there were things they needed to discuss rationally, and so he said, calmly, politely, as if Janet had made her own point reasonably, "What worries me is the cultural problem, the, the..." he paused, sighed. "What I mean is that Luke clearly suffered from being adopted into a traditional British family..." it wasn't a time when "white" was used easily in that context. "He says he never felt at home with them, always felt different."

"That's not it," said Janet, miserably, furiously. "That's not it at all. If I wanted to bring it up, I wouldn't care if it was black or white or anything in between. But I don't, Gordon." She was much quieter now. "I don't want to do that."

"It wouldn't be right," said Gordon. "It wouldn't be right to force it on you."

"It's not as if you'd be any help. You weren't much, the first time round."

He probably wouldn't, Gordon thought. He probably hadn't been, not when the children were little, and he wasn't the sort to shake off the self he had spent decades growing into and metamorphose into a nursemaid as some men did. There was Ewan, on the town council, who had married a much younger woman and now had a three-year-old, and talked about getting home for bath-time and taking his daughter to nursery and who had become volubly indignant when someone had used the phrase "helping his wife". Gordon could not pretend to want that, any of that. He loved his children, he had enjoyed bringing them up, teaching them things, showing them how to do things, but he couldn't deal with all that again, now, and besides, he wasn't sure that Janet was wrong. It wasn't that he believed that Susie's baby would have any sort of inherent problems – Gordon had evolved beyond that kind of thought long ago. It was more that he felt that if it were given a clean slate, if it were placed in family which longed for a child more than anything in the world, it would have a much better chance, a much better life. And what sort of a father could Luke be? Gordon believed, more than anyone, in rehabilitation. He believed that Luke, given the right opportunities, had every chance of living a good life. It was beyond him what Susie saw in him – the sharp little face, the flesh too thin over the bones – but he would not be himself if he didn't fully believe that Luke could live a good life, no doubt beget other children in the future, when he was older, and bring them up quite satisfactorily. But what sort of a life would it be, he said to Janet now, known as the child of a teenager who went straight from care to jail?

"He'd be tarred for life," said Gordon, wondering as he said it if he meant scarred. "He'd have no real chance".

"Or she," said Janet – but the point was that the child had evolved, in their minds, beyond being an "it".

*

Susie had the sense to give herself an alibi, or at least that was how Janet thought of it. Going to visit Arthur, she had for some reason put on Janet's old gardening shoes instead of her usual trainers or wellingtons. These shoes, a pair of suede, once-beige Aqua Skips, were two decades old and their soles were worn completely smooth. Janet did not in fact wear them for gardening, but only to put the washing out and bring it in again. Susie, climbing over the gate on her way out of the paddock, as was her habit, although she could just as easily have opened it, slipped and fell heavily in the lane, where she lay, shocked, with one arm bent awkwardly underneath her and pain shooting up her right leg. As it happened, Gerry Allingham was at that moment driving past on his way home, and he saw her lying there and came to her aid.

Susie sat crying, and the first thing she said was, "I'm pregnant. I'm up the spout," as if her fall had somehow resulted in this condition. Gerry stood and looked at her, taken aback, and then said, "We'd better get you into the car." She was so slight he could practically carry her, and once arranged on the front seat with the twist straightened out of her arm, she looked much better. He drove her the couple of hundred yards which lay between the paddock and Oak Lodge and saw her into Janet's care, without commenting on what she had told him, although later it occurred to him to wonder if her parents knew.

Janet, who was competent in first aid (it was the deeper wounds she could not deal with, said Gina), bandaged up Susie's sprained ankle and wrist solicitously. There was also a nasty graze on her right elbow, which she dressed with a large compress, almost tenderly. Susie looked as if she had been in the wars and walked with a limp. Janet immediately saw the utility of this. If it came to anyone's ears that Susie had refused to get rid of this unfortunate pregnancy – and hospital staff were not always discreet – it could now be safely assumed that she would have lost it naturally in the accident, which could be blown up to ampler proportions. As far as Ashwick was concerned, Susie would have miscarried and there would be no baby.

It was Saturday afternoon. Janet drove Susie into town, where lots of people they knew would be about, on the pretext of taking her to Boots to get something for the pain. When Gerry phoned later to ask after the invalid (he was gentlemanly, whatever else he was), Janet said that it was rather worse than she'd thought, although she was sure Susie would be well enough in a few days. (Gerry took this to mean what Janet wanted it to mean, although she was not aware of this as she had no idea Susie would have told him she was expecting.) Over the next few days, Janet phoned friends on various pretexts, and she mentioned Susie's accident to all of them.

XXVIII

Gordon and Janet drove Susie to Gatwick, with her ankle still bandaged and her wrist in a sling. She had a crutch, and one of the new wheeled suitcases, and, "People will help," said Janet. "They'll see a damsel in distress and they'll sort you out." Susie tried to smile, and for a moment Janet wished it was Gina, who would have been acid and unpleasant to mask her own feelings and who expected nothing of her parents. Janet had given Susie two nice editions of novels by E.M. Forster, *Howard's End* and *Where Angels Fear to Tread* as a parting present. Susie had put these in her cabin bag rather than her suitcase. Was that a good sign? If Janet had been a different kind of woman, she would have admitted, at least to herself, that she wanted to throw herself to the ground and weep when Susie went through to departures. Susie herself was crying, without noise, without fuss. How could Janet let her go?

"Susie needs a lot of TLC," Gordon had said to Felicity on the phone the previous evening, when the final details were being ironed out. "She's not one of these tough young things. Not like some of them are these days. And there's been a lot of upset."

"We'll do our best," Felicity had said, "And we'll keep

you posted." Gordon had been more reassured by this than if she had told him not to worry. They had already talked about telephoning: Janet had factored it into the rate they were paying the Thomsons for Susie's keep. She had drawn up a budget some days before, because it was easier to do something practical than to think about the intangibles.

Felicity phoned the first night, to say that Susie had arrived safely, had eaten her supper – baked eggs, a little chicken and a salad of broad beans, then peach compote (Felicity always liked to give details of her well-chosen menus), had had a bath, with her foot bound up in a plastic bag and hanging over the side (the sling for her wrist was removable), and was now asleep.

"She hasn't changed much," said Felicity, and this too Gordon found reassuring: Felicity had, after all, known Susie as a small child, remembered her, she had said, sitting at Janet's kitchen table in Shakespeare, colouring in a sheet of tropical fish, with her hair bound up in a top-knot to keep it out of the way, but escaping in long corkscrew tendrils down her cheeks. Felicity hadn't seen much, if any, of Susie in recent years, but there was history, she knew who Susie was, where she came from, what had made her. Besides, what else would they have done? Institutions for unmarried expectant mothers had been a feature of Britain until not that long ago, but of course they would never have wanted that for Susie. What Gordon felt, perhaps, was that Susie was better with the Thomson's than at home. But he was not sure he himself had been ready for this point in his youngest child's life. She hadn't even finished her schooling. No, Susie leaving home was something he hadn't got to yet, hadn't seriously envisaged – because, said conscience, you've had your mind on anything and everything except her; and look where it's landed you: you, Janet, Susie and now this benighted baby.

Although over the summer neither Gordon nor Janet had had time for Susie, leaving her to her own devices, the house seemed very empty without her now. It had been different when Gina had left for Durham, she had been so anxious to be gone, so full of her own future. And with Robert it had simply been a relief when he had left for university – there had been the sense that at least he had got in somewhere, found a place by the skin of his teeth, through clearing, so they could at last stop fretting about what would happen if he didn't. And besides, both the elder children had been home for vacations; it had, often, been as if they had never left. But now Gordon missed Susie at odd times: his mind tricked him into believing that he heard her feet running up the stairs. Once he had gone up to her room to check, and of course found it empty, her three old cloth Snoopies heaped on her pillows, gazing straight ahead, waiting patiently for her to come home.

*

Mrs Shaw and Mrs Tredwell had turned up in Tuscany, in the middle of the countryside, trying again with the papers they wanted Susie to sign. A family called Ingram, fairly new to the church but apparently exemplary in their faith and unable to have children of their own, wanted to adopt Susie's baby. It must have been Mary who leaked the information about where she was. There was no other way they could have found out.

Mrs Shaw and Mrs Tredwell had not gone to Tuscany alone: the goodwill of the church had gone with them. In fact, the goodwill of the church paid for their tickets. There had been a meeting of the Elders to approve the mission, then a meeting of the Deacons to disburse the funds, then a special prayer meeting of the church at large to help them on their way. And then there they were, two ladies in their middle forties who had never been out of England. Package holidays were clearly sinful, and the people they knew who had travelled had done so largely as missionaries, to Spain (to save the souls of the Catholics), or, in rarer cases, to Peru. The whole business of obtaining passports (you could still get temporary passports then, and why would they want to go anywhere again after this?), of booking tickets and foreign hotels at a travel agent's in the town had weighed heavily on them, and had seemed like a terrible responsibility, undertaken only in the name of duty and serving the Lord.

They had set off, dressed as usual in clothes vaguely inspired by the coats and skirts of the 1940s, whose principle function was to demarcate them from the common herd of pleasure-seekers and business travellers. Mrs Tredwell had wondered whether perhaps the new leisure suits might be in order, but Mrs Shaw had been appalled at the suggestion, and now the hats were firmly in place, Mrs Tredwell's shaped like an upturned cake tin, Mrs Shaw's a hard, ribbed curve, rising on one side. The hats seemed somehow proof against the worldliness which was all around, in the train, at the airport, in the offer of alcohol on the plane (Mrs Shaw had made a fuss about this, seeing it as an opportunity to witness; Mrs Tredwell had felt it was enough to decline politely).

This new, profane world to which they were so rarely exposed – they were largely domestic creatures, and neither could remember a time, apart from the odd church wives' coach trip, that they had travelled without their husbands – proved exhausting. They didn't know how to negotiate it, had to be taken in hand and shown where to go at Birmingham and Rome, where they changed planes. Arriving at Pisa, they almost forgot that they had to go and pick up their luggage from a carousel, were in the very act of getting into a taxi (they could not be expected to negotiate Italian buses, the Deacons had felt), when Mrs Tredwell remembered their cases. Then the taxi ride had been terrible, the roads winding, the constant blaring of the horn appalling, although the countryside, they admitted, was pleasant enough. At the guesthouse – an actual hotel had been considered a little too secular – they had eaten early and retired to their room. Mrs Shaw wanted them to pray together on their knees before retiring. Mrs Tredwell, who had had just about enough, almost snapped "Must we?" but managed to control her tongue, just in time. So they prayed that Susie in her sin might be guided back to the path of righteousness, but Mrs Tredwell couldn't stop herself thinking about Luke's parents, and wondering whether what they had done counted as sin too.

Sinful Susie had been surprisingly kind to them, when they arrived next day in another taxi, looking, she thought, rather grey, rather unwell. The Elders had told them not to call ahead, because that would give Susie and her protectors a chance to avoid them. If after three attempts, they were unable to find them in, they should give it up, they had pronounced. It would mean it was not the will of the Lord. (Could the Lord not make up his mind beforehand? thought Mrs Tredwell. She was sometimes troubled by these not exactly blasphemous, but unholy, unworthy, thoughts).

Susie and the Thomsons had been having a late breakfast on the terrace of the house. It was not a particularly attractive house, being composed of greying concrete slabs, which had also incurred the scorn of the colleagues they had left behind at Coombe's, but the terrace looked out over vineyards and the sea could be glimpsed beyond. "Tourists, up here?"

wondered Felicity, watching the taxi arrive, and Oliver said flippantly, "Jehovah's Witnesses?" Then "Oh", said Susie, in a tone of dismay. "I know them."

Felicity went inside to get more cups, coffee and biscuits, since however strange the situation she felt that the rules of hospitality still applied, and Mrs Shaw and Mrs Tredwell were invited to sit down. Susie, backed by Oliver – "We are after all in loco parentis" – said no to what they asked, and continued to say no, sweetly and politely, until they rose to leave. She did not say "No, I will not trust you with my baby because of what your church people did to Luke", because she didn't have to. To refuse was enough. She felt almost sorry for them, they were so scared of everything, of sin and sex and leaving Ashwick.

"Do have a safe journey," said Susie. "And give my love to Luke."

Oliver drove them back to the nearest town, where getting a coach to Pisa was a simple matter – he waited with them, saw them on board. "Please don't come again," he said to them, looking directly into each pair of eyes, as they parted. Mrs Shaw phoned the travel agency from the hotel, and managed to get their flights home changed to that evening. She felt they had seen enough.

Felicity phoned England that evening: "We didn't know what to do," she said.

"It sounds," said Gordon, "as if you couldn't have done anything else."

"Anyway, we thought you should know," said Felicity.

Susie hadn't wanted to talk.

Next day, Gordon and Janet made an appointment with their solicitor, to have a strongly-worded letter sent to the pastor of the church, asking them to "butt out", said Janet, although it would have to be put more tactfully than that, reiterating that a private adoption was out of the question, that the thing would be handled by state agencies, who had the know-how and the experience, who knew what to do for the best.

So the visit had misfired badly, and just made Gordon and Janet more certain that bringing the child home, bringing it up in Ashwick, would mean exposing it to a constant battle for its soul.

*

"Those people were very persistent," said Gordon, in the garden in Falmouth, where, incredibly, they were still eating, in a desultory sort of way. They had moved on to the salads. "There was no knowing what they might do."

"You could have left Ashwick," said Gina, in spite of herself.

"Why should we?" flared Janet. "It was our home." Gina allowed herself a glance at Robert, to see if he had noticed the "was", but he was looking down at the table. He seemed to have disappeared inside himself, made himself completely unavailable.

"What you have to understand," said Gordon, who had been indoors to get his pipe and had now lit it, something Gina hadn't seen him do for years, "Is that we thought we were doing the right thing."

"And do you still?" said Gina. "Do you still think that?"

"It's so easy," said Janet, "so easy to sit there and criticise."

"Janet," said Gordon, warningly.

"I'm not criticising," said Gina. "But do you?" She said it gently, without challenge. She was no Inspector to sum up and apportion blame: it was not for her to deliver fire and blood and anguish.

"*Yes*," snapped Janet, without elaboration. She stood up, shook the crumbs off her skirt, walked through the kitchen and went upstairs. Gordon sighed and said, heavily, answering Gina in his turn, "I haven't the least idea."

Gina dimly perceived, in among all the untold chapters of the story, how it must have been: the quarrelling, the consensus, the final sense that there was only one possible thing to be done, that there had been no choice. And then, as the years went on, doubt settling, invisible but toxic, like radiation – Janet fending it off, refusing to recognise that they could have been wrong, Gordon giving in, letting himself become more and more certain that they should have taken the child, should have moved away from Ashwick, brought it up between them, that anything would have been better than this everlasting, irreparable sense of loss.

"We thought the child would have a better chance," went on Gordon, "With people who would love him for himself alone, not know anything about Luke, all the sadness."

"What happened to Luke?" Robert, who hadn't spoken for some time, was the one who asked this. Gina wondered if he was thinking he could do well as a lay-brother at St Agnes.

"It's a sad story," said Gordon.

"Well, now we've got this far you may as well tell it," said Gina, hearing herself sound like Janet.

"In and out of prison," said Gordon. "Dealing drugs, then fraud of some kind. The last we heard he was serving three more years."

Gina's mind ran briefly on how long they had served, she and Robert, and latterly Clara, when they hadn't done anything wrong. It should perhaps have been easier to talk to Gordon in the absence of Janet, but she found herself suddenly threatened by anger, by real fury. It was the word, "fraud". It had unleashed something. Like Janet, she got up abruptly, and went in through the kitchen. "Best leave your mother, for a bit," said Gordon's voice behind her. "I was going to," said Gina acidly, and went up to her room.

Looking at her watch, she saw that it was heading towards four o'clock, an hour after her usual time to text Eduardo. Texting seemed too complicated, now: she found that her hands were trembling. She pressed Call. Hearing his voice on the other end of the line, even with a little echo, a little delay, was like honey smoothed into her soul. She said, finding that her voice, also, was trembling, "Mais tu n'y croiras pas, ce nouveau chapitre de la merde familiale". And saw Clara's little face, withdrawing from the doorway to her room, Clara who of course would have got all that, about a new chapter in all the family shit. That bloody child, into everything, she thought, and then, dear Clara. She apologised mentally for her thought.

When she had finished telling Eduardo about it, and he had, said, finally and wryly, "Families, eh. Who'd have them?" she lay down on her bed, and, most bizarrely, she thought later – although she had drunk far more wine than she was accustomed to in the middle of the day – fell asleep.

Day three: evening

XXIX

Gina woke with no idea how long she had slept. She thought at first, confusedly, that she felt Jupiter nosing at her face, as he sometimes did. Gina had always been taught not to wake a sleeping cat, not to treat it as a plaything, but Jupiter didn't feel the same about his humans and woke them when he wanted company or food. But this was not Jupiter, it was Clara, dabbing at her face with a serviette. "You were crying in your sleep," she said tenderly. "And you shouted something." Robert was there too, looming over her. "What?" said Gina, "What did I shout?"

"'No, no you can't'". And something else I didn't get."

"Oh." Gina felt very exposed. She sat up, and Clara passed her a glass of fizzy water, which she sipped gratefully.

"There's cake, too," said Clara helpfully, and Gina saw that there was, on a paper plate with a fork, on the bedside table. The events of the afternoon unspooled, returned, and she remembered that she had been dreaming that Janet was serving her an egg, hard-boiled when she had wanted the yolk still soft and bright, and the egg was disturbingly attached to a stem; something to do with aubergines, with egg-plants; with Janet, with Susie. She took the plate and dug into a layer of chocolate butter-cream.

"What's happening?" she said.

"Not much," said Robert. "Clara and I went for a walk. When we came back they'd gone."

"Mum and Dad?

"The car's not there."

"Oh. Did they leave a note?"

"Nope."

"It feels," said Gina, on an outward breath, "It feels as if we're in disgrace."

"I know what you mean," said Robert, and they both refrained from saying the whole thing was entirely Nadège's fault, since Nadège's daughter was sitting on the edge of the bed with her big round dark eyes.

"We couldn't not *ask*," said Gina. "Not once... not once it started."

That was how it felt. That it had started, some ineluctable process, like giving birth, or an earthquake.

"What was that," said Clara, carefully – taking her cue from the grown-ups, she did not mention her mother – "What was that about a website?"

"Oh," said Gina. "Part of Me. Yes."

She reached down beside the bed, where her laptop was recharging, nearly losing the cake-plate in the process. Robert caught it, switched on the computer, passed it over.

"I didn't know, er, anybody else knew about it." The computer was old, and the wifi slow, but after a minute or two she got into her favourites, clicked on the familiar site, and logged in.

"Here," she said, showing her page: *Gina*, looking for: *Susie*; country: *UK*; relationship: *sister*; last contact: *unspecified*."

"Why did you put unspecified?" asked Clara, leaning in

so that the long tendrils of hair round her face trailed in the cake.

"Because there always has been contact," said Gina. "Sort of. Writing emails which might or might not ever arrive. You can't say there hasn't been any."

"Why didn't you put photos?"

"Oh, I don't know," said Gina. "It just seemed so indiscreet. Pinning it up for the whole world to see. Especially now."

Robert took the computer, peered, clicked, peered again. He had left his glasses somewhere. Possibly he, too, had been weeping, thought Gina, hoping that it hadn't been in front of Clara. It wasn't that men should not weep, just that it was difficult if it was your father —

"You can leave messages," he said.

"Yes," said Gina. "I have. I did."

Hi Susie,

Gina's inadequate little message ran.

It would be great to hear from you. Nobody is sure if we have the right e mail address and we don't know where you are. You just fell off the edge of the world.

Lots of love, Gina.

"Shall we leave another one?"

"We could. I mean, yes, I suppose so." But saying what?

"Can I do it?" said Clara, surprisingly.

Gina passed her the computer. Clara thought visibly, then after a moment began typing. "French keyboard," she said, going back and erasing. "No, it's ok, Mum's got one. I just didn't know this one was."

"So?" said Gina, after a few minutes.

"It's probably really stupid."

"I expect it's very good. Go on, read it out."

"No, it's terrible. I don't know what to say." Clara read in a monotonous, self-mocking tone,

Hello Auntie Susie, we're all together in Cornwall for three days by the sea and everyone is missing you really a lot so please come next time because Grandma says there will be other times and everyone loves you. And we're really sorry about everything that happened because now we've found out. Love Clara

and then said, as Gina sat shifted her weight and sat up and the laptop almost slid off her knee, "Oh *no*. I accidentally sent it."

"It's nice. It's sweet. Don't worry."

Gina swung her legs off the bed, yawned, stretched, clambered back into older sister mode.

"I'm going to go down and pack up the food," she said. "Then maybe we should go out. It's sort of weird staying around here."

The plan for this last evening had been to go to a beach, somewhere on the north side, "a real Cornish beach", Janet had said, but it would seem more than bizarre to do that now, even if Gordon and Janet did come back.

"What do you think they're doing?" Clara asked, hovering around the table in the garden, picking at the food, as Gina was doing herself while she piled what could be saved back into the boxes. Anything involving salmon or rice definitely couldn't be salvaged – it had been out too long, with the sun high in the sky on what seemed like this endless day.

"I don't know," said Gina. "Talking, I suppose. I hope they're all right."

Had they gone somewhere where they could reclaim their private drama and scream at each other uncensored? Some quiet country lane? Surely they wouldn't have chased after Nadège – they had wanted her gone. Or had one or other of them taken the car and driven off, and was the other, probably Gordon, sitting in a pub drinking whisky, speaking to nobody? Dear God, had there been an accident, was their car skewed across a lane somewhere with both of them unconscious, and nobody around to call for help?

"I hope they're all right too," said Clara. She stopped eating and began to help Gina.

"Do you think we should phone them?" said Gina to Robert, who was standing on the threshold of the kitchen, checking his own phone.

"Maybe not," said Robert. "Or not yet. Give them a bit of time. Get themselves together." And Gina supposed he had more experience of these things, albeit indirectly, what with St Agnes Mount.

"Let's go to the beach round here then," she said. "Then we can get back if we need to. Bring your bathers." And she went upstairs to get her own.

*

They went to Castle Beach, with its little row of beach-huts on a raised walkway, which seemed to offer reassurance and protection. There were several people bathing in the sea, some in wetsuits, some in ordinary swimming gear. The tide was now up past the rocks, making getting in less difficult than it could be, but they had brought the bathing shoes Janet had provided. Clara immediately undressed to her swimsuit and plunged into the water, while Gina and Robert sat on their towels on the sand, as if they were, thought Gina for a moment, her parents. "Don't go too far," called Gina, but the water was completely calm, with only the smallest of waves.

"So," said Gina, knees drawn up to her chin, looking straight ahead.

"So?" said Robert.

"So, where does all this leave us?"

Robert said nothing.

"The whole thing makes me so angry," said Gina.

"What, Mum and Dad?"

"Them. And Susie. All of it. Inflicting two decades of this shit on everyone when they knew how it would be, how it would feel. And it's not as if any of it is our fault."

"Maybe they thought it was for Susie to say. If she wanted."

"And she didn't. But all those lies, from Mum."

"Because Dad didn't want to do the lying."

Gina, whose head was still far from clear, couldn't get into the moral niceties of this, but she suddenly remembered something easier to grasp: "But why would Susie be in touch with Nadège, of all people?" Clara was safely out of earshot.

"I don't know," said Robert. "Something to do with Nadège looking for her father, at a guess. They must have ended up on the same website."

"Ah yes. The mystery man." Gina sifted sand through her fingers. "So do you mind? About Clara's grandfather. Does she mind?"

"Oh Gina, I don't know. I've just made contact with her for the first time in years, we haven't talked about it."

"But do you?"

"No. I don't care who her grandfather is. She's just herself."

"But why wouldn't they say? Nadège's family? What reason could there be?"

"I don't know. Prison, probably. Something like that. Some crime."

"Or she was just illegitimate. Some affair. Or worse."

"Could be."

"But you'll never know."

"I can live with that."

"But not with Nadège."

"Give me a break."

"With Melanie."

Robert said nothing, but sat smiling towards the sea. Gina got up ungracefully, legs stiff, unzipped and shucked off her skirt (she already had her swimsuit on), peeled off her top, and joined Clara in the sea. After a minute or two, Robert did the same. The water, very cold, was salutary. Gina swam out a little, then trod water, looking first at the beach, under this perfectly blue, untroubled, and inappropriate sky, not even now beginning to darken, when really it felt as if it was time for the day to at least begin to end, then at the horizon, across which a small and perfect white sail progressed. Then turning back to the beach, she saw Gordon, also standing scanning the horizon, and waved. She hurried out of the water, grabbing her sandy towel.

"Dad," she said, breathless. "Are you ok?"

"Oh, yes, yes," said Gordon, vaguely. "Not quite what we had in mind when, er..." This sentence had no end. "Are you?"

"Yes. We just came down to the beach. Is Mum all right?"

"She's all right," said Gordon, in a dubious tone. "Went off on her own for a bit. Feeling a bit – cornered."

"Yes."

"Feels we acted in good faith. Did our best." He gave a sigh which sounded almost impatient. "Too late now. Even if we got it wrong."

Gina took her father's terse and telegraphic tone to mean that he was delivering an official statement, on behalf of both himself and Janet. She was anxious to placate. The period of withdrawal which would normally have been marked – weeks, perhaps months, of no contact, followed by a slow all-round thawing – had been reduced to a couple of hours and a quick scene-change, but she could not stay angry. What would it help? So she said, "Yes, of course. Everyone sees that."

What Janet had actually said was that they couldn't go on being sorry forever, that life had to go on, that there wasn't much of it left anyway and what there was she intended to enjoy. Gordon was not entirely sure that he agreed with that, or at least the first part, but he said now, "She didn't want to give her whole life over to it. She didn't want years of endless grief."

Gina said nothing, but watched a sudden image in her head of shallow water fast-flowing over rock. She thought how little people conformed to what they were supposed to be or feel, like Clara saying she didn't care when Robert left.

"There were letters, you know. Susie wrote. Several times. Telling us we'd done the wrong thing."

"And had you?"

"I don't know, Gina. We did what we thought was best." And then, after a silence, "These few days meant so much to your mother."

"We're still having them."

"Shall I get her to come down?"

"Well yes," said Gina. "Yes, of course. It was supposed to be a celebration, today. Of course she should be with us." She was torn between a desire to invoke her own suffering, and Robert's, and the need to protect her parents, who seemed suddenly so much older and more fragile.

"You tell her that," said Gordon. "She'll be pleased."

Half an hour later, Gordon reappeared with Janet, and a picnic bag loaded with the remains of the buffet. Janet was looking courageous, thought Gina, even doughty: although her eyes looked very tired, she was literally putting a brave face on it. She would have liked to go and hug her mother, to feel the frame, slighter than her own, the bones, more fragile now, but she hesitated because she was still a little damp and sandy, and then the moment was lost. Instead she squeezed her mother's hand, awkwardly. "So nice to get together," said Gina, pointlessly, hypocritically, and they sat and ate and drank without saying much, until Gordon cleared his throat and said, as a sort of announcement, "Your mother and I were saying, this afternoon, that the child, Susie's son, will be eighteen next year. In the spring."

"When, exactly?" said Gina, who needed to know, to try to work out what she had been doing on the day Susie had been giving birth.

"Towards the end of April. We've got the date, somewhere. Anyway, the point is that when he's eighteen, he'll be in a position to look for us. Should he feel that need. And maybe that would make it easier, for Susie." Gina was visited by a vision of the boy walking out of the sea from the metaphorical point on the horizon where the waters had closed over Susie's head, something between Jesus and Venus, coming up to them and saying, "Here I am. The story's end."

Clara said, "But he could have looked for you before. On social media."

"As far as we know he hasn't," said Gordon. "And when it comes to it he might not want to go through the official channels either. It may well be that he's perfectly happy as he is and doesn't feel the need."

Nobody said anything. Gina was thinking about

Eduardo's Julia. Had she ever asked about her biological parents? Or was it different when abject poverty was a factor, when it was a case of being not just sent away for a better life, but for the very perpetuation of life? Impossible to bring any of that up now; it wasn't the moment for more revelations. All this sudden truth-telling perversely assured the safety of the more minor secrets, the Falmouth house, Melanie, America. They sat and looked at the darkening sky as it grew slowly violet, and Gina understood that the subject of Susie and her child, at least for now, was closed.

*

"So," said Gina quietly to Clara, in the kitchen, when Gordon and Janet had driven back with the picnic things, and the rest of them had walked. It sounded as if Gordon and Janet had already gone to bed. "Lots of things for your Susie pages."

"Yes," said Clara. "But I don't really know what to say yet. I need to sort it all out in my head."

"Don't we all," said Gina, thinking how prescient this was, for thirteen.

"Do you think she'll get in touch?"

"I hope so," said Gina. "I hope so." For the moment, there were no more words in her.

Falmouth to Paddington

XXX

The next day – the afterlife, the coda, for the three days by the sea had now been spent – Gina, going down to the kitchen for breakfast, found Janet up early, dressed in another of the new, gaily flowered skirts. There was once more a faint smell of bacon frying – the cooker hood was on, the French windows open – and Janet was mashing hard-boiled eggs, looking competent and cheerful. "Sandwiches for your trip," she said. "Egg and bacon, if that's all right. I'm putting in some salad as well."

"Lovely, thanks," said Gina, wishing she could say something more sincere, less mechanical. But the theme seemed to be the restoration of normality, the resumption of daily life, the extinction of drama. So she merely added, "Really lovely." There was no point, Gina thought, going back into it all now. There was much to think about, much to question, but there would be time, time for them all. And, thought Gina, with an upsurge of optimism, they would come together again. This was not an end but a beginning. She poured herself coffee and sat down, then got up to pour a cup for Robert, who had appeared in the doorway. There was still some time before their train.

"Oh, you're up," said Janet, still in the same cheerful tone.

She seemed perfectly authentic, as if she had regenerated during the night. "I've got something to tell you," said Janet. "While you're both here."

Gina nodded encouragingly. The masks were firmly in place.

"We've decided to stay a bit longer," said Janet. "We've actually taken this house for a few months."

Gina gulped coffee while she thought of something to say, but Robert beat her to it.

"So you're retiring." he said. "Down here." He didn't sound surprised, as Gina would have tried to, but then he rarely did.

"The fact is," said Janet, gently, so that Gina's heart lurched, "The fact is, and we're so very sorry, that they've finally decided to demolish Oak Lodge."

How very odd, thought Gina, how strange, that Janet should announce this so kindly, with such regret, after yesterday, after everything. "We didn't know how to tell you," she went on. "We were going to make an announcement yesterday, make the move into a nice thing, so we could all celebrate together."

"But isn't it?" said Gina. "Isn't it a nice thing?"

"Well of course it is, for us," said Janet. "It was you we were worried about."

"No," said Gina. "There's nothing to worry about, Mum."

"Nothing at all," said Robert.

"This is your time," said Gina. She found herself flooded with a sudden wave of love for her mother, uncomplicated, unconditional love, as if Janet were here own child. She was glad she would be having a seaside holiday in Cornwall, forever.

"But can you retire completely?" said Robert, for once practical.

"We did think we'd have to keep on working," said Janet. "Your father was going to do supply, and I was going to get a few clients. In fact I still might. Just for the interest. But with your father's pension, and the settlement, if we're careful, we worked out we won't have to."

"So you get your lives back," said Gina.

"I suppose so," said Janet. "What's left of them."

"There's plenty left," said Gina, roundly. "Plenty. You can travel. You can do what you like." It felt like a very public conversation, like putting something on record. It seemed important to approve her mother's first steps in her new world, as, she supposed, Janet had done for her, for all of them when they were children, even if it hadn't felt like it at the time. Janet had never seemed an approving mother.

"Oh, Mum," she heard herself say suddenly, and then she was getting up and taking Janet, spiky bony Janet, in her arms, as she had for a moment longed to do the previous day. "Good luck with it all," she said, and laid her cheek for a moment against her mother's. Gordon, coming in with Clara in tow, looked very gratified to stumble on this scene.

"Mum's been telling us about your plans", said Robert, by way of explanation.

"Ah," said Gordon. "Yes. It was supposed to be for yesterday. Bit of an announcement. Bit of a celebration."

"They'll come again," said Janet.

"Of course we will," said Gina. "Of course we will."

"I wish you could stay longer," said Clara, which was not a good idea since Gina just at that moment felt entirely spineless, boneless, as if she might simply collapse and be incapable of propelling herself to wherever it was in the world she was now, for some arbitrary reason she couldn't quite remember, supposed to be.

"My ticket," she managed to gasp. "My plane ticket. It can't be changed."

And then it was time to go upstairs and clean their teeth and zip up their suitcases, and get into the car to drive over to Truro, to pick up the London train.

*

The train back to Paddington was much emptier than the train down, much more peaceful. Robert dealt with stowing their luggage in the available spaces, much as Gina had dealt with getting Robert onto the train on the way down. Then they sat opposite each other in facing seats, spreading out while this was still possible, and the train chugged on its unhurried way.

Family life was unbearable, thought Gina, looking out of the window at the green and gentle undulations of the fields, at the sun pouring through rainclouds. There was simply too much pain. She had been right to avoid it. Everyone should avoid it. She longed, with a physical hunger, for Eduardo's arms around her, for her nose pressed into the honey-silk of his neck and for what would follow, for his house, for being silly together indoors, for the way that sometimes it was like being with a sister. And at the same time she hung on to the thought of having Gordon and Janet out to stay by the lake, of showing them Chicago, of ushering them into her America, her new-found land.

Robert, standing in the corridor to stretch his legs, looked out of the window and saw rabbits, and at one point two young foxes playing in a field in a flash of flaming orange fur. Towards Teignmouth, when the track went so near the sea you felt you were almost in it, he looked out and saw someone waving, on the horizon – a figure, which could have been a man or a woman, waving. Or drowning? No, waving, making a sign. He was sure of it. What the sign was he could not tell, but he was confident that it would be revealed.

Acknowledgement

My thanks go to Robert Peett for his extraordinary work and unfailing good humour; to all at the Franco-American Fulbright Commission, and especially the late Arnaud Roujou de Boubée, for leading me to the edge of a new world; to the wonderful inhabitants of Kalamazoo; and to Urias for his constant love and belief in me.

Helen E. Mundler

Helen E. Mundler studied at Durham University before obtaining her doctorate in Strasbourg, and her *Habilitation* in Nanterre. She is currently Associate Professor at a university in Paris (UPEC), and spent 2019 at Western Michigan University as a Fulbright research scholar.

She has published two other novels, *Homesickness* (Dewi Lewis, 2003) and *L'Anglaise* (Holland House, 2018), as well as three critical works, *Intertextualité dans l'oeuvre d'A.S.Byatt* (Paris, Harmattan, 2003), *The Otherworlds of Liz Jensen: a Critical Reading* (Boydell and Brewer, Rochester, USA, 2016), and *The Noah Myth in Twenty-First-Century Novels: Rewritings from a Drowning World* (Boydell and Brewer, Rochester, USA, 2022).

In 2018 her short story 'The Fish' was shortlisted for the Fish Publishing Prize in Ireland.

Recently Helen has been involved in teaching creative writing workshops in Strasbourg and judging a short story competition, and has been instrumental in developing creative writing as a sub-discipline of English Studies in French universities.

At present she is working on a fourth novel, *Clouds Without Shadows*.

Helen E. Mundler

L'Anglaise

'*L'Anglaise* is an intelligent, finely-wrought exploration of what home means to those who leave and those who stay. In graceful prose it speaks of love engendered, lost, mourned and renewed; of shadows cast and cast off; of how time illuminates, and forgiveness sets us free.' Liz Jensen, author of The Ninth Life of Louis Drax, The Uninvited, Ark Baby, etc

"An intense, unsettling and unflinchingly honest novel" James Wilson, author of The Bastard Boy, The Woman in the Picture, etc.

Praise for Helen's previous novel, Homesickness:

'...beautifully and tenderly told...' John Carey; as Booker Prize Judge Chairman, John Carey nominated Homesickness as a book he would have liked to see in the Prize list.

'Mundler writes about sex as it really exists, a physical act freighted with emotional, spiritual and moral complexity... a smart and courageous book.' Foreword Reviews

'Mundler writes beautifully, with a deep understanding...' Time Out

'... a remarkable début.' Manchester City Life

When Ella offers to look after a stranger's cat, she is not expecting her life to change...

At 35, Ella is no longer excited by her academic career in France, and has not found love. Following the unexpected death of her father, she is thrown into crisis, but then she meets the enigmatic Max. Over the course of a summer, their romance deepens –until she makes a discovery which throws everything off course. As Ella's life becomes bound up with the stories of two other Englishwomen in France, she finds the freedom to tread an unconventional path, and to love in her own way.

This is a book about the need to revisit and make sense of the past in order to move into the future.

Ashutosh Bhardwaj

The Death Script:
Dreams and Delusions in Naxal Country

A haunting ode to those who paid the ultimate price—through the prism of the Maoist insurgency, Ashutosh Bhardwaj meditates on larger questions of violence and betrayal, love and obsession, and what it means to live with and write about death.

From 2011 to 2015, Ashutosh lived in the Red Corridor in India wherein the Ultra-Left Naxalites, taking inspiration from the Russian revolution and Mao's tactics, work to overthrow the Indian government by the barrel of the gun. He made several trips thereafter reporting on the insurgents, on police and governmental atrocities, and on the lives caught in the crossfire. *The Death Script* chronicles his experiences and bears witness to the lives and deaths of the unforgettable men and women he meets from both sides of the struggle, bringing home the human cost of conflict with astonishing power. Narrated in multiple voices, the book is a creative biography of the region, Dandakaranya, that combines the rigour of journalism, the intimacy of a diary, the musings of a travelogue, and the craft of a novel.

The Death Script is one of the most significant works of non-fiction to be published in recent times, bringing often overlooked perspectives and events to light with empathy. Praised by India's topmost scholars and critics, the book has already won various awards.

Ashutosh Bhardwaj is a bilingual fiction writer, literary critic, and is the only journalist in India to have won the prestigious Ramnath Goenka Award for Excellence in Journalism for four consecutive years. As a journalist, he has traveled across Central India and documented the conditions of tribes caught in the conflict between the Maoist insurgents and the police.

Publication: **4th August 2022**
(Hardcover) ISBN: 978-1-910688-86-1

Cass J McMain

Rescuing Barbara

'Subdues one into complete and horrified fascination … The effects of a work like this linger for days' *Karen Jennings* (*An Island*)

Ignoring her mother may have been a mistake.

During a bout of sobriety, Barbara implored her young daughter to turn her back on her if she began drinking again. Exhausted by her mother's alcoholism, Cass McMain finally took this advice and ignored everything the woman said or did for many years. She did not return calls, she did not visit, she did not react, send letters, or cajole. She simply turned away and waited for her mother to hit bottom or die trying. But as she discovered, bottom may be much farther down than one expects. Eventually, she is forced to wade in and untangle the mess her mother has created.

A gripping series of moments –painful, loving, desperate – *Rescuing Barbara* is a bitterly funny, and even lyrical true story about the inherent dangers of detachment … and a reminder that predators are everywhere, waiting to fill in the gaps.

Publication: **2ⁿᵈ June 2022**
(Paperback) ISBN: 978-1-910688-40-3

Saleh Addonia

The Feeling House

'There is nothing to forget'

A young girl awakes alone next to a burning truck and befriends a nearby cloud; an Eritrean refugee studies interior design as he attempts to build his new home; a group of illegal immigrants embark on an arduous journey in the city as they desperately seek: Her.

Darting from the dark underbelly of London to the sexually impenetrable home, Saleh Addonia writes stories of displacement and frustration. Tinged with isolation and alienation, each tale strikes the imagination as Addonia weaves the surreal into devastatingly human stories.

"the ultimate refuge for the loss of love and meaning" Xiaolu Guo, author of *A Lover's Discourse* and writer and director of *She, A Chinese*

"a vital project illuminating the realities of human beings on the move across this restless planet," Ian McMillan, Poet & Presenter of BBC Radio 3's 'The Verb'

Publication: **5th May 2022**
(Paperback) ISBN: 978-1-910688-78-6

Saleh Addonia was born in Eritrea from an Eritrean mother and an Ethiopian Father. As a child, he survived the Om Hajar massacre and migrated to Sudan. He grew up in refugee camps where he lost his hearing at the age of 12. Addonia spent his early teens in Saudi Arabia and arrived in London as an 18 year old refugee.

He has been awarded the Literature Matters Awards 2021 by the Royal Society of Literature. The Feeling House is his first collection in English.

Anees Salim

The Bellboy

Latif's life changes when he is appointed bellboy at the Paradise Lodge –a hotel where people come to die.

After his father's death, drowned in the waters surrounding their small Island, it is 17 year-old Latif's turn to become the man of the house and provide for his ailing mother and sisters. Despite discovering a dead body on his first day of duty, Latif finds entertainment spying on guests and regaling the hotel's janitor, Stella, with made-up stories. However, when Latif finds the corpse of a small-time actor in Room 555 and becomes a mute-witness to a crime that happens there, the course of Latif's life is irretrievably altered.

'There's no other way to put it: Anees Salim [...] is one of the most affecting writers working today. As prodigiously talented as he is, he is distinguished from his contemporaries writing in English by his precision in identifying and then mining the deep fatalism that runs through the Indian psyche.'
Mint Lounge

Publication: **July 14ᵗʰ 2022**
(Hardcover) ISBN: 978-1-910688-67-0

Anees Salim's books include Vanity Bagh (winner of The Hindu Literary Prize for Best Fiction 2013), The Blind Lady's Descendants (winner of the Raymond Crossword Book

Award for Best Fiction 2014 and the Kendra Sahitya Akademi Award 2018), The Small-town Sea (winner of the Atta Galatta-Banaglore Literature Festival Book Prize for Best Fiction 2017), and The Odd Book of Baby Names. His work has been translated into French, German and several Indian languages